SUMMER on EAST END

TRIPLE MOON

SUMMER on EAST END

TRIPLE MOON

melissa de la cruz

G. P. Putnam's Sons

G. P. Putnam's Sons
an imprint of Penguin Random House LLC
375 Hudson Street
New York, NY 10014

G. P. Putnam's Sons is a registered trademark of
Penguin Random House LLC.

Library of Congress Cataloging-in-Publication Data
is available upon request.

Printed in the United States of America.
ISBN 978-0-399-17355-4
1 3 5 7 9 10 8 6 4 2

Design by Richard Amari.
Text set in Zapf Intl Light.

For Mike and Mattie, always

And my Witches of East End family
WitchEEs forever!

With thanks to Jennifer Besser and
everyone at Penguin for making a new home
for a little white magic

I was too young that time to value her,

But now I know her. If she be a traitor,

Why, so am I. We still have slept together,

Rose at an instant, learn'd, play'd, eat together,

And wheresoe'er we went, like Juno's swans,

Still we went coupled and inseparable.

—*William Shakespeare,* As You Like It

FADE TO BLACK

$\mathcal{E}$ven by Manhattan private school standards, Bret Farley's party was unforgettable. It wasn't just the bottomless flow of top-shelf liquor or the mounds of gleaming caviar, the world-class sculpture collection and the spectacular views of the city from the Park Avenue penthouse, or the rumors of a hidden elevator down to a clandestine indoor lap pool of black marble. It wasn't the designer drugs or the thousand-dollar stilettos. It wasn't all the fooling around in gilt bathrooms and between silky Italian sheets.

The night of Bret Farley's party was unforgettable because, by the end of it, two of the guests were dead.

The prime suspects behind this tragic turn of events, the Overbrook twins, Molly and Mardi, had arrived at Bret's penthouse a little after ten, bewitchingly identical in their dark features and lush black hair, but oh so different in style. Molly was the height of chic, Mardi the essence of rebellion. Equally gorgeous and equally brilliant.

So why, only moments after taking their first drinks from a caterer's silver tray, did both goddesses start to feel undone?

Molly was sipping champagne, Mardi a very dry Manhattan. This they both remembered. They also remembered that blue-eyed, ultra-suave Bret had flirted with both of them, telling Molly the vintage bubbles and caviar were all for her benefit, then leading Mardi by the hand among the bronze legs of the enormous Louise Bourgeois spider, the crown jewel of his family's collection. The only other of that size graced the lobby of the Tate Modern in London. The twins recalled the body of the spider looming in the apartment's vast entryway, beautiful and malicious.

Each sister had been glaringly jealous of Bret's attentions to her twin. But neither one could begin to remember where those attentions had led.

There was an obscene swirl of luxury: reflective surfaces, sparkling views, high art, thumping music, and shiny beautiful rich kids who were striking poses for their Insta accounts, gossiping, drinking from priceless crystal, and falling down wasted onto one another.

The Overbrook girls were very much a part of this ruling scene, but they were apart from it as well. Because Molly and Mardi weren't simply pretty and privileged; they were supernatural.

With supernatural instincts.

The twins could tell that something was up that

night, something more than just Upper East Side private school mischief, but they found themselves too spellbound to investigate. Was it in their drinks? Or a deep corruption in the atmosphere? If you'd asked them at the party if they thought it would end in carnage, they would have laughed, but not wholeheartedly. They would have let out tinkling, nervous laughs. Laughs that admitted suspicion. But suspicion of what? Of whom?

The last thing Molly remembered, before blacking out, was the sound of Bret's sexy whisper in her ear. "This is all for you, Molly," he was saying, "every flower petal, every flute, every ivory caviar spoon."

Only she didn't want to believe him because she had just seen him with her twin, probably telling Mardi the same thing.

The last thing Mardi recalled was the bronze underbelly of the giant spider. Bret was telling her it was called *Maman*, because the artist believed that spiders were protective and benevolent. "You're the only girl here who could possibly get the reference," he whispered. His arm rested on her shoulder. "You love spiders, don't you, Mardi?" She managed to say, "Yeah, spiders are cool," and then her memory went blank.

The next morning, the legendary Overbrook twins stared at each other across their kitchen table through raccoon eyes. Neither one had taken off her mascara. They were still in their rumpled party clothes. Molly in her cocktail dress, Mardi in her torn black jeans. Somehow they had managed to order coffee and eggs online from the diner down the street.

They were too spent to start their usual argument about whose fault it was that the eggs were over easy instead of sunny-side up and who had been stupid enough to order whole wheat toast instead of sourdough. Somehow, there was no energy for fighting.

When they finally managed to speak, they sighed, in unison, "What happened last night? What the—?"

Then they sank silently into their breakfast, each straining to remember the previous night.

It was several hours before they got the news.

PART ONE

Hot Fun
in the
Summertime

THRIFT SHOP

Mardi Overbrook shifted into fourth gear on the Montauk Highway, gunning to pass what had to be yet another banker's kid in a brand-new black Ferrari. She belted along to Macklemore, singing about the twenty dollars in her pocket, her car vibrating to the powerful beat as it dusted the ultimate Hamptons douchemobile. Sucker had probably paid extra for automatic because he never learned to drive stick.

Her own car was a Ferrari too, but it was far from new—a 1972 red convertible Daytona that had lived many lives. It didn't look anything like Banker Boy's car, and she didn't look anything like his preppie girl-friend either. Mardi had a rainbow tattoo that circled her neck like a python and an emerald-studded barbell through the tip of her tongue, which she stuck out at the astonished driver as she blurred by him, screaming along to her favorite song.

At the light, she glanced down at her phone, which

was sitting faceup on the ebony leather passenger seat. Her social media feed was flowing in a steady stream, showing the streets and interiors of the city she was leaving behind. Unlike the majority of the stuck-up kids at her stupid prep school, she wasn't getting the posts of sunsets in Mustique or cocktail parties in Nantucket. No, her feed was full of the real stuff from after-hours clubs all over the five boroughs of New York City, places without names or defined locations, places that appeared and disappeared in water towers and in abandoned fleabag motels, places she called home because she traveled there in a manic rebel pack that she called family. The pictures were of passed-out teens, teens staggering out into the daylight like disoriented moths, teens in various states of undress. She smiled down as they migrated across her phone screen. Her tribe.

She adjusted the strap of her vintage leopard-skin push-up bathing-suit bra, which she was wearing with a pair of threadbare rhinestone-encrusted denim shorts. The outfit had been left decades ago in the back of a closet by one of Dad's girlfriends from his Studio 54 days. There was great stuff to be pillaged from Dad's past in the Overbrook loft in Greenpoint—if you knew where to look.

Mardi grabbed the phone, puckered her lips, and took a quick close-up, posting it for all her friends back in the city with a tagline: "Don't you dare forget me while I'm gone."

Why in the Underworld was she leaving her life behind? Could someone please remind her?

Oh, yeah—she was leaving her life behind to spend the summer babysitting in a sleepy town lost somewhere on the East End of Long Island. With her princess of a twin sister, Molly, no less.

It was a fate worse than being badly dressed.

As she drove farther out from civilization, the landscape grew more pastoral and the salt smell in the air grew more pronounced, irritating her eyes so that she started to tear up. She was not one to cry, but this summer stretching ahead of her, an endless ribbon of small-town boredom, was a depressing prospect. She hadn't even arrived in North Hampton, and she already felt trapped.

Mardi Overbrook hated feeling trapped.

She gritted her teeth, shifted into fifth gear, and turned the music up, determined not to admit defeat. If she was going to live for the summer in North Hampton, then she was going to make North Hampton worth living in.

A post popped onto her phone, which she instantly knew was from her twin. Not only because it was a phony artistic shot of some sand dune, complete with endangered shrubs and a pensive-looking seagull, that Molly had surely stopped to capture along her route—typical pretentious Molly—but because of the pink gold ring rolling over the image, undulating like soft taffy across the screen.

This was what young witches did lately to wink at one another through cyberspace. They overlaid their static posts with moving images visible only to their kind. Everyone had a symbol, like a living emoji. There were waxing and waning moons, twinkling stars, beating hearts, all sorts of romping mythical creatures. It was a tribal thing. And tribes were the whole point of social networking, right?

Molly and Mardi always had the rose gold ring, subtly carved with a diamondback pattern, floating through their posts, but only the two of them could see it. They had other images for sharing with the general witch population. Mardi used a vaulting rainbow, Molly a galloping thoroughbred horse. Only to each other did they make the golden ring visible. They'd never talked about it. But that's how it was.

So, when Mardi sent the image of her red lips out into the world, Molly alone would notice the symbol of their sisterhood floating across the screen, while the rest of Midgard's witches saw a snaking rainbow and the general population saw nothing but a cherry-red pout and a hint of leopard and lace.

Normally, this notion that she shared something unique with Molly wouldn't faze Mardi. It was no big deal, a stupid twin thing. But today she had to admit that she found it just a little bit comforting that, as she left the known world, there was someone—even if that someone was *the most irritating person in the universe*—who was truly on her wavelength.

The phone rang, and her father's handsome face filled the screen. She turned the music down and instinctively slowed, as if he could see her, although she was still twenty miles over the limit.

"S'up?"

"How about 'hello, Dad'?" Troy Overbrook asked.

"S'up?"

"Are you almost there, my sweet?"

"Honestly, I have no idea. The GPS is acting weird."

"Well, can't your sister navigate for you? I told you it was tricky."

Mardi looked at the empty seat beside her. "Molly's right here, but I'm afraid she's fully occupied painting her nails a lovely shade of lavender and simply cannot be bothered to come to my aid, Your Majesty. So sorry, Your Highness. At your service, My Lord. Deferentially yours, Master. Is that what you want to hear?"

Troy sighed. "Well, at least you girls are together. And what I want to hear is that you are both going to take this summer with Ingrid seriously. She's an old, dear friend of mine, and I'm afraid she may be our last hope. Show her some respect. Take good care of her children. I'm asking you to try. For your own good."

"I still can't believe you're making us do this—for the whole summer!"

"Do it you will. You have no idea how ugly things will get if you blow it."

"Life is an ugly thing, Dad."

"Not as ugly as Hell, my sweet."

A flashing red light appeared in Mardi's rearview mirror.

"Dad, gotta go. I'm being pulled over."

"What?" There was a groan on the other end. "Okay, but I want you to promise me that there will be no funny business. Take it like a mortal. A mortal who deserves a speeding ticket. I'll pay the fine. You have *got* to learn some self-control."

"Okay, promise, Dad. I swear. Okay. Bye."

She hurled the phone onto the floor and downshifted to a perfect stop. Before the police officer could open his door, she had already appeared between the exhaust pipes of her ridiculously powerful cherry-red car.

Her hair was jet black and knotty. Her eyes were dark and defiant, her makeup artfully smudged. Her legs were endless, sprouting pale and willowy from a pair of gladiator sandals covered in bronze spikes. The effect, with her studded shorts and pointy leopard bra, was quite unnerving. Her stomach was so defined and her arms so ripped that she looked hard to the touch, both wildly attractive and severely off-putting at the same time. The green glow emanating from the precious stone studding her tongue gave her the hypnotic quality of a cobra.

"Young lady," said the cop as he stumbled from his car door, "you should remain in your vehicle."

"Noted for next time." She laughed, squinting at him

until he stumbled again. "Next time, I will remain in my vehicle. Promise." Control her powers? Seriously, Dad, what were powers *for*?

"Next time?" he slurred. Then, making a super-human effort to get ahold of himself, he said, "License and registration, please."

"Say 'pretty please.'"

"Pretty ple—wait a second, you're not old enough to be driving a car like this!"

"I'm sixteen. Last time I checked that was the legal driving age."

"License and registration," he repeated, making his syllables yawn in slow motion. Then he said it again, way too fast, three times over, in a high, squeaky car-toon chipmunk voice: "License and registration! License and registration! License and registration!"

"Officer"—she grinned and took a step toward him—"are you harassing me?"

He looked down at his shiny black beetle shoes and clenched his fists, attempting one last time to get a grip on himself in the presence of her overwhelming magic.

"Miss, you were going over ninety miles an hour in a fifty-mile-per-hour zone. License and registration." This time his voice sounded as though he were underwater.

Gleefully, Mardi watched him close his mouth for fear he would start blowing bubbles. This was one of her favorite tricks to play on authority figures: to fill their mouths with so much saliva that they became terrified of becoming human soap-bubble wands.

"My speedometer told me I was right at the limit, Officer," she said sweetly.

He made a sound, but his lips wouldn't part to form words.

She laughed and hopped effortlessly back into her car.

"I'm afraid," she said as she revved the engine, "that you and I are going to have to agree to disagree, Officer."

She left him standing stock-still by the side of the road. She had made sure he wouldn't move a muscle for five minutes and that his memory of the encounter would be as fuzzy as a fading dream.

Sorry, Dad.

Why be mortally weak when she was immortally gifted?

She was the daughter of Thor, after all.

✳ 2 ✳

FANCY

*A*s she made out with Leo Fairbanks in the back of an Uber limousine, Molly Overbrook not so surreptitiously checked her phone over his muscular shoulder. Her feed was flying with the jet-set frenzy that always marked the beginning of the summer season. Her friends were posting from private seaplanes as they hopped between St. Maarten and St. Barths, from yachts in Newport and from villas on Lake Como and the Côte d'Azur. Each image sent a current of jealousy coursing through Molly's gorgeous frame. She hated her "friends."

Molly was not headed anywhere remotely cool. Quite the contrary, she was on her way to the sleepiest town on the Eastern Seaboard. *To babysit.* And to get lectured by some old lady friend of Daddy's named Ingrid Beauchamp about how not to abuse her magic.

Whatever. She had never felt quite this indignant before. Life was totally unfair.

The most galling picture on her feed showed a clique

of bikini-clad vampires from Duchesne, a rival Upper East Side prep school to Headingley, where she and Mardi had just finished a disastrous but wickedly amusing sophomore year. The Duchesne vamps were arrayed on a white-sand Caribbean beach, brandishing exotic cocktails, each of their bodies a gleaming perfection. Vampires could eat whatever they wanted and not put on an ounce. The famous Blue Blood metabolism. A bunch of social X-rays. Not so with witches. A witch could get as flabby as a mortal if she let herself go. There was no justice on this Earth.

Molly unlocked her glossy lips from Leo's mouth and sighed.

"What?" Leo pulled a few inches away and looked into her dark eyes. He was the hottest guy of a certain set in all of New York City, on his way to his summer home in East Hampton.

When she and Mardi had a fight this morning about Mardi's insisting on driving to North Hampton in that ridiculous old car, which had no trunk—i.e., no room for Molly's three giant Louis Vuitton suitcases—Molly went into one of her huffs and tapped out an order for an Uber limo. After, she texted Leo and offered to drop him off at his house on Lily Pond Lane en route, ostensibly so he wouldn't have to take the train but mostly because the idea of being alone with her thoughts in a car for three hours was unbearable.

Of course, Leo, varsity tennis champion at Headingley, jumped at the chance. With her luxuriant dark mane, mesmerizing dark eyes, willowy curves, vertiginous cleavage, and impeccable style, no one could resist her. And she and Leo had been dating on and off all spring, although her interest was waning pretty hard.

Boys were like shoes. Once you owned them and had worn them out once or twice so that all your friends had seen them and done their oohing and aahing, the high was pretty much over. Leo was smoking cute, but he was last season's catch. You might hold on to a guy like him for a while just because he was high quality. But, once the thrill of the conquest was gone, it was time to go shopping again. You're never that psyched about a pair of scuffed shoes, now, are you?

At this image of worn-out shoes, Molly crinkled her upturned button nose. She would never understand how her sister wore those ratty, smelly used clothes. What was Mardi trying to prove?

As if summoned by the negative thought, a post from Mardi popped onto Molly's screen, a shot of Mardi's pucker in that cherry-red lipstick she liked, along with a strap of that leopard-print bra she'd filched from some skanky old flame of Dad's. So gross. Mardi had written a whiny comment asking her low-life crowd not to forget her over the summer. Pathetic. By the end of the summer, most of Mardi's so-called friends would have overdosed or been shipped off to rehab. There would be no one left to remember her anyway.

Despite her irritation, Molly couldn't help but feel a little bit comforted by the sight of the phantom rose gold ring drifting over her sister's mouth, the ring that she alone could see. The twins shared a secret language that might come in handy in the boonies of the East End. At some point, they just might need to shore each other up.

She fiddled with the ring on her finger, the physical model for the image that drifted secretly across the twins' posts. The ring was warm and luminous, its diamond-shaped grooves pleasantly worn, like a kind old woman's face. She and Mardi passed the ring back and forth between the middle fingers of their right hands. The exchange was almost unconscious and totally peaceful. In every other aspect of their lives, from who got the most cereal in her breakfast bowl to who got to control the playlist at a party to which girl got more of Daddy's attention, the twins were viciously competitive. "It's not fair!" was their constant refrain. But when it came to the ring, which they had shared for as long as they could remember, there was simply no issue. It drifted between them. And they had a tacit understanding that one of them would keep it at all times.

Frustrated with Molly's distraction, Leo checked out her phone too. "Wow," he said. "Is that Mardi? She looks hot!"

Spiked with jealousy, Molly pulled him closer and kissed him harder.

"Whoa." He laughed, enjoying her passion after such a tepid make-out session earlier. "I've never seen you take anything so personally."

Molly refrained from replying, locking him in a rage-infused kiss instead. She jammed her tongue down his throat and kept it there until the limo pulled up in front of his family's ten-million-dollar vine-covered house.

Feeling confident that she had erased any impression her sister might have made on *her* boyfriend, Molly waved him off. He stumbled onto his vast lawn, racket bag slung over his shoulder, and in an instant, he crumpled under the bag's weight. She watched, cackling to herself as he squirmed in a helpless puddle, gradually going still. Someone would find him in a few hours and assume he was wickedly hungover. He would remember nothing.

Causing silly boys to black out was a favorite sport of Molly's.

As the limo glided back toward the Montauk Highway, she put her headphones on and scrolled through for her go-to song. Over the blasting music, she yelled to the driver that she hoped he knew where they were going, because she herself had no idea of East End geography. All she had was an address.

He said the GPS wasn't showing him the place exactly, but he was sure they would find it.

She shrugged. She wasn't in any hurry to greet her oppressive fate.

Why was Daddy doing this to them? Why was he so intimidated by the White Council? If the Council wanted to punish her and Mardi, they would have done so already. But Daddy was convinced that, this time, after the havoc they had wreaked on Headingley Prep and the wild accusations flying in all directions, things would be different. If Molly and Mardi didn't shape up and start to use their magic "responsibly"—yawn—Daddy feared they would be hurled into Limbo or some such ridiculous thing. But he was wasting his time worrying. And, worse, he was wasting their precious summer by banishing them to North Hampton, because she and her sister were never going to change their ways. No one could make them. There was no point in trying.

Molly belted along with Iggy Azalea as the green of the Montauk Highway started to give way to the gold of undulating sand dunes. She scrolled down her posts, looking to see if anyone had "liked" the photo she had taken earlier, when it had occurred to her that she should put up something tragic and artistic about her upcoming fate, a tableau of nature to be followed by radio silence. Make them wonder.

She'd told the driver to pull over for a minute, teetered out onto a dune in her stilettos and snapped a shot of a seagull. She hoped Bret Farley would be intrigued, but so far there was no indication he had seen it—no "likes" no "favorites."

Why did she care whether or not Bret saw her post? She repressed an image of his ice-blond hair, blue eyes, and sharp cheekbones, wanting to banish him from her mind like last year's platform shoes. But his memory was haunting her—perhaps because he was the one that got away? Bretland Farley was the ultimate pair of designer stilettos that were all sold out in her size.

For a while she pouted in silence. Then she put her headphones back on.

As the limo eased into a sudden bank of fog, the bright day grew misty and strange, and Molly grew uneasy about what lay before her.

"Are we almost there?" she whined.

She couldn't hear the answer to her question because her ears were suddenly ringing with a full orchestral sound. It was a total rush. She recognized it as the theme music for some famous movie that Daddy was into. *Apocalypse* something. While the orchestra galloped forward, louder and louder, she envisioned helicopters and exploding bombs. She was carried away from the moment in a thrilling fever vision.

Then it was if her soul had been deposited on the other side of a dream. The sky was bright again, everything was calm, and Iggy was rapping again, boasting about how fabulous she was. Molly knew the feeling.

"We made it," the driver chirped with palpable relief as they passed a WELCOME TO NORTH HAMPTON sign.

They drove through peaceful fields of corn and potatoes, a peach orchard. There were quaint farmhouses that probably weren't air-conditioned, a shabby bar called the North Inn, and some beachside restaurants advertising local fare on chalkboards. There was no frozen yogurt, no Starbucks. Molly looked desperately along the road for any brand names she might recognize. At this point, she would have settled for a Duane Reade pharmacy. But there was nothing. She was going to wither and die here.

Her feed had stopped. It was just as Ingrid had warned in her email: North Hampton was not wired for social networking—no Facebook, no Tumblr, no Twitter, no Snapchat, nada. You could text and email here, but that was about it. When you came to North Hampton, your whole being was immersed in the actual place, rather than scattered throughout cyberspace. "In some ways," Ingrid had written, "North Hampton is outside of time. It is the perfect place to reflect."

At the very moment that Molly's limo pulled up to a beachfront colonial house, freshly painted robin's egg blue, with a saltbox roof and white gables, Mardi's idiotic Ferrari screeched to halt in the unpaved driveway. Molly waited for the dust to settle before she nodded to her driver to open her door. She didn't want to ruin her Prada shift. She couldn't imagine that this town boasted a decent dry cleaner.

Molly surveyed the front yard: a swing set, a dome-shaped jungle gym, and a huge vegetable patch. Then she turned her eyes to her sister.

The twins emerged tentatively from their respective vehicles.

"Nice ride," they sneered at each other in unison.

✳ 3 ✳

AMERICAN PIE

$\mathcal{S}$omething about the little family that rushed out of the pretty gabled house in welcome made Mardi wistful, but only for a second. She quickly remembered she had no desire to be here, and no desire to like these people she was stuck with.

She recognized Ingrid, a.k.a. Erda, from old pictures of Dad's, since witches don't age unless they choose to (they had that on the vampires at least). She was fair and slender in a flour-dusted red apron tied over a blue eyelet sundress. Her blond hair was swooped into a loose bun.

Ingrid's daughter, who looked just like her except for two missing front teeth, was also wearing a red apron. In her case, though, the flour was everywhere. The poor kid's hair was practically white.

The mortal next to Ingrid had to be her husband, Matt Noble. He was very fit, handsome, with salt-and-pepper hair and chin stubble. He held a squirming towheaded baby who was wearing nothing but an unbleached diaper. When the baby started to fuss, Matt began to curl him up and down like a barbell, eliciting delighted squeals.

Mardi forced a smile. Playing house with a mortal might be fun for a few years. But eventually, Ingrid was going to watch him age, drool, and die, Mardi said to herself, with the wicked sensation she derived from seeing insects splatter on her windshield. Beneath her evil glee she felt an undercurrent of sadness.

"Welcome to the East End!" Ingrid hugged each girl, while Matt stopped his antics with the kid long enough to reach out and shake their hands.

"I bet you can tell that Jo and I have been baking." Ingrid gestured happily to the little girl's flour-covered hair. "We've just put two pies in the oven. I hope you like pie."

Mardi nodded slowly. "Sure, I like pie." She had never met anyone who actually baked. Or cooked for themselves, for that matter.

Ingrid seemed to know what the girl was thinking.

"You probably don't get to do a lot of cooking with your father in New York, what with all the restaurants he likes to go to."

"I don't think Dad knows how to turn on the stove in our kitchen. We either go out, eat cereal, or get takeout."

"You won't find any takeout in this house," Matt

chimed in. "My mother-in-law, Joanna Beauchamp, who is still in charge of the place even from beyond the grave, wouldn't hear of it."

Ingrid laughed and squeezed his arm. "My mother equated eating takeout with being depressed," she said, quickly adding, "But, of course, everyone has a different perspective—and different circumstances." Obviously, she didn't want to seem critical of the twins' bachelor lifestyle right off the bat. "Come in. Come in."

The house was more spacious and hip inside than one would expect. Walls had been knocked down to create an open kitchen and living space. The wide-planked wooden floors were painted white. The furniture was midcentury modern mixed in with some Italian leather pieces and a smattering of well-chosen antiques. Windows had been enlarged to create great pools of light.

Mardi, who had been envisioning an overstuffed French Provençal nightmare, was palpably relieved. Glancing at Molly, she could tell her twin felt the same.

Matt noticed them looking appreciatively around and explained that his architect brother had helped them remodel the place when they moved in ten years ago.

"And the spirit of Joanna Beauchamp didn't mind all the changes?" Mardi quipped.

Not at all, Matt said. Joanna herself had been a compulsive remodeler and redecorator. She believed houses were alive and should always be evolving. It was only where home cooking was concerned that she was a deep traditionalist.

Speaking of which, thought Mardi, the pies were starting to smell amazing.

Matt offered to take Jo and Henry on a walk to give Ingrid and the girls some time to get to know one another.

As soon as he and the kids were gone, Ingrid shifted her tone slightly, becoming more serious, piercing almost. Before the twins knew it, they were sitting side by side on a white leather sectional, holding glasses of herbal iced tea full of lemon wedges. Ingrid faced them, ramrod straight, on a chocolate-brown ottoman.

"Girls," Ingrid began, "your father sent you to me because he is worried about you. Thor—I mean Troy—is one of my oldest friends, we've known each other for years, give or take a century here and there—and I've promised him I would try to help you learn to use your magic."

Molly interrupted her, "What I don't get is why Daddy doesn't want to deal with us himself. What's he doing that's so important that he has to, literally, farm us out? Commercial real estate deals in Brooklyn?"

Mardi glared at Molly, willing her to shut up. It would be so much smarter in this situation to fly under the radar than to be confrontational. This wasn't some mortal moron they were dealing with. This witch was as powerful as they were, if not more.

Ingrid seemed unfazed by the interruption. "Troy tells me you are completely out of control, that you are hexing and wreaking havoc out in the open all over New York City, and that there was even a certain fatal situation among your classmates. I understand the White Council is threatening to send you to the Underworld, pending the results of the mortal police investigation. If anything like the Salem witch trials occurs in Midgard again, we could all be punished." She let that sink in. Mardi squirmed and felt Molly doing the same next to her.

Mardi didn't want to think about what had happened just a few weeks ago. The accident on the night of that half-remembered party at Bret's. The fatal one that Ingrid had just mentioned.

"Listen, the Council could reimpose the Restriction of Magical Powers that we suffered under for centuries before it was lifted only ten years ago. Every one of us could be condemned to a life in the shadows. And you two could be banished forever to the Kingdom of the Dead. Am I making my point?"

The girls looked at her blankly.

Ingrid sighed. "Your father warned me that none of this seems to trouble either of you. Can one of you at least tell me what's been going on? What happened with those kids who fell onto the subway tracks? Please tell me that wasn't you."

"Of course not!" cried Mardi.

"It wasn't our fault!" whined Molly.

"Molly, let me explain!"

"No, wait, Mardi, I'm talking!"

"Girls"—Ingrid remained calm—"may I remind you that you are sixteen years old? You're bickering like toddlers."

Molly smirked. "Point taken. Mardi, why don't you do the honors?"

Mardi was suddenly furious. As soon as Molly didn't want to be the one explaining, then neither did she. She realized she had been tricked, left holding the burning potato.

"Fine, whatever," Mardi snapped. "It's true we maybe have a little too much fun with our powers sometimes. But we had nothing to do with what happened to Parker and Sam. We were at the same party on the Upper East Side, at Bret Farley's, but . . ."

The problem was that, while both twins clamored instinctively to have the last word, neither one of them could remember what actually happened the night Parker Fales and Samantha Hill fell onto the tracks in front of an oncoming 6 train.

"We mess with people. But we don't *kill* them." Even as she was sure she was telling the truth, Mardi was nervous because she intuited that they had been involved at the scene of the crime somehow. She wished she could remember that night with any kind of clarity, but there was a gray fog around her memory.

Mardi looked to her sister for help, but Molly appeared as confused and uncomfortable as she did. She was fiddling anxiously with the rose gold ring on her right hand. She slipped it off and handed it to Mardi, who put it on her own hand without missing a beat.

Ingrid, sensing the girls' discomfort, softened her tone. "Listen, don't worry about the sequence of events right now. We have all summer to get the bottom of it. Let's just establish some practical boundaries for the time being, okay?"

"Okay," said Mardi, relieved to be off the hook but also dreading the rules that were about to be laid down.

"First of all, my family. Matt, as you must know, is mortal, and he's the chief of police. He knows I'm a witch and that I use my magic primarily to help people in town with medical and emotional issues, but we have an understanding that there is no magic in the house. We try to keep things as normal as possible. When the Restriction was lifted, the deal was that we witches could practice magic, *as long as we didn't draw too much attention to our supernatural abilities.* Matt"—she cracked a smile—"is a rules guy."

"What about the kids?" asked Mardi.

Ingrid explained that Jo had definitely inherited her powers but that they weren't sure about Henry yet. He certainly seemed to emerge unscathed from some pretty hairy situations, but maybe he was simply a lucky boy. Matt was hoping his son would take after him, but for now, only time would tell.

"So, keep it on the down low, here in the house and in town as well. What we are going to work on, girls, is using your magic for good. And using it with subtlety, which," she said as she smiled at their brash and contrasting outfits, "doesn't appear to be a strength yet."

4

ROYALS

You little . . . ! You spilled raspberry fruit goo on my Alexander McQueen top! This was one of that last pieces he designed before he killed himself!" Molly looked desperately down at the large spot spreading over her neckline and glared at Henry. "This piece," she said, her voice trembling with indignation, "is a treasure . . . or at least it *was* a treasure."

Molly recoiled to a safe distance from the boy's filthy hands. He squealed with delight at her distress, the organic red sludge dribbling down his chin. At least he was contained in his high chair and couldn't come after her to do more damage.

Matt, Ingrid, Jo, and Mardi all milled around the kitchen island as if nothing had happened, making macaroni and cheese ("homemade, never from a box!") and nibbling on the remains of the otherworldly delicious strawberry rhubarb pies that Ingrid and Jo had baked to welcome the twins into their home. Nobody seemed remotely concerned that this devil in diapers had just ruined a priceless top, one of the linchpins of Molly's wardrobe, a classic in cream-and-black-striped silk with a built-in corset. McQueen had designed it expressly for his muse Annabelle Neilson. There were only three in existence, Annabelle's, Giselle's, and Molly's.

Molly was in shock. And the "no magic in the house" rule meant that she couldn't do anything to lift the stain until she got outside, by which time it would probably be too late for her powers to save the situation.

Matt and Ingrid were going to a party that night at Fair Haven, which they described as a glorious historic mansion on its own private island facing the town. Gardiners Island it was called, after the Gardiner family, the oldest and wealthiest of North Hampton's clans. Supposedly the house had just undergone a fabulous renovation and this party was to be the unveiling. There were at least three hundred people invited. Matt and Ingrid hoped the girls wouldn't mind if they went out on the night of their arrival, but they couldn't resist the chance to see what the Gardiners had done with the place.

Molly couldn't believe she was going to have to sit at home with these kids while there was a party going on where she actually might be able to show off some of her wardrobe and have a bit of fun. After only a few hours in this godforsaken place, she was already feeling totally deprived.

Affecting dignity in the face of her tragic situation,

she announced that she was going upstairs to her room to change into something more appropriate for the evening at home. But as she started toward the staircase, she was struck by a brilliant, if obvious, idea.

"Hey," she said. "Ingrid, Matt, you really don't need *both* of us to babysit, do you? I mean, I'm sure Mardi could handle it. She's *great* with kids. She tells *awesome* stories. You don't mind if I come with you, right? Meet some people? It's not like I'm going to hang out at that skanky North Inn bar."

"The North Inn is where my sister Freya works," said Ingrid matter-of-factly.

Molly felt Mardi's hard black eyes on her, scornful and victorious. Mardi loved it when Molly made a fool of herself. Needless to say, it was mutual.

"Well, I'm sure it's a cool bar." Molly tried to back-pedal. "I mean, how can it not be? All I'm saying is that I would love to check out Fair Haven and meet some people." She was already thinking about what she would wear. She could see that Ingrid and Matt weren't going to mind. It all hinged on her sister now.

Ingrid stirred a big lump of butter into some whole-wheat penne with grated cheddar and poured the mixture into an earthenware baking dish. "Well, I suppose it's fine with us, right, Matt?" He nodded, sprinkling bread crumbs, freshly crushed from a day-old baguette, onto his wife's pasta mixture.

They really were a team, thought Molly. Bummer that it would only last a few decades. What was Ingrid thinking? Mortals were to be played with, but not married. Hadn't Ingrid gotten the memo? Wasn't she supposed to be the smart one here?

"Do you mind if I go, Mardi?" Molly asked testily.

"You think I want to go to some silly Gatsby-style party?" Mardi made the finger-down-throat gag-me sign.

"Okay! Thanks! I'll go get dressed." Phew.

"But you owe me one!" Mardi's voice followed her up the stairs.

Molly decided on a buttery suede miniskirt that zipped up front and back, purchased this past spring during a long weekend in Paris. Daddy had taken her along on a business trip but of course had had no time for her and had given her his credit card to assuage his guilt. Such an easy target, her father, so much guilt for never spending any time with them. She paired the skirt with a simple blush-colored silk top and silver mules that her personal shopper had sourced for her from an image she'd seen in Italian *Vogue*.

As Molly, Ingrid, and Matt crossed the bridge to Gardiners Island in the family's maroon Subaru wagon, Molly's spirits lifted. The dunes surrounding the mansion of Fair Haven were lit up to a fiery gold with giant torches. The house itself burned bright and beckoning. This might not be such a lame summer after all.

After a valet whisked their car into the twilight,

they started up a blazing path bordered with iridescent white peony bushes in full bloom. The crowd, Molly noticed immediately, was well-dressed for the most part, in a clubby, preppy sort of way. Not too shabby. This was more like it.

Through large picture windows, she could see what looked like a ballroom hung with baroque chandeliers, alight with wax candles. Somewhere out of view, a band softly tuned its strings. A rogue flute trilled and then went silent.

As a waiter handed Molly a flute of champagne and she waved away a tray of hors d'oeuvres, she felt a pair of eyes gazing upon her with startling intensity. She blushed inside. Before she knew it, a graceful hand had whisked away her glass and handed her another. Its champagne had fewer bubbles than the first. The color was darker, more like honey than wine.

"Try this instead," came a suave voice. "It's vintage. You are much too beautiful tonight to be drinking brut."

"Too beautiful *tonight*?" Molly's flirting instinct surged. She flipped back her silky curtain of blue-black hair to look squarely at her interlocutor. "Why only tonight?"

"Not *only* tonight. But *especially* tonight." The voice belonged to a stunning young man of about seventeen. He was olive skinned with jet-black hair and chiseled cheekbones. His blue eyes twinkled in striking contrast to his dark features. He wore a navy blazer over a bespoke shirt of white linen with a discreet monogram on its cuff: the initials TG in delicate silk of the deepest red. Could he be one of the Gardiner brothers who owned Fair Haven?

As if reading her thoughts, he introduced himself. "Welcome to Fair Haven. I'm Trystan Gardiner. Call me Tris."

"Molly Overbrook." She held out her hand for him to shake. She was surprised to find herself a tad nervous. Usually, she was the one who intimidated all the boys. But Tris was utterly cool, calm, and gracious, while she had butterflies in her stomach. He was so formal, yet so familiar. As she clinked her champagne flute with his, her hand trembled ever so slightly. "Beautiful house," she managed.

"Yes, it's wonderful to come back to. My family was away from it for ages. Until about ten years ago, Fair Haven was a relic. There was no one on this island except the ospreys who nested all over our beaches. They still do make their home here, of course."

He was in boarding school in England, and his older brothers had overseen a complete restoration of the house and grounds. They were off again, traveling the world, and he lived in the house with their stepmother. He gestured a few feet farther up the torch-lit path to an immaculately groomed older woman wearing a summery Chanel suit and two-toned pumps, who was deep in conversation with Ingrid and Matt, most likely about finishes and light fixtures.

"So," Molly asked, "how are you dealing in North Hampton? Is there anything to do here?"

He looked her over appreciatively, her glittering blue-black eyes, cascading hair, calf muscles taut in her silver mules. It was as if he were sculpting a masterpiece with his sharp blue gaze.

Molly had never felt quite so beautiful, and that was saying something.

"Hm." He repeated her question: "Is there anything to do here?" His smile was both wicked and winning. "Well, there certainly is now that I've met you, Molly Overbrook."

* 5 *

RESCUE ME

*O*nce the grown-ups had pulled out of the driveway, Mardi took Jo and Henry to the beach in front of the house. She tossed a blanket over the silver sand, and they sat down and watched the sunsct with Fair Haven lit up on Gardiners Island across the bay.

Henry had a bucket that he filled with little fistfuls of sand. He dumped it out over and over, with no signs of boredom or slowing down. Kids were so weird. Mardi supposed she was going to have to give him a bath after this to get the sand off his body before putting him to bed, and she shuddered at the drudgery of it all. She was never having children.

Jo kept running her finger over Mardi's rainbow tattoo, murmuring, "It's so, so, so pretty!" It was all Mardi could do not to swat the little girl away from her neck.

Finally, she pulled herself to standing and suggested they go put their feet in the water.

"Sure," said Jo. "But will you tell me why you have a rainbow bridge on your neck?"

Startled, Mardi inhaled sharply. "Why did you call it a bridge?"

Without answering, Jo demanded, "Tell me the story of the rainbow bridge! Molly promised you tell good stories!"

Frigging Molly, thought Mardi with a grimace. Molly was across Gardiner Bay, probably sipping champagne and nibbling caviar toasts and smoked salmon, while she was stuck babysitting.

Obviously, Jo wasn't going to leave Mardi alone until she talked about her tattoo. She might as well get it over with. It was a story their father had told them when they were young, when they asked the usual questions about their family and where they came from.

"I'm surprised your mom hasn't told you! You see, my rainbow bridge, like you called it, is actually the Bofrir Bridge, a magical bridge built by the king of the gods so that all the other gods could travel from Middle Earth, which is the ordinary world where we all live now, to their palace in heaven, a castle called Valhalla, which was built using the labor of dragons."

"Neat!"

Phew, the kid seemed satisfied. Mardi had always liked that story about Asgard, she thought as she twisted the ring on her finger.

Suddenly, she felt a brush of soft fur on her ankle.

She looked down to see Jo scooping up a black kitten.

"Midnight!" Jo cried out in delight. "Midnight, where have you been?"

Mardi understood immediately that Midnight and Jo had a magical bond. "Is Midnight your familiar?" she asked wistfully.

"Yes. Are you a witch too?" Jo's question was completely without guile.

"Yes, I am." There was no point in lying.

"And your sister?"

"Yes."

"So, then, where are your familiars? Why didn't they come to live here with you?"

"Our dad made us board them for the summer." Mardi felt a pang for her Siamese cat, Killer, who was stuck in an overpriced pet hotel in SoHo. She missed Killer's steady companionship, her knowing gaze, and deep purr.

Killer had an archenemy in Molly's Fury, a small Löwchen dog, with the typical long feathery hair in front, smooth hindquarters, and upturned fluffy tail. Of course Molly would be shadowed by a specimen of one of the priciest dog breeds on the planet, and one that required heaps of grooming to maintain its absurd hairstyle.

For the most part, the two animals despised one another. Fury yapped at Killer. Killer hissed at Fury. They sometimes even peed in one another's water bowls. But every once in a while, for no apparent reason, they would curl up together and nap, their eyelids fluttering in unison as if to the same dream.

"Henry!" Jo screamed out to sea, shattering Mardi's reverie. "Oh, no!"

Mardi followed the little witch's anxious gaze to discover that the baby boy had somehow managed to launch himself in an orange kayak and was drifting off into the twilight at an alarming rate.

"No!" Mardi screamed, yanking off her sandals. "Jo, stay right here! Don't move! I'll get him!"

As she ran into the water, Mardi watched in horror while the kid stood up, wobbled, spread his arms, and jumped out of the kayak as if he thought he could fly. Then Henry disappeared under the water.

Mardi swam faster than she ever had in her life, knifing through the darkening sea toward the spot where she had seen Henry disappear. Her heart was pounding. Her arms and legs tensed with the muscle memory of the thousands of laps she had swum this past year as a way to calm her anxiety and steady her racing pulse. She had to remind herself to breathe.

She reached the kayak and began diving around it, waving through the water with her arms and legs in the desperate hope of touching a little limb. Nothing.

Then she heard the distinct chime of baby laughter. Miraculously, Henry's chubby fingers were grasping the front tip of the kayak. He was hanging there, feet dangling in the sea, cackling to himself. She grabbed him and held him close.

"Henry, why on earth did you do that?"

By way of answer, he stuck his thumb in her mouth to touch her emerald tongue stud. "Wowie," he squealed. As far as Mardi could tell, his vocabulary consisted of four words: *Mama, Dada, more,* and *wowie.*

The rush of gratitude she felt toward the universe was intense. She burst into tears, then realized she should wave to reassure Jo, who was standing motionless in the surf. Had Jo used magic to rescue her brother? Or was he simply really lucky and really coordinated? Or was it something else?

Mardi lifted him into the seat, grabbed the back of the kayak, and kicked her legs like an outboard motor, propelling it to shore. As she pulled it up onto the wet sand and let Henry scamper out, vowing never to take her eyes off him again when he was in her charge, a gorgeous dark-haired figure appeared on the beach.

Mardi was not easily impressed by physical beauty, but this woman was a total fox. Her hair was dark with red-gold highlights. She was small, more petite than the long, lanky Mardi, and much curvier. She was barefoot in skinny jeans of an iridescent, opaline black that perfectly cinched her tiny waist, along with a silver and bronze silk bustier that would have been cool in any decade over the past thousand years. Her breasts were mesmerizing, perfectly full and high. They should have seemed disproportionate to her tiny frame, but they looked as right and natural as full blossoms on a slender stalk. Her cheekbones popped, and her large green up-slanting eyes twinkled in the light of the rising moon. She didn't look remotely troubled by the fact that the baby had just been pulled from the jaws of the sea.

Mardi recognized this creature instantly as one of her tribe, a goddess from Asgard stuck in Midgard, or Middle Earth, for all eternity after the bridge connecting the two worlds was destroyed centuries ago. Here in Midgard, the gods lived among humans as witches and warlocks. Molly and Mardi's own father, Troy Overbrook, was once known as Thor, god of thunder. And this gorgeous woman on the beach, exuding ripeness and sexuality, had to be Ingrid's sister, Freya, goddess of love. She had reached her eternal age of about twenty-five and would not grow physically older until the end of time, unless of course she chose to.

As if to confirm Mardi's hunch, the young woman held out her pretty hand, smiled blinding white, and said, "Hi, I'm Freya Beauchamp. You must be one of Troy's girls. Ingrid told me you guys were here this summer. Welcome!"

"Thanks. I'm Mardi."

"Nice to meet you. That was an impressive rescue just now. You're a good swimmer."

"I spend a lot of time in the pool back home." Mardi was still wearing her leopard bra and short shorts, which were soaked now. The black dye from the leopard spots was running, streaking her six-pack. This was one of the problems she ran into, wearing clothes of dubious origin.

As if reading Mardi's thoughts, Freya said, "Let's get you guys into some dry clothes. You're shivering, and it looks like Henry's diaper has absorbed half of the water in Gardiner Bay. It's sagging down to his knees. Poor kid."

Inside the house, Mardi toweled Henry off, put him in a dry diaper, then asked if Freya would keep an eye on the kids while she ran upstairs to change.

"Wait a second, are you the only one here? Did they all leave you with Jo and Henry to go to the party on Gardiners Island? That is so uncool. I was stopping by so that we could all head out together."

"No big deal. I didn't want to go anyway. Preppy is not my scene."

Freya let out a silvery laugh.

"Honey, preppy is only the surface of it. You have no idea. I cannot tell you how much fun I've had through the years at Fair Haven. The Gardiner men are something else. Killian and Bran are out of town right now. You might say they're both on hiatus from me. But there's some fresh Gardiner blood in town. Now, get yourself dressed to go out."

"But what about Ingrid's kids?"

Freya was tapping out a number on her phone. "I've got that covered. Ingrid's housekeeper lives down the street, and she loves Henry and Jo. I don't understand why Ingrid didn't call her to come in the first place."

"I think," said Mardi, "that Dad told her to give me and Molly some responsibility. He has this idea that he's going to make good little witches out of us here."

"As if Troy was ever a good boy himself!" Freya gave an ironic smile. "Give me a break."

"I don't want Graciella to put me to bed!" Jo shrieked. "I want Mardi to stay! I want more rainbow stories! Auntie Freya, don't go!"

"Don't be like that, Jo," said Freya firmly. "There's nothing less attractive than a little self-witch. Mardi is going to be here all summer. You'll get plenty of stories. Now, let's take her to the attic and show her our dress-up clothes, shall we? Let's get her ready for the ball."

As they walked up to the attic, with Henry and Midnight crawling up the stairs at their heels, Freya explained that when her mother and father "died," her mother left Ingrid the house because it was obvious that Ingrid was going to have a family. Freya liked children fine, but not half as much as she loved her freedom. Since Matt was moving in with Ingrid, Freya bought his bachelor pad from him. It was a little ways out of town on an isolated strip of beach, a sleek all-glass house that was a peaceful refuge from her busy social job at the North Inn bar. It was perfect for her, except for one thing: there wasn't enough storage space to accommodate the overflow from her epoch-spanning wardrobe.

She had filled every closet. And all the shelves and surfaces were piled with her clothes. It was enough to make minimalist Matt wince whenever he paid a visit to his old home. All this to say that she still used the attic at the Beauchamp homestead as a backup closet, and she was sure they would find something here that Mardi would approve of.

As they opened the house's uppermost door, Mardi gasped. Freya wasn't kidding about quantity. This was a treasure chest of the sexiest fashions from the past hundred years or so, with a focus on the 1920s, '60s, and '70s, and a few throwbacks to much earlier times when undergarments could be spectacular. There were dozens of tiny beaded flapper dresses, suede fringe skirts and tops, rhinestone encrusted micro-minis, corsets and garters, all hanging on bars that went around the four walls of the large room. The space was illuminated by skylights through which the moon poured its glow, so that the pearls, beads, rhinestones, and sequins glimmered like stars. There were rows and rows of shoes, mostly heels, arranged around the room by color. It was as if the attic were encircled by some exotic, multistriped snake.

"What's your pleasure?" asked Freya.

For the first time in her life, Mardi had no idea what she wanted to wear. Her mother had disappeared when they were young, and her sister had a totally different aesthetic, so she'd never had anyone to help her pick out clothes. She had always relied on her innate sense of eclectic thrift-shop style. But this was too much for her to process.

"I'm having total sensory overload," she said with unaccustomed shyness. "You're gonna have to pick something out for me."

"Are you serious?" Freya clapped with glee.

Mardi nodded her coal-dark head.

"Awesome! Jo, help me out here. This is going to be so much fun."

"Nothing pretty, though," Mardi hastened to specify. "I don't do pretty."

"Don't worry, we've got it covered."

In no time, Mardi was outfitted in a pair of denim hot pants with a silky Bengal tiger appliqué across the butt, tall patent boots, a cutoff Lou Reed T-shirt, a light-weight black pigskin vest from back in Freya's New York City days, and an arm's length of black rubber bangles.

Graciella arrived and swept the kids under her wing. Freya declared that the Ferrari was a way cooler ride than her Mini, and the witches screeched off into the night.

* 6 *

I KNEW YOU WERE TROUBLE, PART ONE

$\mathcal{M}$olly sat cross-legged on one of the deep-red velvet poufs strewn throughout the immense candlelit ballroom of Fair Haven in order to receive the weary bodies of its dancing guests. There was an ethereal band playing salsas, tangos, and merengues. She and Tris had been twirling across the floor for seven numbers, and she had sent him to get her another drink as she sank into the plush cushion and let the breeze from the open windows waft over her. The scent of lilacs from the lavish bushes just outside filled her senses. She was deeply content. For about five minutes.

Where the Hell was he? Okay, so he had made a cute comment about needing some extra time to track down another bottle of vintage champagne. But there was no excuse to leave her alone for this long. It *was* his house, wasn't it? Shouldn't he have unfettered access to the best of the booze and a direct line to the staff? If he wasn't back soon, she was going to leave the room, and he would have to search for her if he wanted to see her again this evening. No one kept Molly Overbrook waiting.

She looked around her at the swirling couples and began to feel a familiar itch to perform one of her signature party tricks, like slipping potions into drinks to remove all inhibitions or breaking spaghetti straps with the force of her gaze so that cocktail dresses fell to the floor. She especially liked to undo the work of Botox over the course of a few minutes so that dozens of women, unbeknownst to themselves, would erupt in wrinkles, creases, and worry lines. Each one of them would start smugly thinking how all of her "friends" had suddenly aged, and each would feel great about herself, until she got home, looked in the mirror, and screamed. By the morning after the party, the spell would have worn off, the offending wrinkles would be frozen again, and the whole thing would feel like a distant nightmare. But it sure was fun while it lasted.

Molly, of course, would never need Botox. She and Mardi would remain fresh-faced ever after. Daddy was forever just shy of fifty. And Ingrid would always present between twenty-seven and thirty-two. Molly wondered, though, about the half-mortal kids. Would they go one way or the other? It was a complicated question, and Molly was not one to enjoy thinking too hard, especially when she was alone. Where was that Tris Gardiner? If there was one thing she hated, it was being taken for granted.

A waiter kneeled in front of her pouf, proffering a silver tray with a full caviar service, a generous mound of shining black beluga surrounded by blinis, sour cream, minced red onions, and finely diced hard-boiled eggs. He handed Molly a china plate, and she went about delicately assembling two perfect blinis, trying to stave off the sting of rejection.

As the rich salty burst of flavor swirled through her mouth, a fresh vision from the past rose up inside her, vivid and urgent. There had been an obscene amount of caviar that crazy night in New York at Bret Farley's. The luxurious taste, along with the plush feel of velvet on her skin, sparked her senses, giving rise to whole new layer of memory. As the music and dancers blurred around her, she began to recall more of the buried details of that fateful party. That cool April night, the first buds out on the trees lining Park Avenue, came flooding back to her.

Both Molly and Mardi suspected that Bret was one of them. A warlock. There was something supernatural about his charm. But he hadn't given them any clear indication, and so they all three danced around the possibility.

The twins had never been attracted to the same guy

before, and Molly couldn't imagine that Mardi would be interested in someone as mainstream rich as Bret. But he seemed to know how to engage Mardi, and Molly didn't like this fact one bit.

That mysterious night, searching to ground herself with a familiar sensation, she had felt her right hand for her ring. It wasn't there. Had she passed it to Mardi without noticing? This had happened before, of course, since the ring slid so automatically between them. But she was positive she had been the one wearing it when they left for Bret's party, and she had no recollection of coming close to Mardi since they arrived. Certainly not close enough to slip a ring on her finger. Weird. She must have drunk that first champagne too fast.

She tried to steal a look at Mardi's hand through the doorway, but Bret and Mardi were now talking to a couple of juniors from Headingley. Parker and Sam, she thought their names were. They were a freshly minted couple, hanging all over each other. Their conjoined bodies blocked Molly's view of her sister.

After this, her mental image of the party grew fuzzy again. Her vision began to ebb. The last things she felt with any clarity were her frustration at not being able to check Mardi's hand to make sure she had the ring, and her insane jealousy of Bret's attention to her twin.

Later, of course, Parker and Sam would end up dead, crushed by a subway train in the early hours of Sunday morning, and Molly and Mardi, infamous for their pranks at school, would be prime suspects. But

Molly knew she and her twin had nothing against either Parker or Sam, and she had no memory of the accident. Her sole lingering sensation was one of strange powerlessness.

Emerging from her vision in the middle of the ball at Fair Haven, Molly looked down at her empty plate. In the throes of her involuntary memory, she had eaten all of her beluga. All around her, the Fair Haven ballroom came back into focus. The candles, the velvet, the dancers, the sparkling drinks, the scent of lilacs through the open windows. It was all perfection. Except for one thing. Tris Gardiner was still not back at her side. Annoying!

Like her sister, Molly had a quick temper. She looked around the ballroom for a suitable object on which to take out her rage. She envisioned shattering the lead plate windows that had been the most expensive aspect of the renovation, according to Tris. Or she could send one of the brand-new Swarovski crystal chandeliers crashing down amid the dancers. Or she could pierce the giant silver punch bowl on the buffet table with a hundred tiny holes, turning it into a strainer so that the bloodred liquid would flood out all over the freshly finished ebony floors. Perhaps she could set that sweet-smelling lilac bush outside aflame. That would be kinda fun.

But then another idea occurred to her, an idea so

good it simply took over and became stronger than she was. Before she could stop herself, everyone dancing at the party—and there were at least a dozen of them—grabbed their stomachs and started to heave violently, turning the dance floor into a slick of vomit. The band clanged to a stop amid mass screaming. "It's the oysters!" "It's the scallops!" "It's the shrimp!" "Somebody call an ambulance!"

Molly surveyed the ensuing chaos with the calm of one who had given expression to a violent impulse and no longer felt any pressure building inside. Her pent-up anger released, the world felt light again. Nothing could touch her. Certainly not some vain, ridiculous boy.

Breezily, Molly rose from her velvet cushion and sauntered among the black-clad staff rushing to the scene with mops, buckets, and towels. The guests, bewildered, were looking down at their ruined dresses and shoes. Molly chuckled to herself. It wasn't everyone who could cause sudden stomach flu.

"What do you think you're doing, young lady?" Ingrid was blocking Molly's path, shaking her head so hard the blond strands were falling from her bun, giving her an ironic beauty in the midst of her anger.

"What are you talking about?" Molly twirled her thick gold chain and batted her dark eyes in a parody of innocence.

"I may be many things, Molly, but I'm not stupid. I know that was you," Ingrid whispered furiously, taking Molly by the arm and leading her firmly into the garden, out of earshot of the traumatized party guests.

Quelle buzzkill.

Molly realized there was no point in trying to lie to Ingrid. So she took a different tack: "Okay, look, I'm sorry. I can't always control myself. I was dealing with some negative feelings just now. Some really tough stuff with Daddy that I have to work through. Sometimes the magic just flows, you know."

"Actually, kid, there is really no excuse for making people vomit in unison. None whatsoever. I don't care how miserable you are."

"Obviously, you have no sense of what it's like to be raised by a single parent."

"In truth, dear, I do. But that's another story. And it's not what we're talking about here. We're talking about the fact that you need to learn how to control your magic. We can't have vicious spells erupting from you girls every time you get bored at a party."

Eye roll.

"I can imagine that Troy isn't always the most present father, although I know he loves you very much. You girls are going through something difficult, with that investigation in New York and the Council on your backs. Which is why it is all the more important that you stop acting so frivolous right now and get a grip on your powers. Am I making myself clear?"

"Sure." Molly wanted out of this conversation pronto.

She was no fan of lectures. "Fine, I promise, no more magic for the rest of the party."

"The rest of the party?" Ingrid flared. "As far as we're concerned, this party's over."

"But we've only been here for about an hour! Look, I swear, I'll be good. You and Matt can't be ready to leave already."

"Actually, Matt has a headache. He'll be glad for an excuse to go."

"A headache. Really? God, it must suck to be mortal."

Ingrid simply glared at her, refusing to dignify her comment with a response.

Molly started to squirm. "You're really going to drag me home like some little kid?"

"We're going to treat you like a little kid until you stop acting like one."

✳ 7 ✳

EVERYBODY EATS WHEN THEY COME TO MY HOUSE

As a wildly impressed valet whisked the Ferrari off to the large clearing in the dunes that served as a parking lot for the Fair Haven party, Mardi looked up the torch-lit path toward the spectacular old mansion. Night had fallen, and the lush grounds were mostly in shadow so that the trees and bushes appeared as dark figures, like spirits hovering in the gloaming. Mardi got a strong vibe from this place, not spooky exactly, but charged. Gardiners Island was definitely a place that spanned two worlds.

As she and Freya started up the path, all eyes on their stunning figures, Mardi was startled to see Molly, Matt, and Ingrid heading toward her with hanging heads.

"Hey, guys!"

They looked up, startled. "Freya! Mardi! What are you doing here?" Ingrid was trying to look pleased by the surprise but was obviously confused. "Who's watching the kids?"

Matt's expression of alarm perfectly mimicked his wife's. It was as if they spoke as one, Mardi thought with a twitch of sadness that she quickly squelched. Ingrid had made her own bed by marrying a mortal man. Why did Mardi keep feeling sorry for her?

"I called Graciella," Freya explained. "I stopped by to see if we could head to the party together and found poor Mardi stuck at home. It didn't seem fair."

"I guess you're right," said Ingrid. "We should have left both of them home."

Whoa, Mardi thought, noting that her sister had a "busted" look all over her face. *What did she do?* Mardi was dying to know. A pleasure in party tricks was something the sisters actually shared.

"They obviously aren't ready to handle adult situations yet," Ingrid fumed.

"Lighten up, Ingrid," said Freya. "If you and Matt are tired and want to head out, I can chaperone both of them."

"No, we'll take Molly," Ingrid said decidedly. Then she remembered her manners. "Oh, Molly, this is my sister, Freya."

"Cool skirt," said Freya, holding out her hand. She had finished her skinny jean and metallic bustier outfit with six-inch python heels and a python belt, and she looked even more stunning than she had back on the beach.

"Thanks. Cool shoes!" said Molly, clasping Freya's fingers as if they could somehow hold her back and save her from the ride of shame home in the family Subaru.

"Time to go, Molly," said Ingrid. "You girls can continue your lovefest some other time. I'm sure Freya's closet is big is enough for all of you."

Molly cast Freya a thanks-for-trying look as she sulked off behind her captors.

Mardi couldn't help but feel a tad gratified at her sister's misfortune. There was some relief at having this beautiful summer evening all to herself. With her twin gone, Mardi didn't have to compete all night. Now she could relax into her own skin and really check this crazy place out.

"Don't mind Molly," she said to Freya. "She's spoiled selfish."

"You really think you're that different from her?" Freya asked.

"Totally!" Mardi shot back. She was caught completely off guard by the question.

Freya frowned thoughtfully. "Ingrid and I might be very different, but we're the best of friends. One day you'll be glad you have a sister who has your back." She grabbed them each a glass of champagne from a passing tray.

Biting her tongue, Mardi accepted the champagne

gladly. While she was normally utterly unconcerned with what others thought of her, she found that she really wanted Freya to like her. Freya was so cosmically cool.

They clinked glasses in the moonlight as a band somewhere inside Fair Haven struck up a waltz. The music swayed out through the enormous open windows of what looked like a chandeliered ballroom. Notes poured over the vast front lawn, enticing the crowd to come inside and dance. Freya and Mardi were carried on the tide toward the house.

As they walked up the path, they reached out to one another and clinked glasses again.

"Champagne really isn't my thing," said Mardi. "It's more Molly's style, as you can probably figure. But this stuff isn't so bad."

"Don't worry," Freya stage-whispered, "I know where they stash the tequila around here."

"Awesome," said Mardi. "You're a bartender, right?"

"That's right. I'm the queen of the North Inn. My drinks are known as love potions. I've created a menu of drinks: Infatuation, Irresistible, Unrequited, Forever . . ." Her mouth shaped the cocktail names as if they were juicy pieces of fruit bursting on her tongue.

Mardi was equally attracted to—and equally wary of—both sexes. Her dad, who was rabidly heterosexual, couldn't understand how she could flow so freely in her appetites. Couldn't she go definitively one way or the other? Mardi looked down at her boots and snarled just thinking about how binary he was. How limited. Freya was probably the sexiest girl she'd ever met, but she was also sort of like an aunt, or an older sister, so that was, um, weird.

"Love potions, huh?" she asked.

"Mardi, the trick to being a—quote unquote—good witch, here on Middle Earth, is to twist your sense of mischief to spreading the love."

"I'm not so sure that spreading love is in my nature. Rage is more like it."

"You'll see." Freya winked a feline eye and turned to say hello to a conservatively dressed middle-aged couple.

Mardi took a step toward the front door. There was an odor of roasting meat wafting from the house. Her nostrils flared. She realized she was starving.

But as she took a step toward Fair Haven's luminous entryway, with its promise of dinner, she was immediately stopped by a silken male voice. "You must be Mardi Overbrook." Someone was blocking her way.

She couldn't stand it when people, men in particular, messed with her freedom of movement. It made her blood boil. "Yeah," she said, pushing around him. "That's me."

"What's the hurry?"

She looked up, annoyed. He was about seventeen, in ripped jeans, a T-shirt, and a beat-up leather jacket. His hair and skin were dark like hers, but his eyes were as brilliant blue as hers were deepest brown. She could see his lean form through his thin T-shirt. His arm muscles rippled in the moonlight; he must be a swimmer like her.

She was taken. But to his face, she said, with all the coldness she could muster, "If you must know, I'm headed to the buffet."

"Do you want me to show you the fastest way?"

In spite of herself, she cracked a smile. "I'm sure I can find it. I know how to take care of myself."

"That," he said, "is perfectly obvious. Just think of me as a means to an end. Your support staff. I know where the kitchen is, and I have friends here on the inside."

"Do you work here or something?"

"I live here. Or I could live here if I felt like it. It's my house. I mean, my brothers are the ones who brought it back to life for the family, and my stepmother is really into it now. She gives garden tours and stuff."

"So how come you don't live here if it's your family's house?"

"I like my brother's boat better. It's a fishing yacht called the *Dragon*. I spend most of my nights there, on the water. I'm Trent Gardiner, by the way."

"Hi, Trent," she said.

"Hi, Mardi."

"How do you know who I am?"

"Freya told me about you and Molly coming to town for the summer."

"You're tight with Freya?"

"She's close to my older brothers, Killian and Bran. Close to both of them, if you know what I mean. She's got a lot of love to go around."

"So I gather."

As they talked, he guided her into the house with a hand on the small of her back. Normally, this would have driven her crazy with the urge to hex him, to web his hands into duck feet or make his gums bleed profusely, but somehow she didn't mind. There was nothing condescending or controlling in his touch, it was firm, gentle, protective.

The buffet in the crystalline ballroom, with its huge windows open onto fragrant gardens, was lush and bountiful. Jaded as she was from Manhattan excess, Mardi still couldn't help but be impressed. She wasn't so much struck by the cost of the food—she knew well from her private school world that there was no limit to what people could spend—as she was touched by the loving attention to detail. There was a suckling pig turning on a spit over an open flame, a perfectly rare prime rib and a glimmering lacquered duck breast. There were duck-fat potatoes; truffle risotto; green beans tossed in an almond pesto; a salad of local tomatoes, grilled peaches, and feta, sprinkled with basil from the Fair Haven garden; and another salad of shaved fennel and fresh fava beans. Even though she knew it had been expensively catered, Mardi could tell that someone had given this meal a lot of thought.

"Is your stepmother a foodie?" she asked over the music as she filled her plate.

Trent laughed. "My stepmother lives on saltines, gin, and Fresca. I'm the foodie. This is my menu," he gestured to the spread. "What do you think?"

"I'll let you know when I've tasted it."

"Make sure you get some of the risotto. I stirred it myself."

"You cook?" She nearly spit out the champagne she was swallowing.

"Why so surprised?" His eyes twinkled mischievously.

She thought about it. "I shouldn't be. Everyone watches the Food Channel these days."

"Ah, so now I'm just like everyone?"

"No you're not, actually. I know lots of people who watch cooking shows, I don't know anyone who really cooks."

"Follow me," he commanded softly.

Instead of bristling, she happily trailed him, sensing that he was taking her somewhere she would have chosen to go on her own. Balancing their laden plates, she and Trent meandered through a labyrinth of passageways and down a pine staircase into a vast basement kitchen with large French doors framing a sunken herb garden. There were so many copper pots hanging from the ceiling that Mardi had the urge to take a soft mallet and play them like gongs.

The staff smiled at Trent fondly. No one skipped a

beat when he opened a double-wide Sub-Zero—another part of the renovation, he explained—and pulled out a stash of foie gras terrine. He said he had made it himself. "And you have to have some of this cherry compote with the foie gras. I did it with cherries from our orchard."

Was this gorgeous boy really talking to her about compote? About how he didn't use a cherry pitter because he preferred the sensation of pitting the cherries with his fingers?

"Why are you looking at me funny?" he finally asked.

"I've never met a domestic person before." She almost added, *especially one who looks like you*, but she figured he could read this aside in her eyes if he was paying attention.

"North Hampton will do that to you," he replied. "I wasn't into this stuff when I got here either. I always liked good food, but I thought you bought it. I guess there's some kind of connection to nature here. Or to the past. It's kind of a wormhole that way. You know, Freya's an awesome cook."

"Really?" It was hard to picture Freya in an apron. "I can't see Freya over a hot stove. But her sister, Ingrid, makes great strawberry rhubarb pie. Too bad she's so uptight."

Trent walked Mardi through the herb garden around the side of the mansion to a restored eighteenth-century greenhouse. He unlatched the door and led her inside, where he gave her a quick tour of the twisting palm trees, *Agave ferox*, African violets, Swiss cheese plants with bright lacy fronds. There was a reflecting pool where pink and white water lilies floated in harmony. Interspersed with the larger plants were the herbs Freya used for her potions at the North Inn: damiana, burdock, feverfew, valerian, catnip, and angelica root, to name a few. Trent told Mardi that his brother Killian had planted them for Freya. "Ten years ago, this place was a ruin. Killian brought it back to life for her."

They sat on a bench, and Mardi attacked her plate.

He watched her and smiled, amused. "You don't eat like a girl, do you? I'm sorry, was that sexist?"

"Sort of," she said, "but I agree. I hate the way most girls eat. Like my sister, for example. It's either tiny bites of caviar and sips of champagne or nonfat frozen yogurt and Diet Coke. The only time she actually eats is when she sees I have something I really like and she insists on taking 'her' half just so I don't get it all."

"Sounds like you guys have a really healthy relationship." He grinned. "Do you want 'your' half of my foie gras?"

Without waiting for her to say yes, he popped a piece of brioche toast, slivered over with foie gras and drizzled with cherry compote, into her mouth. From someone else, it could have been a forceful, annoying gesture. But it was exactly what she wanted from Trent.

"Wow. Thanks for sharing. And by the way, you said Freya had told you about Molly and me coming to North

Hampton. But how did you know which sister I was when you saw me?"

Trent searched her face with his sea-deep eyes. "Freya had the lowdown on you both from your dad. She said you were the cool one."

Without giving her time to respond, he leapt to his feet and pulled a metal box out from among the stalks of some long green plant whose leaves were clamped shut like smirking mouths. He opened the box, pulled out a pair of long metal tweezers, extracted a writhing worm, and held it up to one of the bulbous leaves. The tight green lips suddenly parted wide. Trent dropped the worm into the heart of it, and the leaves snapped shut on its prey.

"Venus flytrap," he said. "We're not the only carnivores around here. I promised Killian I would feed them while he's gone."

"Can I have one of those to take home?" Mardi asked breathlessly, fantasizing about how much fun it would be to feed Molly to it piece by piece, first her fingers, then her toes, then her wicked tongue, all the way down to her black, black heart.

"Sorry to interrupt, guys, but I'm low on catnip for the bar," Freya said, appearing in the moonlight carrying a small wicker basket and pair of gardening scissors.

As Freya kneeled to clip, Mardi saw that she was not only a glamorous goddess but a nurturing one. If Mardi hadn't happened to like Freya so much, she would have hated her for being so perfect.

"As long as I'm here, I'm also going to grab a little angelica root."

"Go nuts," said Trent. "It's your greenhouse."

Once Freya had gathered her ingredients, she told Mardi they should probably take off. "We don't want Ingrid on our case," she said.

Trent walked them to their car and gave them each a good-night kiss on the cheek. His faint stubble set Mardi's skin aglow. He squeezed her hand, pressing her ring softly into his palm.

"See you around?" she asked.

"It's a small town," he replied with a smile.

As Mardi shifted the old Ferrari from first gear into second, heading away from Fair Haven toward the bridge to the mainland, she checked her rearview mirror to see Trent's strong dark figure silhouetted against the starlit sky. He was smoldering, yes, with those soul-melting eyes and that hard body, but he was also sweet. Something about him felt like home. A home she had never had.

✳ 8 ✳

YOU BETTER WORK, B★TCH

*W*hy on Earth do I have to get a job, Daddy?"

"Because it's character building."

"I have plenty of character already."

"Touché, Miss Molly, but you're still getting a summer job. There's got to be something to amuse you in North Hampton. What else are you going to do all day? Shop?"

"Do you realize that doing menial labor for two and a half months will barely net me enough for a new handbag this coming fall?"

"I realize that, yes. But many wealthy families who give their kids everything still have them do low-paying jobs as teenagers. These jobs are a part of their education. They teach the value of work."

"So you admit that it's a total pretense."

"Sweetheart, if you and your sister don't learn to integrate better, you are going to spark a modern-day Salem witch trial. Did you read the papers after those kids were killed? Did you watch the news? You have got to start 'pretending,' if that's what you want to call it. We need all the pretense we can get right now."

"But, Daddy, I'm a goddess. Goddesses don't have paper routes. They don't waitress. Or pump gas."

"You're a goddess who is cut off from her natural world. You can only use your powers if you assimilate into this one. Look at the Beauchamp sisters. Ingrid is a librarian. Freya bartends. They inhabit a disorienting space where nobody quite notices that they never age."

"Are you suggesting that I live here in this backwater forever to keep the mortals off my trail? Are you banishing me? That is a fate worse than death, Daddy. You must know that."

"Relax, relax. New York City is a plenty disorienting enough space for you to spend eternity in without anyone batting an eye. I'm not worried about geography. I'm worried about the human authorities accusing and convicting you so that our own higher authorities banish you to the Underworld. I don't want to lose my babies for all eternity. Can you blame me?"

"Okay, okay, okay, fine, I'll get a job, but can we make it fun? Can I be a sleazy, jet-setting, sleight-of-hand real estate tycoon like you?"

"Molly, you're sixteen." Troy sighed. "And I'm not that sleazy, am I?" he asked, sounding wounded.

"No, of course not. You're awesome Daddy, you know that. Look, I can dress way older. Totally pass for twenty. And you should see the inventory out here. All these places with fabulous bones screaming to be fixed up. And so, so undervalued. And the land, Daddy, utterly wasted on potato farms and fruit trees. It's scandalous."

"Molly—"

"Just listen! I could be the force behind the development and marketing of the next Hampton. We just need to put this place on the map, take down that stupid force field that old Joanna Beauchamp put up a few centuries ago, give North Hampton a train station and a Jitney stop, and we're golden. We're the new gem of the East End."

"Can you try to understand, Molly, that the point of this summer exercise is for us not to draw attention to ourselves? To fly under the radar? To be normal?"

"You call disappearing from the face of social media normal?"

"Please, will you just get a job? The kind of basic job that kids your age do during the summer? As we've established, even trust-fund kids do it. It's the American way."

"Maybe."

"That's my girl. I knew you'd see reason. Tell your sister I said hi, doll face. I've got to run. I have to make a call."

"What else is new?"

"Don't sass me, kid. And take care of yourself, okay? Have some chowder for me. Manhattan clam chowder. The tomato-based kind. I swear it's not fattening."

Molly put her phone down on her bedside table,

opened her window, and leaned out into the bright morning. Her room faced the water. There were sand toys scattered on the beach below, and a couple of kayaks. Matt was out on his paddleboard, moving swiftly across the bay. She supposed he was trying to stay fit as long as he could for his immortal wife, poor guy. Good luck with that.

Molly could see Gardiners Island in the distance, with Fair Haven stately in its lush green grounds, ringed with golden dunes. Somewhere on that island was Tris Gardiner.

Why had she blown it at the party the night before last? She had such power and such strength, yet she had so little control over it. Was it possible that Daddy and Ingrid were right? Did she really need to learn some discipline? She shuddered at the thought.

She supposed she should get ready for the day. She stepped into her small en suite bathroom. It had a Scandinavian feel to it, blond wood, white tile, a single skylight. She showered and dressed in a fitted white sundress and a pair of wraparound cork platform sandals. She wanted something fresh yet beguiling for her job search. She kept her makeup light and chose a pale lipstick.

Downstairs, she found Mardi in an oversized Sigur Rós T-shirt, slumped at the kitchen island over a pile of three steaming blueberry pancakes. Next to Mardi, Jo sat dreamily staring at her rainbow tattoo. The little girl had already finished eating and was absently running a finger in circles through the maple syrup puddled on her plate, lifting it to her mouth and licking it. There was evidence of Henry's breakfast smeared all over his high chair, but he was thankfully absent. For now, the white dress was safe.

"Pancakes?" Ingrid chirped, handing Molly a plate of two.

Molly didn't really want to be eating pancakes, but she couldn't keep herself from blurting out, "Wait a second. Why does Mardi get more than me? I only have two. She has three."

"Four actually." Mardi yawned. "I already ate one."

"Sorry," said Ingrid. "I'm afraid that's the last of the batter."

"You snooze, you lose," Mardi said.

If no one else had been in the room, Molly would have snatched a pancake from her sister. But since she had an audience, she made a show of sitting up very straight on her barstool to contrast her posture favorably with Mardi's slovenly slouch.

After breakfast, she announced that she was going to cycle to town to look for a job. Could she please borrow Ingrid's bike?

Ingrid had a three-speed painted a cheerful red, with an oversized wicker basket hanging from the handlebars, "for trips to the farmers' market." As Molly pedaled it through bucolic North Hampton toward the Main Street, she wondered how much trouble she would get into if she used her fake ID to gain employment at Ocean Vines, the high-end wine store next to the town's old-fashioned, third-run movie theater. At least that way she would learn something about wine to add to her culture and patina.

She imagined that Tris Gardiner was a frequent patron of Ocean Vines. He certainly seemed like a connoisseur. She pictured him coming in for advice on the perfect white Burgundy to accompany a romantic sunset picnic with a certain girl on the beach. She would play along, pretending he was referring to someone else, until the last minute, when he would break into a sexy laugh and tell her he would be picking her up at six.

Why couldn't she get him out of her mind? It was driving her crazy. She squeezed down hard on her handlebars in frustration and felt the press of the gold ring on the middle finger of her right hand. Last night after family dinner at the local fish-'n'-chips place, while they watched television with Ingrid and Matt after the kids were in bed, Mardi had slipped Molly the ring in a barely perceptible moment of sisterly bonding. Ingrid and Matt had not noticed a thing. They had been cuddling, which was sickening to watch. Old people should not do PDA as far as Molly was concerned.

Molly sighed as she rode past Ocean Vines, but she was immediately distracted by the charming, gingham-framed picture window of a gourmet shop two doors down called the Cheesemonger. Her eye was caught in particular by a display of a red-lined picnic basket with leather straps and big brass buckles. There were pretty metal plates, with a floral design that mimicked fine china, and pearl-handled cutlery. Inside the basket was an array of gourmet foods: wild boar sausage, cloth-wrapped aged Cheddar, veiny Roquefort, artisanal crackers, a tin of shortbread, a farm-stand pie, a bottle of local sparkling cider. It made her want to lie on a blanket and hear opera under the stars. And she didn't even like opera.

At least, Molly thought as she leaned her bike against a tree, *I will feel civilized in a place like this.*

It never occurred to her that there might not be a job for her at the Cheesemonger, and it certainly never occurred to her that she might not be a suitable hire.

If she'd been honest with herself, she would have had to admit that this twee, "charming" sort of shop was not at all up her alley. She usually made fun of any person, place, or thing that tried to appear homespun. While she knew this deep inside, she didn't want to acknowledge it. She didn't want to question the fact that, for some inexplicable reason, the Cheesemonger was pulling her inside with a magnetic force.

As she entered the narrow store, a bell tinkled behind the counter and a pretty, long-lashed elfin boy with huge cornflower blue eyes popped out from behind a door that presumably led to a storage room.

"Well, hello," he said with a cheerful goofiness. "How can I help you?"

Molly smiled, sweet and blinding. This was going to be easy. She decided to give herself the "challenge" of getting herself employed on the strength of her charms alone, without resorting to magic. Although of course she would do whatever it took. She was not one to follow rules too closely, not even her own.

"Actually," she said, "I was hoping *I* could help *you*."

"I—I'm sorry?" He began to fiddle nervously with a cheese knife in his right hand. He had sandy hair and mild, pleasant features.

She reached across the old-fashioned register and steadied his hand with hers. "Don't worry, I won't bite you," she said. "I thought you could probably use some help around here. I'm sure you're expecting a huge influx of customers over the summer, and I have great retail experience." She neglected to mention that all of this retail experience was on the consumer side, and not in sales. It hardly mattered. She knew what people liked.

"Oh, I get it now. You're looking for a job?"

She nodded, bouncing her dark hair seductively against her slender neck. "I'm spending the summer in North Hampton, and I'd like to do something productive with my time. I'm very interested in a restaurant or boutique hotel career. I'm exploring my options. And I would like to deepen my understanding of the gourmet food business. I'm thinking my ideal hours would be from eleven to six or seven, during the part of the day when one doesn't want to get too much sun." She laughed. "That's probably your busiest time anyway," she added, gesturing around the empty shop.

"A-actually," he stammered, "I'd love to hire you, but—"

"But what?" She withdrew her hand.

"Well, it's actually my mom's store, and she's left me to work here for a few months. She didn't really give me the authority to make this kind of decision."

"That doesn't make much sense, now, does it? I mean she left you in charge, didn't she?"

"I suppose she did, but I'm not sure we have the budget to—"

Molly was beginning to itch with impatience. She figured that if she worked on him long enough, she could get what she wanted the "normal" way. But Molly Overbrook was not known for happily biding her time. And with such powerful forms of persuasion at her disposal, why subject herself to this silly back and forth, when she knew the end result would be the same no matter what?

Before she had time to consider what she was doing, she had whispered an incantation that had him handing her a neatly pressed blue-and-white-striped apron to match his, with the Cheesemonger logo, a mouse with a beret and curled mustache, embroidered on the front.

He invited her behind the counter in order to show her how the displays were organized. "The cheeses are by country. From left to right, we have France, Spain, Italy, and the US. The meats are over here by France. The prosciutto, salami, and roast beef are all from local farmers. Do you know how to use a meat slicer?"

"Of course," she lied.

"And, in this case, we feature a few salads that I source and make myself, along with a daily quiche. I also make muffins and scones. And over there are the pies and cakes I buy from a wonderful woman down on Dune Road. People sometimes come and stay for lunch." He gestured to two wrought-iron tables, each with two chairs, at the back of the store. "Finally, the breads and other baked goods are in these square baskets back here."

He seemed to gain confidence as he moved through his familiar little universe. He took visible pride in his wares. Within his limited sphere, she remarked with a certain degree of appreciation, he appeared almost passionate. It was sort of attractive, she had to admit.

Suddenly he stopped talking and flushed. "I'm so sorry!" he exclaimed. "I have no idea how we've come this far without an introduction. Marshall Brighton." He looked down at his Converse high-tops as if her beauty was too dazzling to look at.

"Nice to meet you, Cheeseboy, I'm Molly Overbrook. And I start tomorrow."

9

THE DOCK OF THE BAY

$\mathcal{M}$y mommy is a librarian, and my daddy is a police-man," Jo practically sang as she spoke. She and Mardi were curled up on the couch, with Midnight napping between them. "So, what job are you going to get, Mardi? Mommy says you need to get a job."

"I think I'm going to work on a fishing boat," said Mardi. She had been racking her brain to find some way to escape Ingrid's controlling gaze. It had to be physical work, work that would numb her frustration and tame her anger. She pictured herself hauling nets full of stripers across wave-swept decks, diving with a harpoon to spear swordfish and tuna. She would be one of the guys, in her short yellow slicker and high rub-ber boots, going out for beers at the North Inn after a hard day's work.

"How fun to be a fisherman!" Jo closed her pretty eyes. "You'll be like a silver mermaid on the prow of the ship. The fish will see the shiny green light from your mouth and the pretty rainbow on your neck, and they will be under your spell. They will come flying out of the water onto your fishing boat just to be your friends. And by the time the sun rises, you will have so many fish on the boat that all the other fishermen will love you and crown you their queen."

"You're a great storyteller." Mardi smirked. However, her face fell as her mind snagged on six little words from Jo's vision: *by the time the sun rises*. What an idiot Mardi was. Fishing boats went out before dawn. Mardi hated the morning. Unless, of course, she was seeing the sunrise after a night of clubbing, in which case the morning might as well be the evening, since she was heading straight to bed. The notion of vigorous exercise in the ocean spray was a whole lot less appealing when she had to consider setting her alarm for some ungodly hour. Never mind. She had to think of something else physically punishing enough to expend her energy.

"So, what do you know about potato farming?" she asked Jo.

Before Jo could answer, Ingrid came in and suggested that Mardi help clear the breakfast dishes.

Man, did Mardi miss her online delivery services. But she bit her tongue, rinsed the plates, cups, and silverware, and loaded them into the dishwasher. Although she hated to admit it, dishwashing actually wasn't that bad. She felt a simple satisfaction in the domestic chore. The running water on her hands was hypnotic. As she worked, she noticed that her ring finger was bare. She faintly remembered slipping the ring over to her twin while they were watching TV with Ingrid and Matt, but she could no longer picture the actual moment of the exchange. She and Molly could recall their ring exchanges for a little while, the way you hold on to a vivid dream, but eventually the images would fade.

"So Jo tells me you're considering a fishing career?" Ingrid smiled as she gathered her things to go to work at the library. Since the children had been born, she went only part-time, three afternoons a week, during which time Graciella, the housekeeper, watched Jo and Henry.

"Yeah, I was considering doing fishing. Until it occurred to me that I would have to get up at some crazy hour. So I've scratched that career path. But it would be cool to find something to do with water." As she spoke, she realized how drawn she was to the sea. "And I guess that if I'm going to work on controlling things in myself, I need to be pretty active. Otherwise, if I don't, you know, move my body a lot, stuff builds up inside me, and it all starts busting loose."

"Sounds like you've been doing a bit of thinking," said Ingrid with barely concealed delight. "Funny how that happens when life slows down."

Mardi smarted a bit at Ingrid's self-congratulatory tone. "Well, I guess I'm off to the docks to see if I can find a job that'll keep Dad off my case and keep me from killing someone this summer."

With that, she went up to her room, pulled on a 1965

black-and-white-striped minidress, and slipped into a pair of dark gray Vans that she had illustrated herself in black Sharpie, with an intricate pattern of skulls and bones. She waited to go downstairs until she heard Ingrid's car start and then fade into the distance. She had had enough advice for one morning.

As Mardi pulled out of the driveway, she was terrified by the thump of little Henry landing in the passenger seat beside her, as though he had dropped out of the sky.

"What the—!"

She slammed on the brakes and looked up to see that he must have fallen from the branch of the oak tree above the car. How had he gotten up there? And how had he chosen this very moment to let go, when she happened to be passing under to break his fall?

She didn't want to know, and she certainly didn't want to deal with explaining what had just happened. She didn't need people accusing her of recklessly endangering a child right now. She turned off the car, scooped him up, and carried him back to the house.

She knocked on the front door and handed him to Graciella. "I found him wandering in the driveway," Mardi claimed.

Not waiting for a reply, she rushed away with the distinct sensation of Henry's silent gaze tracking her every movement from the safety of Graciella's arms.

Without looking back, she sped to the North Hampton harbor, where the Ferrari drew curious and appreciative looks. She parked and began to walk along the docks, not quite sure what she was looking for but somehow certain that she was in the right place.

"Hey," came a familiar voice, "fancy meeting you here."

"Trent!"

His hair was wet, and his thick lashes sparkled with tiny crystals of salt. He must have been fresh from the water. He had on deep green board shorts, flip-flops, and a worn blue T-shirt with the words THE ONE THAT GOT AWAY in faded lettering across the chest.

"Who's the one that got away?" she asked.

"It's the name of a local fish place. A friend of mine runs it. It's awesome. Best bluefish I ever had. They do it with fennel, olives, and orange rind. Maybe we can go sometime."

How could he look so studly and be talking about fennel and not seem totally ridiculous?

"Yeah, sure. I do bluefish sometimes."

"Cool . . . So, it's good to run into you here. Want to see my boat?"

"Oh, that's right. You live on a boat here. Now I remember. The *Dragon*, right? Your brother's boat?"

"You got it. Come check it out."

When Trent took her hand in order to lead her to his mooring, she didn't snatch it away as she normally would with a virtual stranger. In fact, she liked the feel of his sun-kissed skin. He played with her hand. "You have a ring tan right there," he said, amused at the white skin around her fourth finger.

"Yeah, my sister has the ring on now. If I'm not wearing it, you can be sure she is, and vice versa. That ring is basically the only thing we know how to share."

Trent gave a sunny laugh as they approached a long sleek white boat with a high mast and gleaming teak decks. With childlike delight, he explained that the *Dragon* was considered a midsized sport fishing boat, that it had twenty-foot outriggers and a seventeen-foot high beam, and that it could cruise at up to forty-four knots at 2,330 rpm.

He started Mardi's tour up top, on the exterior gallery with its mezzanine-style cockpit replete with tackle, coolers, and a fridge full of beer.

"What are you doing here anyway?" he asked.

"Looking for a job," she said.

He nodded. "Want a cold one?"

"Sure."

He popped the tops off two icy pale ales and handed her one as they headed down a flight to the second tier, the flybridge and peninsula style console. There was starboard and forward seating, with bright orange-and-white-striped cushions.

"And finally, down here," Trent announced, opening a solid teak door onto steps leading to the interior gallery, "is where I lurk." Belowdecks, the walls, cabinetry, and built-in beds were all of cherry wood. The counters were black granite. The upholstery was leather, chocolate with cream piping.

Mardi looked around for a few minutes, then whistled. "No offense," she said, "but I didn't picture you living somewhere quite so . . . well . . . fancy. I got the impression you were escaping all that by hiding out on the *Dragon*. But this here is pretty flash."

"It's not my boat, remember. This is all Killian's doing. And Killian was all about impressing Freya when he bought it. I'm nothing but a squatter on the *Dragon*." He took her hand again. This time, he did not let go. "But a squatter has squatter's rights." He winked. "Which means I'm entitled to visitors whenever I want."

She turned around so he wouldn't see her blush. Then she made her way back up the stairs.

Back in the daylight, she told him more about her job search, that she wanted something physical, on or near the water, but that there was no way she was getting up early to work on a fishing boat. Did he have any ideas?

"I'm sure we can think of something," he said. "But why the urgency to get a job? Can't you relax for the summer?"

"I'm sort of in trouble," she blurted out, not sure why she was trusting him with this information but unable to hold back. "Molly and I both are kind of screwed, actually. And we have to make a show of cleaning up our acts and pretending to be normal so that the authorities will leave us alone."

"What happened?"

"I don't really want to talk about it," she said.

"Fair enough," said Trent. "But I'm all ears whenever you're ready." He led her back to the deck, where they looked out to the sea through a forest of masts and billowing sails.

"Thanks," she said.

"So, about a job," he said calmly. "You look pretty strong to me. How do you feel about loading and unloading cargo?"

* 10 *

C IS FOR COOKIE

*O*nce Freya found out that Molly was working at the Cheesemonger, she made a habit of stopping by on the way to her shift at the North Inn for her favorite sandwich of cave-aged Gruyère, salted butter, and cornichons on a crusty baguette, always followed by a brownie studded with walnuts and pecans.

"I've inherited my mom's sweet tooth," Freya complained. "Ever since she left this world, it's as if I've taken on her curse. I can't go a day without chocolate. It's a good thing I'm running off my feet for eight hours a night."

Molly looked across the tiny round café table at Freya. The brownies didn't appear to be doing her an ounce of harm. She was flawless in a tight black jumpsuit with a scooped back, her tiny waist cinched by a gold rope elaborately knotted at her navel. Her toenails glimmered a wicked purple in peeky-toe heels. Her lips were impossibly glossy, and her cheeks glinted as if by the light of their own private moon. She exuded magic from every pore of her body. *How*, wondered Molly, *did she keep it in check?*

"You should stop by the bar sometime, Molly," Freya suggested. Then she turned to Marshall, who was behind the counter, dicing cucumbers for a Greek salad. "You too, Marsh. I won't card you guys if you don't tell."

Marshall graced Freya and Molly with a shy but knowing smile. Molly had to admit that there was something endearing about him. As he loosened up around her, he was beginning to banter and make jokes. His cracks were often self-deprecating and amusing without being mean.

He liked to make up little songs while he worked. Her favorite was "Mangoes on My Mind," to the tune of "Singing in the Rain," which he sang as he prepped the mango salsa for the crab cakes.

Marshall was cute, but she was much too impressed with Tris Gardiner, who loomed large in her mind's eye from the Fair Haven party, to give Cheeseboy any serious consideration. It might be fun to have him follow her around like a puppy, but he was nothing compared to Tris.

"Tell me"—she leaned in close to Freya—"what do you know about the youngest Gardiner brother? Is he really bad news? Or do we sort of like him?"

"Well, well, well." Freya raised her eyebrows playfully. "So we've met young Trystan, have we?"

"Maybe. And maybe he's been texting me."

"Really?" Freya asked, raising an eyebrow. "But I thought . . ." She frowned.

"Why? Is that so hard to believe?" Molly asked, annoyed.

"No. I guess I just had him pegged wrong, then," Freya said.

"What do you mean?"

"Nothing. Forget I said anything."

"Anyway, he's pretty hot," Molly admitted. "I mean, he's certainly a catch in this town. But it's not like there's fierce competition."

She stole a glance at Marshall and saw that he had stopped chopping.

"Molly," he said softly, running his hand nervously through his fine sand-colored hair, "can you mind the store for a few minutes? I forgot to pick up my heirloom tomatoes at Jasper Farms. I'm going to ride my bike over right now. I'll be back soon."

"No problem," she said, standing up, retying her apron and making a show of going to stand behind the counter.

Freya gestured to Marshall with her chin. "I think you might have hurt his feelings. I think he likes you."

Molly rolled her eyes. "Does it look like I care?" But she felt a small, unfamiliar twinge of regret for her harsh words.

She got up and manned the counter. It was close to July, business was picking up, and Molly found she enjoyed the ritual of entertaining the Cheesemonger's customers. There was a certain elegance to the activity of slicing, wrapping, and serving beautiful foodstuffs in pretty packages and charging a lot of money for them. She enjoyed the feel of the register keys on her fingertips. The job was like playacting, and she was quite good at it. It was even fun, until someone was rude, impatient, or, God forbid, belligerent. Unsavory customers would often find their picnics infested with red ants, their cars covered in seagull droppings, or their sunglasses mysteriously shattered in their cases.

For the moment, though, the Cheesemonger was empty, except for Molly and Freya, who was sipping a double espresso with the last of her brownie. Molly seized the opportunity to ask the question that was really on her mind.

"The Gardiners are warlocks, aren't they? Tell me I'm right. I get the impression that they are divine, like us. I got such a magical vibe the other night. Am I onto something?"

"There's no point in trying to tell you otherwise if you already sense it," answered Freya, serious all of a sudden. "Yes, they are like us. Fair Haven sits on the seam between two of the nine worlds of the Known Universe: Midgard, where we are destined to live out our days, and the Land of the Dead. It's the joining of the living and the twilight words. Somewhere inside that mansion is a crucial entry point into the skeleton of the universe. I used to know where it was, but the refurbishment has obscured all that. It's a mystery again."

"Wow." Molly's eyes widened. She was not easily impressed, but this was intense.

Freya continued. "Our mother, Joanna, placed a powerful containment spell on the house centuries ago. Ingrid and I are the spell's guardians now. Believe me, you don't want to be messing with those boundaries, especially in your delicate situation. You really don't want to be rocking the boat at this point."

This was getting too heavy for Molly. It was time to bring it down a notch. "All I want to know is whether or not you think fooling around with a Gardiner brother is a good idea."

"Fooling around, my dear, is always a good idea, especially if his last name is Gardiner." Freya laughed, appearing relieved to change the subject and to leave the spooky territory of the gloaming behind in favor of happier concerns. "You don't need my approval for that!"

"That's great news because I did actually text him back and—"

At that moment, the bell to the store's entrance tinkled, and in walked Mardi, wearing a pair of cutoff OshKosh overalls over an electric yellow tube top.

Molly gave Freya a meaningful look and put a finger to her lips. She did *not* want her sister in her business.

"Hey, guys," she said. "What's good today? I'm ravenous. I've been lifting crates of sardines all day."

Molly sniffed the air, crinkling her tiny nose. "I can tell."

"Hey, I showered after work."

"Where? In the public bathroom?"

"If you must know, I showered on a yacht."

"Which yacht?"

"None of your business."

Freya burst out laughing. "I thought Ingrid and I were bad when we bickered. You girls put us to shame. If you don't watch out, you'll scare away all of Marshall's customers." She downed the final sip of her espresso, gave each twin a kiss on the cheek, and drove off in her pumpkin-colored Mini Cooper to begin her night of charmed mixology at the North Inn.

"Freya invited me to come to her bar sometime. She's not going to card me," Molly boasted once she and Mardi were alone.

"I'm sure she won't card me either. No one ever cards me."

"That's because you cheat with your magic."

"And you don't?"

"You got me there," sighed Molly. There was a shift inside her, something about the way her sister's rainbow tattoo caught the afternoon light as it slanted in through the Cheesemonger's picture window, which made Molly want to let up and enjoy this moment. She found that she didn't feel like fighting anymore. "I'll admit that I use my magic on bouncers, bartenders, and door guys all the time too. So we're even. Truce? Want a sandwich?"

"Sure."

"Roast beef? It's rare like you like it. And we have this gorgeous purple mustard. It's purple because it's made from the must of wine grapes."

"*Gorgeous* mustard?" Mardi teased, but with no sting in her voice. Molly could tell Mardi's heart wasn't in it, and so she didn't take offense.

"For once, can you please trust me? Try it."

As Molly sliced focaccia, spread the purple mustard, layered the meat with crumbles of Gorgonzola and arugula leaves, a question began to form in her mind. She didn't know exactly what the question was, but she knew it had to do with that fateful night back in April, with the party at Bret's house, the lost hours, the tragedy. It wasn't until she handed Mardi her sandwich with a bottle of high-end root beer that the words came out fully formed: "Did you have the ring on that night?"

Mardi, of course, knew exactly what night Molly was referring to. The twins were symbiotic. This was the precise reason why they were also the bitterest of rivals. Intuition is not always an easy thing to share. But there were moments like this when they both relaxed their guard and searched for common ground. Together, they were circling the idea that maybe their ring was more than just a private symbol between the two of them. It had some kind of power. After all, it was the only thing they had left of their mother.

"I don't think so. No, I didn't have it on at Bret's. I did wake up wearing it, weirdly. But I didn't have it when I was checking out that awesome spider sculpture with him. I remember feeling for it and thinking you must have had it."

"But I didn't," said Molly, instinctively checking her right hand to make sure the ring was still there now. "I remember thinking *you* must have had it."

"Well, one of us has to be wrong. The ring never disappeared, obviously, because it was still there in the morning."

Molly bristled. The brief interlude of sisterly bonding was so over. "Well, it's obviously not me who's wrong!"

"Are you implying that it's me?" Mardi tore into her roast beef furiously. "Because it can't be me. There's no way. I am so much higher functioning than you."

"Oh, so I'm supposed to be the ditzy one?"

"Well, since I'm *not* the ditzy one, it goes without saying that you must be."

"You're the one who was wearing it the morning after! I think that proves that *you* spaced, not me!"

The girls were interrupted by Marshall, returning with a small wooden crate of green, yellow, and orange tomatoes in all kinds of funky, nonengineered shapes. He'd obviously recovered his spirits and was all freckled smiles from behind his colorful heap of summer bounty.

"Have I stumbled on an epic battle?" He grinned.

"Sort of," Molly and Mardi answered as one, starting to laugh in spite of themselves.

"Great," Marshall said, putting his vegetable crate

down on top of the cheese case, "because deflating massive conflict happens to be my specialty. Did you ladies know that I have ten-year-old identical-twin half brothers? Whenever I go to visit them in Philly, they make me wear a cape with a capital *P* sewn on the back. *P* stands for Peacemaker. That's my superhero identity."

"Where is this going?" Molly asked, cracking a reluctant smile.

"You'll see. Now, I don't have my cape here, so you'll have to use your imaginations. You've got to picture me flying over the counter, like so." In an agile leap, he cleared the counter to land right in front of the cookie basket. He took an oatmeal chocolate chip cookie—both sisters' favorite—laid it on a small plate with a knife, and put the plate on the counter. "Here's the twin challenge," he said, somehow maintaining eye contact with both of them. "One of you gets to cut the cookie in half. The other one gets to pick her half first."

"This is my store," Molly said immediately. "I work here. So, I get to decide. And I want to cut the cookie," she insisted.

"Okay, that works out great," Mardi quipped, "because I want to choose my half first."

"Wait a second, never mind. You can cut. I'm picking! It's my store, remember?" Molly knew they were bickering like children. It was even worse here in North Hampton than back in the city. It felt like someone had hexed them with a curse of discord. Why did they have no control of themselves?

"That is so unfair!" Mardi grabbed the knife. But instead of turning it on the oatmeal chocolate chip cookie, she pointed it at Molly's face.

Molly laughed. "Marshall, as you are my witness, my own sister is threatening me with a knife."

"A butter knife, I might add," Marshall said, totally deadpan. "Ladies, would you like to witness my earth-shattering peacemaking skills in action?"

Mardi lowered the knife, and they both stared at him in disbelief as he began to eat the disputed cookie himself.

He began to sing a song from *Sesame Street*: "*C* is for cookie. That's good enough for me—"

"Are you channeling the Cookie Monster right now?" Molly couldn't help but smile at Marshall. She was melting inside.

"Scrumptious," he sighed, by way of an answer. "My mom's secret recipe. I'm the only soul on Earth she will ever trust with it." He took a long, languorous bite, then he took two more cookies from the basket and handed one to each girl. "The moral of this story is all you ever have to do in life is realize there is *always* enough to go around. That full basket has been there this whole time."

The girls chewed in silent contemplation. *He was sort of right*, Molly thought. And sort of adorable. And he baked killer cookies.

"Would you girls like some strawberry lemonade?" They nodded.

Marshall poured three tall glasses, stirred in fresh mint leaves, and handed them around. "Ladies, I would like to propose a toast to Peace. With a capital *P*."

In unison, they raised their lemonade. "Peace!"

Molly gave this happy new state of affairs about five minutes. But she supposed it would be sweet while it lasted.

11

REHAB

𝒜my Winehouse was singing about not wanting to go to rehab, and Mardi was singing right along with her. She hated anything that smacked of an intervention, and this scene had all the elements.

She and Molly were sitting side by side on the couch in the living room of Freya's spare modern house, the one she had taken over from Matt when he got married, piling it high with her excess clothes. In this glass and steel setting, the clothes, stacked by color, looked like abstract expressionist art rather than clutter.

Presumably, this out-of-the-way location, with its unfettered views of empty beach and open sea, was a neutral spot, the exact sort of place where interventions were staged.

Mardi trailed off a lyric in the face of Ingrid's admonishing glare. Even Freya looked dead serious beside her sister. For once, her neckline gave no hint of cleavage. The two women sat cross-legged on a sleek leather-upholstered bench.

Most ominous of all was the dapper older man whose lanky frame was folded into a camel-colored Eames chair. He appeared every bit the Upper East Side shrink in a bespoke gray suit complete with a red pocket square. He had a faint mustache and goatee. His bald brown head was shiny under the light.

"Girls," Ingrid began, "this is our dear friend Jean-Baptiste Mésomier. He has been very helpful to us through the centuries. The most recent time he came to our aid was about ten years ago when we had our last crises of memory threatening the community. In order to speak to you, he has kindly agreed to travel up from New Orleans back into our midst."

"Jean-Baptiste," Freya chimed in, "Molly and Mardi Overbrook, Troy's girls."

"It's a pleasure to meet you both," said the old man in a light French accent. "Now, how may I help you?"

This sounded suspiciously like the kind of open-ended therapy question Mardi despised. "Could you start by telling us what exactly we're doing here?" she retorted.

"Mardi!" Ingrid looked mortified. "Please be respectful. You are speaking to the god of memory himself."

"He's come to help you with your amnesia," Freya added helpfully. "We're starting to think that someone has been messing with your memories. There's no reason for you both to be so vague about what happened the night those kids were killed in Manhattan. We suspect foul play."

"You mean we didn't just black out because we were wasted?" Mardi was in the depths of a dark sarcastic mood. "Why do you guys have to tease everything out to make it so *meaningful*? Why can't we just be ordinary kids who do ordinary stupid things at parties?" She knew she was being disingenuous, but she couldn't stop.

"But, Mardi," Molly interjected, "we can't be ordinary." She pronounced the word *ordinary* as if it were toxic. "We're extraordinary by nature. We're not like other kids. We're—we're . . ."

"We're legendary!" exclaimed Mardi, intending to be sarcastic, but realizing as she pronounced the words that they were absolutely true. Her father was the god of thunder. The mortals had named Thursday after him. That was her family heritage: the days of the week were named after her forebears. Who else could claim that?

"Yes," the old man purred, "indeed we are legendary. We are all myths and legends. Powerful ones, I might add. And, as my great friend and countryman Voltaire once said, 'With great power comes great responsibility.'"

"I thought that was Spider-Man," said Mardi, genuinely perplexed.

"Actually I think it was Thomas Jefferson," Molly chimed.

"Regardless of who said it, it pertains to the two of you," said Jean-Baptiste.

"Girls," Ingrid sighed, "this is serious. Please pay attention and try to focus. Here's the problem as we see it. You two have been creating quite a stir in and around your high school in New York. You are wanton with your spells and hexes—making girls' hair fall out in clumps, causing sworn enemies to make out with one another in broad daylight, rewriting test questions to make them—quote, unquote—less dry, inducing temporary paralysis in your rivals, and the list goes on."

"Way to go, girls!" Freya interrupted with irrepressible glee. "I turned a teacher's eyebrows purple once because she told me I wasn't trying hard enough in geometry, and once, I made my elementary school principal loudly declare his undying love for our class's pet lizard. He got down on his knees to propose and everything. I can't remember what lifetime that was, but it was a good one."

"Awesome," cried Mardi, high-fiving Freya.

"Cool," Molly echoed.

"Come on, Freya," Ingrid chided. "You're not helping our cause here. You and I live in North Hampton, a disorienting space that doesn't exist on any map and is protected by strong spells. It would take a heck of a lot for us to be persecuted here in this day and age.

"But you twins, on the other hand," she continued, looking squarely at Mardi and Molly, "have been living large in the public eye. Granted, New York City can absorb massive amounts of weirdness. Which is all the more reason that we have to hand it to you. It's quite a feat on your part to have the mortals who live there actually beginning to suspect witchcraft and enchantment. It's saying a lot in today's skeptical, electronic age . . ."

Ingrid seemed to lose her train of thought for the moment. Freya took up the slack: "The rumor about that young couple who died is that the two of you somehow put a spell on them and used your powers to force them onto the tracks in front of an oncoming train. If that rumor turns into a formal legal accusation, we're in big trouble. The one thing the White Council has forbidden is another witch hunt. They won't tolerate any more trials or convictions. So, if it's not true that you killed them, you've got to cooperate with us to help us figure out what really happened. You have to let Jean-Baptiste help you to retrieve that night."

"What do you mean, 'if it's not true'?" Mardi's blood rose. "Of course we didn't kill them. We barely even knew them. We ran in totally different crowds. But that's beside the point. We would never kill *anyone*. I've never even killed a roach with my magic." She paused to gather her thoughts. "Okay, maybe we express a little uncontrolled anger here and there. But mostly, we have fun with our powers. Believe me, we don't murder people. We don't even really hurt people. We sometimes toy with them is all."

"Yeah, mostly we just embarrass them," Molly added.

"Molly, Mardi." Jean-Baptiste rolled their names off his tongue with calm authority. "Or, rather, I should call you Mooi and Magdi, for those are your true given names, Thor's daughters, twin goddesses of strength and rage: you will both grow serious now, if you please. And you will both please close your eyes."

Before she had time to raise an objection, Mardi's lids dropped thick and leaden over her eyes. Instantly, the cubic beach house was blacked out. She no longer felt she was sitting in the light, airy living room on stilts over the beach. Gone were the pale wood, the brushed steel, and the glassy views of the gray green sea. Instead, she saw a swirl of lush, garish colors: bloodred, royal blue, burnished gold, all tinseled over with sprays of silver. She sank into a decadent and disturbing dream.

There was water here too, but it was not at all the vibrant water of the ocean. It was the overheated water of an interior lap pool encased in black marble. She was swimming in somebody's private pool, in a dimly mood-lit room. Along the shining black rim of the deck were half-empty glasses of alcohol in varying shades. The drinks were sloshed everywhere. For all she knew, what looked like the white flakes of a snow globe, swirling around the filter, were the remains of spilled cocaine. The water was too warm to actually move in, and the pool was much too small for real laps. One flip turn and you would be halfway across it. Mardi felt herself stewing, like a lobster in a pot over a flame, slowly losing her will to live.

As her senses grew more acute and the picture of the pool in its luxurious setting came more sharply into focus, she realized that she wasn't alone in the water. Molly was there too. And Molly wasn't wearing a swimsuit. Mardi looked down at her own body. Neither was she.

They were skinny-dipping. And there was a boy with them. He was chasing them in a half-playful, half hostile game. There was much splashing and flirting, but also a bit of fear. Was it Bret? He had Bret's sharp features and platinum hair, but she couldn't be sure. She couldn't remember.

Molly seemed to be teasing the boy, whoever he was. "It's so, so powerful. You know you want it! But the ring is ours. You can't have it. And you can't have us."

Mardi's every intuition told her they should get out of this water and run. But her body was lulled by the warmth, and it was all she could do to dodge Bret-not-Bret's unwelcome caresses as he dove after her and her sister. When was this farce going to end?

Then the boy was shouting at them. Except his voice was different from Bret's, higher-pitched and whinier, but oddly familiar. She knew she had heard this voice recently, but in the confusion of her fugue state she could not match it to a face.

Finally, Mardi's frustration boiled over. Tapping into the anger at her core, she was able to break through whatever curse was blurring her mind.

"Get away!" she screamed. The desperation in his movements made her feel physically sick. Fitfully, he grasped for the girls' limbs in the dark water of his private Manhattan pool. "You bitches are going to burn in Hell!"

Mardi despised him as she had never despised anyone before. "Leave us alone! Don't touch me! Don't touch my sister! You can never have our ring!"

The power of her own voice brought her back to her senses. She opened her eyes to find herself back on the couch in Freya's stark modern living room, surrounded by kindly, curious, and concerned faces. She looked at Molly, who was also blinking and who appeared deeply confused. Molly was shaking, pale, and drained.

Mardi had the urge to take Molly into her arms and cling to her. What was it that they had been through together? Who was that weird guy in the pool with them? Why did he want their ring? What was so powerful about it?

"I think," said Jean-Baptiste from the depths of his leather seat, giving Freya and Ingrid a meaningful look, "that that we have certainly done enough work for one afternoon."

After they were released from their session, Mardi and Molly stood together on the empty beach in front of the house, catching their breath and comparing visions. They found that they had been in the same black marble pool, taunted by the same creepy guy with the bizarre whining voice. He had wanted their ring, and they had been trying desperately to keep it away from him.

"Did you see whether or not he finally got it?" Mardi asked.

Molly shook her head. "I'm not even sure which one of us had it that night."

"It must have been you because you woke up with it, right?"

"I guess. It's all so vague . . . But I remember clearly from the vision that it was really important to us to keep the ring away from him. I remember sensing that it was super powerful."

"Yeah, I remember that too . . . Maybe the ring is more than we've always thought."

"You mean more than just something between the two of us?" Molly lifted her finger. The rose gold caught the soft light of the setting sun. The diamondback pattern shimmered.

"Yeah, Molly, it's definitely bigger than we are." Mardi took a thick platinum box chain off from around her neck. "Maybe we should wear it around our necks for a while? That way we'll be more aware of it, and of who has it, instead of slipping it on and off our fingers without always remembering. It'll be safer. Here, take this chain."

Molly didn't argue. She took the chain, unclasped it, slipped the ring onto it, and put it on. The ring hit her just below her clavicle.

As Mardi looked at her twin with the rose gold gleaming against her chest, she had the distinct impression that she was gazing into a mirror at her own dark features, her own black hair, and her own uncertain future.

12

RUNNING WITH THE DEVIL

What are you doing tonight?

With a surreptitious glance at the phone in her bag, since she was supposed to be minding the kids, Molly read Tris's text yet again. She appreciated his restraint in not using abbreviations. Nothing was more of a turn-off than being referred to as "u." Tris was obviously a product of good breeding. She approved.

She started to compose an answer in her head. This was no easy task. She wanted to see him again, but she didn't want to seem overly available.

"Jo," she asked, "if you want someone to want to be your friend in kindergarten, what do you do?"

Molly was walking the children to the lunchtime story hour at the North Hampton Public Library, pushing Henry in his all-terrain stroller while Jo skipped beside her. The plan was for Molly to drop them off and then head to her afternoon and evening shift at the Cheesemonger.

The library was about a mile from the house, on a

leafy green square with a stunning view of the water. When it had almost been torn down a few years ago to make way for condos, Ingrid had spearheaded the effort to have it landmarked, thwarting developers in order to preserve the character and integrity of the town. She still talked a lot about that battle, about getting the mayor on her side, the petitions and the fund-raisers. Ingrid, Molly thought, faintly baffled, was one of these people who actually took pride in bettering the world around her. Was Ingrid a different species of witch from Mardi and her? Molly couldn't imagine herself ever taking in two obnoxious teenagers for a whole summer out of the kindness of her heart. Come to think of it, *was* there any kindness in her heart?

There had to be, didn't there?

"If I like someone and I want them to like me back, then I ask Mommy to help me bake some brownies to give them," Jo said matter-of-factly. "We always bake our brownies from my grandma Joanna's recipe. I never got to meet my grandma, but Mommy says she still loves me and that her magic is still in the house, and that's what makes all our sweets taste so good."

This answer cut Molly to the quick. She had no idea who her own mother was; their father never talked about her—he was too sad—and no one had ever baked with her in her life.

Hating to feel sorry for herself, she scrambled to find the humor in the situation.

"I don't think," she smirked, "that brownies are the fastest way to his heart."

"To whose heart?" asked Jo.

But Molly didn't answer. She had veered into strategy mode. The trick to hooking Tris, she decided after several false mental starts, was to blame the fact that she was free tonight on the dullness of North Hampton. She should imply that, had Tris tried texting her back in the city, he would have had to get in a long, long line . . . Now that she had her message, she had to come up with the actual words to convey it.

Having handed Henry and Jo off to their mother, Molly went another mile to the Cheesemonger. Her crisp white bandeau-top sundress would easily transition into night if she were to meet Tris for a late dinner. She was wearing flats but had heels in her tote. Since Mardi had given her a ride home last evening from work, Ingrid's bike was still parked behind the shop. Molly had aligned her stars so that nothing could get in her way. Getting what she wanted was a specialty of hers, she thought with pride, having completely recovered her confidence after her unexpected moment of doubt on the street with Jo, that sweet little witch.

Inside the Cheesemonger, Marshall was singing a song about the runner beans he was busy trimming. He waved a handful of beans at her and belted out a song about running with the devil.

It was the head-banging Van Halen song that Daddy still liked to blast through the house when he was feeling spry. It was so incongruous with Marshall's boy-next-door looks that she burst out laughing.

"What?" He smiled. "What's so funny?"

"It's just that you don't look like you could run with the devil for a second."

"Looks can be deceiving." He shrugged his shoulders playfully. "Take, for instance, these very runner beans. They look pretty misshapen, and they have a few brown spots. Their color isn't uniform. If you were looking for perfection in a gleaming supermarket, you might turn up your nose at these particular beans. But these particular beans are actually fantastic, bursting with flavor. All of their color and beauty is on the inside. So you have to know them in order to love them. Do you want to try one?"

"Sure. Can I eat it raw?"

"Absolutely," he said.

Molly suddenly felt shy as she took a bean from his outstretched hand. He had been keeping his eyes mostly on his work, and this was the first time he was really looking at her. "Um," he said, watching her face for signs of appreciation as she chewed. "You look pretty today. I mean, you look especially pretty today. Because you look pretty every day." He grew flustered and looked down at the floor, where he obviously latched on to the first thing that caught his eye. "I like your shoes."

"Thanks. I like your beans. You're right, they taste way better than they look. I guess this is another one of your life lessons, right?"

He shrugged. "Do you want to help me slice them? It would be good to get ahead on prep work before people start coming in for dinner stuff on their way home from the beach."

"Good thinking. Sure I'll help you. Why not?"

Because Marshall assumed Molly wanted to be helpful, she found she actually did. It was like he drew a sweet shape for her to step into. She found herself in a cheerful role she had never quite imagined before.

As he was showing her how to slice the runner beans, humming the Van Halen song again, he placed his right hand on top of hers over the paring knife. "Try to do it diagonally, like this," he said gently.

"Okay . . . So you think I'm pretty, huh?" she asked with a wicked smile.

Under normal circumstances, she would have tortured and humiliated a guy who tried to flirt with her like this when he should have known he had zero chance. But either she was starting to lose her edge, or she kinda liked him, because she was definitely flirting back.

The doorbell tinkled with the beginning of the late-afternoon rush. For the next few hours, she and Marshall worked together, side by side, until about seven, when business started to taper, since everyone in town knew that the shop closed at eight.

At one point around five o'clock, she stole into the bathroom, pulled out her phone, and finally answered Tris. To be honest, I'm not quite sure what I'm doing tonight. The possibilities are so endless in this town that I don't know where to begin. Any advice?

After that, she checked her phone between customers and sometimes even in the middle of preparing an order. Why wasn't he texting her back? Who did this guy think he was?

The irritation she had felt back at the party over a week ago overtook her again. If anyone in the shop even thought about messing with her, if anyone asked for their turkey sliced a bit thinner or for light dressing on their line-caught tuna salad, she was afraid of what she might do to them. But the evening customers didn't cross any lines, and Marshall stayed buoyant throughout. Molly found no excuse to blow her top, which made the waiting all that much harder.

Finally, as she was hanging up her apron and Marshall was starting to switch off the lights, a message flashed on her phone.

Have you finished your shift at the Cheesemonger?

How did Tris even know she was working there? They hadn't seen each other since the party, and she hadn't mentioned her job in any of her texts to him. He must be watching her from afar. Spying. How sexy.

Yes, she typed. She certainly was finished with the shop for today. Assuming he would now offer to pick her up and take her somewhere for the evening, she started fishing in her giant bag for her heels.

"Hey, Marshall," she said, "do you mind leaving the lights on for another minute or two? I'm going to pop into the bathroom and freshen up."

"Of course. I'll wait for you. You have Ingrid's bike here, right?"

"I do."

"I—well—I have my bike too. And I was wondering, wondering . . . wondering if you wanted to take a ride together over to the North Inn. You know, the bar where Freya works?"

Marshall was seriously getting ahead of himself. He was nice and all, but she would have to put him in his place. The rush of haughtiness that filled her soul reminded her of who she really was. She was Molly Overbrook, and she was unattainable by ordinary means. She had been playing at being sweet to this cute, but very ordinary boy. But no more.

"Some other time, Cheeseboy. Sorry, I have a date tonight."

"Oh. Okay."

Although he looked disappointed, he was not as crestfallen as she would have liked, which meant he might try to ask her out again. She was coming up with something else to say when her phone beeped.

It must be Tris saying he was on his way. She felt a rush of victory. Marshall became the last thing on her mind.

She darted into the bathroom, pulled out her makeup bag and began to curl her eyelashes. The lighting was terrible, overbright, so she did a little dimming incantation. "That's much better," she sighed to herself. When she had finished with her lashes, she took a look at her phone to see where she should wait for him and was miffed to read that he wasn't actually coming for her.

Can I expect you at Fair Haven within the hour?

What, was he *summoning* her? How cosmically conceited of him! It was all she could do not to crack the bathroom mirror.

Somehow, she steeled herself and managed to walk out of the shop and hop onto her bicycle without wreaking any havoc.

"Well," said Marshall, locking the door to the shop, "good night, Molly. I look forward to seeing you tomorrow."

She waited for him to pedal off before she started riding in the direction of home. Because there was no way she was heading to Fair Haven and giving Tris the satisfaction of answering his booty call.

Or was there?

Was there, perhaps, more than one way to look at this situation? Molly could, of course, decide that Trystan Gardiner was an arrogant bastard who didn't deserve a moment of her attention. But, following her own logic earlier about how lame this town was, she could make the case that an invitation to Fair Haven was as good as it got. He was offering her a private tour of his mansion, without any of the hangers-on who had been clamoring to check out the latest renovation at the big party last week. He was letting her in on an exclusive basis. As his date. Considered in this light, his invitation grew quite appealing. Besides, she was lonely. She wasn't used to going this long without male attention. And Cheeseboy didn't count.

Slowly, Molly turned around. Instead of going home, she steered her red bicycle toward the bridge to Gardiners Island.

Summoned, indeed.

✳ *13* ✳

MEMORY MOTEL

𝓜ardi hadn't even kissed him yet. She and Trent had come close a couple of times on the *Dragon*, within fractions of an inch, but their lips had never touched.

He had given her keys to the *Dragon*'s cabin so that she could shower at the end of the day or grab a drink during a break from her hard physical work. Often she would bump into him on his deck or on the docks, where he was helping a friend renovate a clam shack into a farm-to-table restaurant. They always had charged exchanges. And, without being pushy, Trent made it quite clear with his body language that he would be open to more than just talking. But he hadn't made a move.

Usually, Mardi hated nothing more than to feel pressured, so she was grateful for Trent's restraint, but she was growing frustrated too. She was going to have to make the first move. Again. When she actually liked someone, she always did. Probably because she was so intimidating with her tongue stud and her tattoo that boys didn't want to blow it. But she could tell Trent wasn't cowed by her. She hadn't been this intrigued by a boy in a long, long time.

She had been beside Trent most of the day, unloading lumber for the new restaurant, and her body was aching for him. Wasn't it time now to give him the signal to pull her into his arms and down into the *Dragon*? It wouldn't take much.

He was only an inch away, sitting beside her on the dock, dangling his bare feet next to hers. There was a now-familiar hint of salt on his skin catching the late-afternoon light. In order not to stare at him, she looked out to sea.

"Do you have any plans tonight, Mardi?" His voice was insistently sexy, yet gentle.

There. He'd made his move.

But all of a sudden she was terrified.

She turned to face him and immediately felt herself swimming in the beauty of his bottomless blue eyes. She could drown in them. Lose herself.

It was tempting. Too tempting. She was able to hold his gaze for only a few seconds before she had to look away again. It was as though she were being sucked into a riptide. She had to protect herself from her own attraction. "Thanks, Trent, but I have a date with Freya at the North Inn."

As soon as she said it, she felt a sting of regret. Along with a huge sense of relief. She liked this guy too much to get close.

"That's cool." He sighed, crinkling those gorgeous eyes into the sunset. "Well, maybe some other time."

"Yeah, some other time."

Now that she had pushed him away, Mardi was able to look at Trent again and take in the full picture of what she was denying herself: the broad shoulders and ropy arms, the strong hands, the high cheekbones and full lips, and the deep eyes sparkling now with something like sadness. What was wrong with her?

"You'll like the North Inn," he said. "It's a cool place, and Freya really lights it up. Maybe we can go together sometime soon?"

"Sure. Maybe."

He flashed a smile. "I'm going to go out on a limb and take that as a yes, Mardi Overbrook."

"Maybe it is."

As Mardi left him behind on the dock, she felt her body being pulled back in his direction with a magnetic force. It was all she could do to rip herself away and run to her car. Man, did she need a strong drink to distract her right now.

Freya had more than once hinted at the possibility of tequila shots. And she'd said she thought Mardi would dig the rock-'n'-roll vibe of the North Inn. Too bad Mardi wasn't wearing something with more of a '70s feel tonight. Her black denim cutoffs and vintage Black Sabbath T-shirt were pretty basic, but she was going to give the place a try. Freya would be happy to see her. And Freya would probably also have some advice for her on how to loosen up around Trent.

As she was figuring out which way to turn to get to the North Inn, Mardi's headlights suddenly illuminated a red bicycle pedaled by none other than her sister. Who else but Molly would be riding a bike through a beach town in four-inch stilettos?

Mardi pulled the convertible over and waited for Molly to ride up to her.

"Where are you going in those shoes?" Mardi asked.

Ignoring the question, Molly asked, "Where are *you* going?" She appeared flushed and distracted.

"To check out Freya's bar. Wanna come?"

"Thanks, but I'm on my way to Fair Haven."

"What for?" Mardi's curiosity was instantly piqued.

Molly answered with nothing but a smug smile.

"Well, if you're going all the way to Gardiners Island, you really should have a light on your bike." Ever since the session with Jean-Baptiste, Mardi had been feeling protective of her twin.

"Don't worry." Molly laughed. "I have reflectors on my tires, and, more importantly, I've put up a repellent shield against drunk-driving lowlifes as well as blind old ladies who shouldn't be allowed behind the wheel. So don't sweat it, sis. I'm not going to end up as a splotch on the road tonight."

"You should still be careful . . . . You can't tell me who you are going to see at Fair Haven?"

"I can. But I won't."

With that, Molly pedaled off into the night.

Mardi gritted her teeth all the way to the North Inn. Why did her sister have to act like such a brat at a time when they should be sticking together? It was so frustrating that they couldn't get along right now. The friction was even stronger than usual. A real curse.

And why was Molly being so secretive about Fair Haven? The only person of interest who had anything to do with Fair Haven was Trent. But Trent was never at the house, so it couldn't possibly be Trent that Mardi was going to see, besides which, Trent would never look at Molly, and Molly would never look at Trent. So what the Hell was Mardi stressing about?

She parked the Ferrari in between a pickup truck and a Volvo in the North Inn parking lot. This was probably going to suck.

But once she was inside the bar, Mardi was pleasantly surprised. The jukebox was playing "Memory Motel" by the Rolling Stones, another of Dad's favorites that she had unconsciously learned by heart.

Mardi wasn't the only one familiar with the song. Half the patrons were singing along as they drank. There was even a couple slow-dancing. The place, which was totally unpretentious, its wooden booths carved with years' worth of names and messages, managed to be mellow and relaxed while at the same time giving off a charged party vibe. It was as if the North Inn orbited its own interior sun. And that sun's name was Freya.

Freya was warm, brilliant, and life-giving. Even when her customers weren't looking directly at her, they were inspired by her presence. Mardi wasn't the only one who was half in love with her. Freya was wonderfully steady, and yet she was always in motion, vibrantly shaking and mixing drinks, calling everyone by name, cranking the tunes.

This feeling of entering a private universe when she came into the bar was instantly familiar to Mardi from her endless nights and early mornings at after-hours clubs. Even if the people here were older and a thousand times less hip than her crowd back in the city, they formed a similar pocket of belonging.

"Mardi, great to see you!" Freya handed Mardi a drink right away. As soon as she tasted it, Mardi realized it was exactly what she wanted, mescal with pomegranate, jalapeño, and some other unidentifiable flavors that Mardi imagined came from herbs out of the greenhouse at Fair Haven, where she and Trent had shared their dinner. The memory felt distant already. How long exactly had she been in North Hampton? Time here was freaky.

"How did you know I would love this drink, Freya? Do you read minds?"

"I do where matters of the heart are concerned."

"That must get pretty weird on occasion."

"Mmm-hmm. It can be a little TMI sometimes."

"Still, it must also be cool to see into people's hearts."

"*You* could see into people's hearts too, Mardi, if you chose to focus. You have a seer's gift. I sense it. If you quieted down, you could see everything I see."

"Really, I feel like I can't see anything right now. I feel like the blindest kid in town." She took a long appreciative drink, licking the peppery rim of her glass to get the full intensity of its flavor. "What do you call this drink?"

"The Omnivore. I mixed it just for you. And I'll never pour it for another."

Mardi smiled. Freya was too awesome. "Freya, what do you think of Trent?"

"You mean Trent Gardiner?" Freya's green eyes came into sharp focus.

"Yeah, the guy we were hanging with in the greenhouse at Fair Haven the other night."

"What about him?" Freya asked. "He's great. One of my favorite people. He's basically like a brother to us. We sort of adopted him since he's all alone this summer."

"Cool."

"Have you mentioned him to your sister yet?" Freya asked.

Mardi shrugged. "No. Why should I? She's being such a pain lately."

Freya looked as if she wanted to say something more but had decided against it.

✳ *14* ✳

KISS

*A*s Molly rode across the bridge to Gardiners Island, her excitement was tinged with a slight foreboding. The house was not nearly as well lit as it had been the night of the party. Only two windows, one upstairs, one down, shone out into the night. The rest of the mansion appeared as a dark mass against a moonless sky. She could not help but recall Freya's words about the place being built over a seam between this world and the Land of the Dead. She began to feel vulnerable on Ingrid's bicycle, with black water on either side of her. Her protection spell would work against stupid human drivers, but would do nothing to save her from being swallowed up into the deep, were she to fall off the bridge and through some portal into a parallel world. Suddenly Daddy's warnings about Limbo didn't seem quite so frivolous. Maybe she should turn back?

Yet despite her fears, she was pulled toward the

island, with its promise of Tris, as if by soul-attracting magnet. She *had* to go; she had to see him again.

Once she was safely across the water and looking for a spot on the grassy dunes to lay her bike, a light rose at her back, illuminating the sand in front of her in a large glittering circle. For a second, she felt like an escaped convict who had just been caught at the climax of a dramatic manhunt. But, after a beat, she decided she appeared more like a pop star in the limelight, with her killer heels and freshly applied lipstick. Or at least that's how she should play it. After all, she wasn't sneaking around. She had been invited here.

She turned to the source of the light beam to see Tris holding a brass lantern above his head in order to spotlight her to maximum effect.

"Molly." His voice was deeply welcoming, an intimate stage whisper that carried across the dunes. "I'm so glad you came."

"I was curious to see the house without all those random locals crowding around."

"Fair enough." He took a step toward her. He was wearing crisp white jeans and a white linen shirt with his TG monogram in gold thread, gleaming rich and subtle on the cuffs. His bare bronzed feet rested comfortably in the sand. He was every bit the young lord of that manor in casual attire.

"Anything else you're curious about?" He smiled as he took her hand. "Aren't you a vision," he said as he took her waist and spun her so that the skirt of her white dress flared out into the night. "Come to the house. I'll mix you a drink. I can already tell we have much to celebrate."

This guy was too much. Yet Molly couldn't call him on it, and she allowed herself to be guided up the misty path to Fair Haven.

Molly was not accustomed to being spellbound. She was supposed to be the spell*binder*. This passive walking like a clueless bride being led to the altar was absurd. She had to get ahold of herself. However, she simply didn't feel like taking her accustomed control of the situation. Not quite yet.

Tris brought her into a small, mahogany-paneled library that she had not seen on her first visit. One wall was composed of floor-to-ceiling shelves of leather-bound, gold-lettered volumes. Between the wood panels on the other walls was hand-painted wallpaper in a striking William Morris floral design. Molly recognized it from an internship she had done last spring with a world-class interior decorator. The internship had started out well, as Molly had "a good eye," according to her employer, but ended abruptly when said employer asked Molly to pick up her dry cleaning one too many times and her boss arrived at a client meeting to find all her fabric samples in shreds, smelling distinctly of fried garlic.

"What are you smiling about?" Tris asked, ambling over to a gleaming bar cart.

"Just recalling a little prank I played a few months ago."

"Oh, yeah? I like pranks." He raised his eyebrows, so startlingly black over his bright blue eyes that she caught her breath. "Tell me about it," he said.

"It's not the sort of thing a girl like me is supposed to share." Buried in her refusal was the hint of a question. She was testing this young warlock. She could tell he knew she was a witch. And she was pretty sure he was aware that she was onto him too. But she wasn't going to be the first one to drop the façade.

"After one of my dirty martinis, you won't be able to keep it from me. In fact, you won't be able to keep anything from me."

"Dirty martinis are so housewife," she snorted.

"Is that so? Well, if you're after something with lychees or muddled mangoes, you've come to the wrong establishment. No toothpick umbrellas at Fair Haven, I'm afraid."

"I'm not even going to respond to that. I like my martinis without brine. Brine makes me think of mud. And I don't want to drink mud. Do you have any St-Germain?"

"I think I can manage a little elderflower."

"Good." She watched with pleasure as he began to do her bidding. "So, what're you doing in North Hampton?" she asked.

"I could ask you the same question."

"But you won't," she retorted, unstrapping her delicate sandals and letting them fall to the floor as she folded her smooth legs underneath her on the soft leather seat of the armchair.

"Okay, I won't. I pretty much do anything a beautiful girl tells me to do." For the first time, Tris lost his cockiness, and she felt herself truly vulnerable to his charms. Trying to resist his flattery was like swimming against a current. She knew there was no point in tackling it head-on. When you are caught in rip, Mardi always told her, you want to go at an angle.

"I'm still waiting for my answer," she deadpanned.

"Cheers first?" He handed her a golden martini and then raised his own "dirty" glass to hers. "Please, Molly Overbrook?" he asked, almost anxiously, as though he was worried she might disappear were he to say the wrong thing. "Drink with me?"

She had been prepared for the arrogance and the charm, but this vulnerability was potentially disarming. She wanted to give in, but she knew she shouldn't.

"Okay. I'll take one sip, if you'll tell me what you're really doing hiding here in East End instead of living out in the world," she said.

"Deal."

As they clinked glasses and drank deeply, he settled himself with feline grace on the arm of her chair, his toes grazing her bare thighs.

"I'm on Gardiners Island because I'm in a little bit of

trouble, I'm afraid. I think you might know what I'm talking about. We're the same, you and I."

She nodded. "Are you being punished by the Council too?"

He bristled just perceptibly. "Not exactly punished. But I need to lie low for a while."

Molly felt a thrill of recognition. She and Tris were prisoners of the same fate.

"Trystan Gardiner"—she locked eyes with him—"if this is an act, it's awfully convincing."

"Molly Overbrook, you are the most amazing and beautiful witch I've ever met. Not to mention one of the smartest. If this were an act, you would see right through it. Now, kiss me."

Molly wanted to understand more of her newly revealed soul mate, but she also wanted to stop thinking and to simply succumb to his embrace. The evening's riptide was suddenly taking her exactly where she wanted to go. Resistance was no longer necessary. She saw nothing but his deep blue eyes, his strong chin, and his muscular arms as he leaned in toward her and pressed his mouth against hers.

15

WILD HORSES

$\mathscr{B}$ack at the North Inn, Freya's delicious, spicy cocktail gave Mardi a brief sense of belonging. She downed it fast and instantly craved another. But as she started in on the second one, the drink began to take its true effect, and she surged inside with a deep longing for Trent. She looked across the bar at Freya, who shot her a quick smile and a complicit wink as if to say, *My mixology never fails to unveil my customers' true desires. Now, go out and find that boy of yours.*

"Thanks, Freya," Mardi whispered. With her second cocktail unfinished, she left a twenty-dollar tip under her glass and stepped out into the fresh air. Behind her the jukebox was blaring the Rolling Stones' "Wild Horses."

Slipping into the Ferrari, she opened her bag to fish for her keys and found the twenty she thought she had left on the bar. It was origami-folded into the shape of a heart.

"Freya, you are a keeper," she exclaimed into the salty night air as she revved the engine and took off for the docks.

Pulsing with expectation, Mardi approached the *Dragon* sometime after midnight. Her mind was alive with visions of Trent emerging sweetly from sleep at her touch, his bare muscular chest outlined in a soft white sheet. She pictured his eyes opening, his gaze alighting on her face, his arms outstretched in a wordless embrace. This was as corny and romantic as she had ever felt. She blamed Freya and her love potion, even if she wanted this boy as never before.

She walked up to the boat, but the *Dragon* was locked and empty. Trent had told her that whenever he was on board, he left the cabin door open. He didn't like the idea of shutting himself in. Of course it was just another way to say, *Come see me anytime—I'll be waiting.* Well, she was here now.

Except he was nowhere to be found. Had she missed her chance? Had she put him off for too long? Had he given up on her? Was he in bed with someone else at the very moment she wanted to be with him?

She sat on the dock and let the night hours roll over her, and her mind drifted back to the shaky memories of that awful night at Bret's house with the giant bronze tarantula, the "crown jewel" of the family's priceless sculpture collection. Had she and Molly really been na-ked in that slick black indoor pool, with the Valkyries singing opera on a giant flat screen while some creepy guy chased her and Molly through the water? Or had that ancient Creole memory god slipped them some peyote the other day in Freya's living room?

Through the predawn darkness, Mardi heard a rush of bicycle wheels coming off the Gardiners Island Bridge and guessed that Molly was racing back to Ingrid and Matt's house in time to make a show of being there in the morning. In spite of herself, she began to harbor a paranoid vision of Molly and Trent together. It seemed impossible, but then again, he wasn't here on his boat, and Molly had just spent the night at Fair Haven. Okay, so Trent wasn't exactly Molly's style of guy. She didn't go in for rough around the edges. But then again, he was a gorgeous, rich heir, no matter how he dressed.

Mardi winced into the breaking dawn. Her mind was racing. Molly *was* her identical twin. If Trent couldn't have Mardi, would he go for Molly? Would Molly be all in? Her sister wasn't known for her scru-ples where other people's crushes were concerned. Could this be their idea of a sick joke? Mardi tried to stop herself from thinking about it, but her skin crawled with suspicion.

The horizon started to a burn a faint rose gold. The first glimmer of dawn found Mardi dangling her feet over the side of the dock beside the empty *Dragon*. There was no sound except for the gentle lapping of the water against the sides of the boat. She felt her anger rise along with the sun.

She didn't exactly know what her dad expected her to take away from this summer of exile, but she feared that whatever his hopes were, they were going to be dashed. She was as dark, mad, and frustrated inside as ever.

One thing that happened when you entered a new microcosm, especially one as limited as North Hampton, was this: no matter how petty and lame you thought its social hierarchies were, you found yourself caring where you fit into them and whether or not you were having as good a time as everyone else. It was more than a competitive instinct; it was a desire to belong. Even in the lamest, preppiest, stupidest, most backward town on the planet, you didn't want to be alone.

Mardi stretched, took a final look at the vacant *Dragon*, and stood up. It was time to go home, put in a couple hours of sleep, and stop freaking out about her sister hooking up with her crush. Suddenly, she was exhausted. She craved the guest bed back at Ingrid and Matt's. In a few hours, a big load of kitchen equipment for the restaurant would arrive, and she would need some energy to get through the day. She figured it would be good for her to work blindingly hard. It would help numb her frustration.

As she was getting to her feet, two familiar voices approached her. She recognized Jean-Baptiste's gravelly French accent. It was as if she had conjured him with her thoughts about her and Molly's vision. And Jean-Baptiste was talking to none other than . . . Trent Gardiner.

"Lovely to see you again, young man."

"I'm glad we talked, Jean-Baptiste. Thank you," Trent said softly, as if to respect the sacred quiet of the dawn. Mardi realized as he spoke that she would know his melodic voice anywhere. It had burrowed deep inside her and lodged like a secret treasure. She hoped beyond hope that he hadn't been hooking up with her twin.

The men betrayed some surprise when they came upon Mardi stretching next to the *Dragon*, but neither one of them lost his composure.

"Why, Mardi!" Jean-Baptiste, dapper in an off-white linen suit, made her name sound like trickling notes of music. "How lovely to see you here, and how unexpected." It was impossible to know whether he was truly pleased, shocked, or annoyed. He was as unreadable as any good shrink.

Mardi didn't know whether she was more stunned to run into Jean-Baptiste on the docks at five-thirty in the morning or to realize that he was on such friendly terms with Trent, who was standing comfortably beside him in the green board shorts she liked so much, sipping coffee from a metal thermos. The coffee smelled like heaven.

Reading her mind, Trent held the thermos out to her. "You look like you need this as much as I do. This gentleman here does not know the meaning of rest. We've been talking all night."

"You have?" She tried not to sound too happy. "You've been with Jean-Baptiste all night?"

"Yep." He grinned. "All night."

She took his coffee gratefully, inhaled its steam, and felt her head clear so quickly that she looked at him with a start. This was no ordinary brew. Trent was no ordinary guy. And here he was hanging out with the god of memory. He *had* to be one of them. That would explain so much. But she wasn't quite ready to ask him openly what his divine status was. Their dance was not far enough along yet.

"I see that you two are acquainted," Trent said, looking from Mardi to Jean-Baptiste.

"Yes, thanks to my lovely young friends Ingrid and Freya Beauchamp. They have convinced me to spend the summer here, to escape the New Orleans heat and to help Mardi and her twin sister, Molly, with a project they have."

"A project?" Trent looked mischievous. How much, Mardi wondered, did he know?

Mardi took a deep breath and began to explain without really explaining. "You see, Jean-Baptiste is part of the doomed effort to reform Molly and me. You should know, Trent, that the two of us, the terrible twins, have been sent here by our father, who fears we are out of control. Dad thinks a summer in the town that time forgot, with normal jobs, life in a stable family that doesn't live on takeout, and sessions with Dr. Mésomier here will somehow set us straight." She was trying to be sarcastic, but her words had no barb. She was too happy to see Trent and profoundly relieved to see he wasn't with any other girl, let alone her twin.

"Well," said Jean-Baptiste, "I'd best be getting back to the Rose Cottage, my charming if overstuffed, overchintzed bed-and-breakfast. My hostess, Mrs. Ashley Green, is a lovely woman, but she does tend to worry about her guests. Besides, I'm rather spent after an evening keeping up with this one." He gestured to Trent.

"You look less tired than either of us," Trent said. It was true. After a presumably sleepless night, Jean-Baptiste was as crisp and bright as his violet pocket square, while Mardi and Trent were both yawning as they passed the coffee back and forth.

"Nevertheless, I shall leave you two," Jean-Baptiste said with a quiet, knowing smile. Mardi and Trent locked eyes for a moment, and by the time they looked around again, the old man had evaporated.

"This coffee is fantastic," Mardi said, enjoying his intense gaze on her as she drank.

"Have you been here long?" he asked.

"I was at the North Inn for a while, hanging out with Freya, and I thought I'd stop by the *Dragon* on my way home—even though it's not really on my way home—and see what you were up to."

He nodded.

She noticed his eyes drawn to the rainbow snake around her neck. He looked at it with such interest that she shimmered inside. No one had ever taken her in so fully before. Yet she still hadn't opened up about who she really was. And neither had he.

"Look, the sun is coming up," she said, looking out at the first rays.

He came up behind her, wrapped her in his arms and nestled his chin on her shoulder. "It's so peaceful, isn't it?" he whispered in her ear.

"Mmmm." She leaned back into him.

"Mardi, I don't want to push you, but I want you to understand that I really care about you, and I can tell you're in some kind of trouble. Jean-Baptiste didn't tell me much. He feels he can't. But he gives me the impression that your struggle is more than a simple discipline problem. You're not just some spoiled brat from the big city. I want you to know. . . ." He trailed off.

"Know what?"

"That I'm just like you," he whispered, and she knew exactly what he meant.

"I thought so" was all she could manage.

"You're not the only one who's exiled here," he continued. "I need Jean-Baptiste's help as much as you do."

She turned around to face him. There was hardly a

breath of space between them. For a few beats, she simply looked into his eyes. Then, because her feelings for him were, yet again, too powerful for her to understand, she pulled away. "I should go," she said.

Gently he took her hands in his. "Wild horses can't drag me away," he said, as if he had read her mind earlier. But he released her and turned toward his beautiful boat while she wandered back to her red convertible, her heart full of hope and confusion.

*

PART TWO

SUMMER NIGHTS

*

16

WE ARE FAMILY

Although it was profoundly bucolic, North Hampton was not devoid of progress. The once decrepit, faintly sleazy motel on the outskirts of town had recently been gussied up into a boutique establishment, complete with vintage photographs in burnished frames and Jonathan Adler throw pillows in nautical colors. Not to mention the historic estate of Fair Haven, which, as the whole town knew, had just been renovated with central air, induction stoves, and radiant heat in its bathroom floors. Among the local clam shacks and candy stores, a traveler could now also find some of the same gourmet food that was flooding the rest of the Hamptons.

The Cheesemonger carried several brands of hand-crafted crackers at ten dollars a box. An ambitious young local named Joshua Goose was opening a restaurant whose menu would explain the provenance of every beet green and beef cheek without a trace of irony.

But these were superficial changes. They gave North Hampton the illusion of keeping up with the times when, in fact, it was shrouded for eternity in a spell of timelessness. How else could its inhabitants fail to notice that the Beauchamp sisters, Freya and Ingrid, never aged? No one had ever noticed as their mother, Joanna, felt her wrinkles go smooth, her gray hair go brown, and her belly swell in order to give birth to them again all those years ago. North Hampton, despite its nod to the occasional trend, was a place of oblivion.

It was also a place that prided itself on its traditions, one of which was Manhattan clam chowder, made with clams from the bay and chunks of potato, onion, and tomato from surrounding farms. So when Marshall suggested that they try making and selling New England clam chowder, the kind made with cream instead of tomatoes, Molly was skeptical. "People here wear the same brand of Top-Siders from the cradle to the grave, Cheeseboy. I can't really picture them suddenly going for a new soup. Especially since Manhattan chowder is their specialty. They're so proud of it."

"You're the one who told me they keep inventing new bagel flavors in New York. And what's more New York than a bagel?"

"Are you really going to compare North Hampton to New York?"

"I guess you're right. North Hampton has so many distinct advantages."

She laughed. "Like?"

"It has fewer roaches. Fewer rats. And it has outdoor opera on the Fourth of July, which is tomorrow night by the way. In case you don't have plans. How about some Wagner under the stars? I make the best picnic in town."

"Am I dreaming, Cheesefriend, or are you actually trying to ask me out again?" Her joking tone took the edge off. "Are you one of those people who doesn't learn from experience? Like the mice who keep reaching for the electric shock button even after the hundredth time? Because the button looks like a piece of cheese?"

He laughed. "Are you really calling your boss a lab animal?"

You had to hand it to Cheeseboy. Against all odds, he remained playfully persistent.

"Oh, my God, I forgot you're my boss!" She covered her face with her hands in mock drama, peeking through long manicured fingers at him as he dropped handfuls of parsley into his creamy chowder. "I depend on you, *Mr.* Cheeseboy, for such a huge part of my up-keep!" She gestured up and down the multicolored designer sundress that had surely cost more than a week's paycheck from the Cheesemonger. "I mean, this job almost covers my sock budget. Not stockings. I didn't say stockings. That would be asking too much. Besides, they don't sell Wolford in this town. But it pretty much covers my athletic socks. So, I guess I better not blow it and alienate you. I guess I have to say yes to your date. So, what time is that opera thing tomorrow? And what is it again? Wagner? Do I like Wagner? By the way, does this count as sexual harassment? Because you're my boss and all."

Partly, she wanted to make Tris a little jealous, since he hadn't mentioned any plans for the Fourth of July. Although in all fairness, they hadn't done much talking once they had started making out the other night. But partly, Molly couldn't help but find Cheeseboy cute, even if he was, you know, Cheeseboy.

She could see that he was so stunned and happy by her acceptance that he had to pretend to be absorbed in his cooking while he scrambled for a comeback worthy of her banter. After a few seconds, he said, "I think you'll like the Wagner a lot. The concert is a little, um, cheesy in that it's a 'greatest hits' of the Ring Cycle. So it's sort of high art meets Americana. But that's sort of how I think of you. You're an exquisite, yet all-American beauty."

"You think of me as 'high art meets Americana'?" She was trying to hold up her end of the conversation, but something about the words *Ring Cycle* was throwing her. Her body surged with the same otherworldly tingling she had felt during that creepy memory therapy session at Freya's house when that old Frenchman with the cool pocket square, Jean-Baptiste, had taken her and Mardi back to that weird night at Bret's. Scared that she was losing her balance, she gripped the counter.

Marshall didn't seem to notice. "Do you want to try my soup?" he asked.

"I guess," she managed. "Do I have a choice?"

He held out a spoon to her mouth. As she leaned toward it, she felt herself swoon. There was heavy music pounding in her head. Images of her and Mardi's ring snaked across her field of vision, and she lost her balance.

"Are you okay?" Marshall yelled as he saved her from face-planting into the chowder pot.

The next thing she knew, she was draped across the shop's gingham-upholstered window seat with a cool wet washcloth pressed to her forehead. Marshall was standing above her, slowly coming into focus as her nausea ebbed. From below, his ordinary features appeared reassuringly familiar, but also strikingly handsome.

"I don't know what happened," she said, slowly sitting up.

Just then, her phone rang. It was Daddy. His ringtone was "We Are Family" by Sister Sledge, which always brought an ironic smile to Molly's glossy lips, because she, Daddy, and Mardi were hardly a traditional family. They were no more than three strong-willed individuals bound up together, with no rhythms, no traditions, no center. Living with Ingrid, Matt, and the kids, with their aromas of home cooking and their chore lists taped to the fridge, was really bringing this fact home.

Marshall handed her the phone.

"Thanks, Ch—I mean, Marshall."

"You're welcome."

He was so kind. And not bad-looking either. Cute, really. Something was melting inside her.

"I really mean it. Thanks."

He winked and went back to his place behind the counter.

"Hi, Daddy," she sighed into her phone.

"Sweetheart, you sound upset. You must have heard the awful news. Did Ingrid tell you?"

"Daddy, I can't deal with your hysteria right now. I'm not feeling so great. Can we talk later?"

"Molly, this is serious. There's a formal accusation by the dead girl's parents. They have testimony from some of the kids and teachers at school about your outrageous pranks. The word *witchcraft* is actually being used. It was in the *Post* today."

"Daddy, this is the twenty-first century. No one is going to get tried for witchcraft in New York City." She tried to sound blithe, but she was starting to feel some of his anxiety. Her usual steely self-confidence was beginning to falter. So she did what she always did when she felt threatened. She said something mean.

"You live in an ancient fantasy world, Daddy. We're never going to be able to return to Asgard, and the mortals of this world think you wear a red cape and hold a hammer, okay? I gotta go."

Molly wasn't stupid. She knew that if there was a trial it would end up being about what mortals considered "facts," and not about witchcraft. But she also knew that the witchcraft thing could easily take hold in the public imagination, that people could start talking and asking questions, and that the White Council would not be remotely psyched about this, which was why Daddy was so stressed. Even if he was an absent single father, she had to admit that he did have some protective instincts. Maybe he was acting so crazy now in an attempt to make up for lost time.

To reassure herself, she felt for the ring on the chain around her neck.

But it wasn't there.

She panicked and began to look around frantically.

"Are you all right?" Marshall sounded concerned from behind the counter.

"I'm fine. It's nothing," she said, beginning to tremble. Was it possible that she had unhooked the chain and slipped it onto Mardi's neck, or that Mardi had taken it and slipped it on her finger? She didn't have the faintest memory. She would have to discreetly check Mardi's neck and hands later. Still, all of Molly's intuition told her Mardi didn't have it. No, Molly had misplaced it herself. But where? And when?

It came to her. It must have somehow fallen off in Tris's library while they were hooking up. Her memory of the evening was hardly sharp. The thick chain was long enough to fit over her head without unclasping it. It must have come off when other things were coming off.

Trembling, she felt the empty spot on her chest where the ring had lain. Although she did not know exactly why, she knew that losing her mother's ring could be disastrous. How could she have been so delirious?

She would double-check tonight that Mardi did not have it. And if it wasn't around Mardi's neck or on her hand, then she, Molly, would go back to Fair Haven and find it.

Soon.

* 17 *

TAKE ME TO THE WATER

The smell of chocolate cake was growing stronger and more delicious by the minute, filling the house with a sense of promise. Mardi had never baked before, and she was amazed by the simple pleasure of mixing the sugar, butter, eggs, flour, chocolate, and buttermilk under the tutelage of Ingrid and Jo, while Henry licked utensils. She had always thought you bought cakes at bakery counters, usually at the last minute when you remembered it was someone's birthday. This experience of actually making one with her hands unveiled a whole new realm of magic to her.

"Smells good in here," Matt sang out as he came through the sliding glass doors that opened onto a deck on the beach. He was wrapped in a towel after a swim. "Looks good too," he said to Ingrid, giving her what Mardi couldn't help noticing was a deep kiss. *Maybe they weren't so uptight after all,* she thought. And then it occurred to her again that because he was mortal, he would die before their passion did. That sucked.

Jo and Henry came running up to their father. Henry leapt into his arms, and the family portrait they made was so charming that Ingrid's choice was beginning to make some sense.

"Daddy!" Jo squealed, "We're baking a Fourth of July cake for our picnic! It's going to have whipped cream frosting and red and blue sprinkles. That makes red, white, and blue! Get it? Mommy, can we decorate it soon?"

"It has to come out of the oven and then cool first, sweetie. *Then* we can frost it." Ingrid smiled as she went to answer her ringing phone, wiping her hands on her apron so as not to get flour on the phone. "Hello? Oh hi, Troy, how are you? . . . You're kidding." With a furtive and anxious glance at Mardi, she went out onto the deck, sliding the glass door behind her, and began to pace as she talked.

Matt went upstairs to take a shower, leaving Mardi to watch Henry and Jo, who were wild with excitement about the picnic tonight with the opera on the big town green overlooking the sea. Poor kids had no idea they were going to be subjected to a bunch of fat people screeching in German all night.

Mardi was relieved that she wasn't going to the concert. Trent had invited her out on the *Dragon* to see the fireworks up close—they were going to be launched from a barge off Gardiners Island.

Mardi felt sure that tonight was the night they would finally kiss. It would be just the two of them, with a bottle of wine and one of his delicious meals, watching the rockets fire and the colors rain through the night sky. She'd foraged a great outfit from Freya's attic closet: a dress from a '60s love-in, made out of an American flag with peace signs graffitied between the stripes. It was sewn into a toga, a very short toga, with fringe. To match it, she had star-spangled garters from Freya's vast lingerie collection. It was going to be a good night.

Henry broke her reverie by squealing one of his few words over and over: "Beach! Beach! Beach!" He tugged her out the door, past Ingrid, who was still on the phone, in an apparently stressful and all-consuming conversation. Impatiently, she waved Henry and Mardi past her on the deck, then ignored Jo asking her when the cake would be out of the oven.

After about fifteen minutes of halfheartedly helping Henry load and unload a plastic dump truck full of wet sand while Jo worked on a sand castle, Mardi saw a stone-faced Ingrid heading toward them.

"Jo!" Ingrid snapped. "How many times do I have to tell you, no magic sand castles!"

Jo was busily constructing a latticework palace with simple waves of her shovel.

"Use your hands like a normal kid," Ingrid went on relentlessly. "We don't do 'special' in our family."

"But that's so boring," Jo whined as she watched her beautiful construction crumble into a heap on the ground.

Ignoring her daughter's complaint, Ingrid gave Mardi a long and serious look. "I just spoke with your father," she said. "Things in New York are not looking good." She proceeded to explain that there was a formal accusation against the Overbrook sisters by the family of the dead girl, Samantha Hill. Mardi and Molly were accused of brainwashing with an intent to kill, but the subtext was witchcraft.

When Mardi tried to interrupt in her own defense, Ingrid told her that there was another development. Right before calling her, Troy had received a warning from the White Council. The Council was concerned that the twins were not only wantonly disrespectful, but that they were unleashing a rash of bad magic into Midgard.

"What exactly did the Council's message say?" Mardi asked as they headed back toward the house with the kids in tow.

"It said, 'Beware the storm of retribution.'"

"Well, that could be a metaphor for almost anything," Mardi laughed nervously.

"No," Ingrid corrected her, sliding open the screen to the deck. "It could be a metaphor for almost anything *negative*. We're going to have to do another session with Jean-Baptiste as soon as possible to figure out what happened that night and clear your names."

Coming into the house, they were assaulted by a burnt smell and a haze of smoke.

"The cake!"

Henry and Jo both burst into tears. Mardi tried hard to stifle a grin. These people were so earnest.

Ingrid and the kids ran to the oven. Dropping the pretense of oven mitts, Ingrid pulled out the blackened cake with her bare hands. It was a sad sight, a steaming lump of coal.

"Please, Mommy, please fix it," Jo begged, while Henry gazed at her with huge imploring eyes.

Mardi watched carefully as Ingrid caved, her face melting into a smile. "Okay," she said, "I'll do it for your grandmother Joanna. She would have loved you so much. And spoiled you so rotten." As she murmured an incantation over the pan, the smoke cleared, the delicious odor of chocolate returned, and the cake rose again. Jo and Henry squealed with delight. Promise was restored to the day.

Ingrid gave Mardi a sheepish smile as she put her finger to her lips. "I know, I know. All right. You got me. Why don't you go get ready for your date."

Mardi slipped into her vintage red, white, and blue. Then she gunned the Ferrari down to the docks, trying to banish negative thoughts brought on by her father's drama queen antics. What the Hell was a "storm of retribution," anyway? A lot of hot air was what it was. Dad might even have been making up the whole White Council thing to freak them out. Since he had no control over his daughters, he was always trying to get higher authorities to step in and parent for him. A summer at Ingrid's with the threat of divine punishment if she and Mardi didn't shape up might well be nothing more than his latest desperate stab at being a father. Pathetic. Not for the first time, she wondered what her mother had been like.

It took her a while to find Trent. When she finally did locate him, he was sanding a countertop in the kitchen of his friend's soon-to-open new restaurant. He was shirtless. His back was sculpted, every lean muscle defined, alive, and alert. His chest and stomach were toned by swimming in the ocean and working on the docks rather than lifting weights. His beauty was unconscious, carefree. It was all she could do not to run her fingers up and down the grooves of his muscles.

"You look incredible," Trent said when he saw her. He apologized for not being quite ready to set sail and promised that there was wine and a killer picnic on the boat if she wanted to go wait for him on the *Dragon*'s deck.

She went to hang out on the boat for a moment, thinking she would enjoy the calm of the sunset and the distant strains of the orchestra tuning as all of North Hampton gathered on the town green for the annual Fourth of July concert. But instead of feeling peaceful as she sat on the *Dragon*'s cushions, leaning on a pile of orange life jackets, she felt a tempest brewing inside her from the White Council's warning. It was so unfair! They hadn't done anything. Every gentle lap of the sea against the side of the boat set off a flurry of furious reverberations in her soul. She was like Jo or Henry on the verge of a tantrum. Only instead of pounding little fists on the floor, she had the urge to set fire to every boat in this harbor, to watch the sails go up in a vast conflagration of her own making, and to feel herself burn among them. She hated the White Council. They had nothing to do with her life, and yet they were threatening to wreck it.

She hadn't done anything to those kids back in the city. She and Molly were spoiled rotten, wild and selfish and heedless, but they weren't murderers. Except she was beginning to wonder now how well she actually knew herself and just how much evil she might be capable of. What had Jean-Baptiste called them? Twin goddesses of strength and rage? Of course since Thor was their father it made sense. But did that make them She-Hulks or something? Maybe she and Molly had bewitched and killed those kids. Maybe they *were* evil.

"Mardi, are you all right? You look upset," Trent said, with a worried look on his face.

"What are you talking about? I'm fine."

"All right, then, look what I stole from the cellar of Fair Haven." It was a 1999 bottle of Château Lafite Rothschild. "A very special year."

"I was born in 1999," she said, impressed.

He winked as he uncorked the bottle and poured two glasses. The ruby liquid sloshed a bit more than usual. Everything around her seemed to be surging with secret power, even though the night was beautifully calm.

You're projecting, she thought. Aloud she simply said "cheers," as he started the motor.

After a short ride, they anchored off Gardiners Island at a safe distance from the barge that would set off the firework display that the Gardiner family organized every year for the citizens of North Hampton.

Trent had put on a light blue linen shirt. As he set out their picnic of smoked bluefish, oysters, and lobster salad with tarragon from his greenhouse garden, the breeze began to pick up so that his shirt billowed in a pale blue cloud and her American Flag dress flew up to reveal Freya's funky garters.

Trent raised his eyebrows in amusement and wolf whistled.

Mardi tried to meet his smile head-on, but felt a momentary shyness. She looked down at her bare feet only to be surprised by a sudden wave washing across the deck over her toes. She scanned the water for a big vessel that might have caused the surge, but saw none. Then she noticed Trent doing the same, a tinge of anxiety in his eyes.

"Isn't the weather supposed to be perfect tonight?" she asked.

"Everything about tonight is supposed to be perfect," he said over the howling rising wind.

* 18 *

DAS RHEINGOLD

Cheeseboy had gone all-out on his picnic for Molly. He had brought a plaid cashmere blanket, the chic wicker basket, overflowing with delicacies, that had first attracted her to the Cheesemonger's window, and a cooler packed with oysters and champagne. He had shucked the oysters before her eyes, arranging them on a bed of ice as the orchestra tuned.

She commented on the rough sea and darkening sky. What was going on with the weather? Wasn't it supposed to be a beautiful evening?

Of course it was a beautiful evening, he said almost defensively, filling two champagne flutes, acting as though she were wildly exaggerating the effect of a gust of twilight breeze. He obviously didn't want some surprise storm to ruin the effect of his long-planned evening.

As the overture to the Ring Cycle began, an expectant hush came over the crowd on the green. A single note repeated, at first only on the strings. As the rest of the orchestra progressively joined in, and the note took on volume, there was a thunderclap from the east. The sound of pounding surf from the nearby beach competed with the percussion section to dominate the rhythm of the music. It was as though a battle were rumbling to life.

The tune was hauntingly familiar, although Molly couldn't think why. She wasn't exactly an opera buff. Once, she had gone to a benefit at the Metropolitan Opera House because the chance to wear her favorite floor-length Versace gown was too good to pass up. She couldn't even remember who the composer was. Mozart? Verdi? They all sounded the same. The only thing she clearly recalled was that she had fallen asleep during the first act and made her date take her home early.

For some reason, though, this music was echoing deep inside her, connecting with her unconscious. "What's this opera about, anyway?" she whispered.

"See those mermaid-like creatures 'swimming' on the stage?" he said, referring to three large, lusty singers in big iridescent dresses floundering around in billowing sheets of blue plastic that Molly assumed were supposed to represent water.

"Yeah?"

"Those are the Rhinemaidens, and they possess something called the Rhinegold, a magical gold. Whoever forges a ring from the Rhinegold will have immense power."

Shivering in her sheer wrap, Molly felt instinctively for her ring on the chain around her neck. Nothing. It was really lost. And this silly opera plot was randomly driving the point home.

"And see that guy who just rose up from the 'crack in the Earth'?" Marshall went on enthusiastically.

She nodded. There was a stocky bearded man pursuing the Rhinemaidens through gusts of steam coming out of the floor while everyone sang loudly in incomprehensible German.

"That's Alberich, the Nibelung. Since the Rhinemaidens won't love him, he's going to steal their gold to forge a powerful ring. It will make him lord of many lands, and, most importantly, it will allow him to subjugate the women who have hurt him, to take revenge on the female race, and—" Marshall was interrupted by more thunder and a wild streak of lightning as the sound system died with a fierce screech and the music was replaced by a crashing rain and screams from the crowd.

The lights on the boats, which had gathered around Gardiners Island for a close-up view of the fireworks, were darting up and down on the suddenly hectic sea. Several of them were sending out flares of alarm, which flickered, barely visible, in the rain-blackened sky. A coast guard siren blared as rescue boats sped out toward them. People everywhere were screaming, running from the green with their picnic blankets flapping behind them like ghosts.

No weather news source had predicted this. Nature was throwing a tantrum. Unannounced.

"Let's go!" Marshall yelled over the din, taking her hand and pulling her toward town. "We can be inside the store in five minutes."

But Molly could not take her eyes off the raging sea. She stood, drenched, fixated on the lights of the stranded boat. "My sister's out there!" she cried.

Mardi had been making obnoxious comments for the past couple of days about how she would be seeing the fireworks from the deck of a yacht off Gardiners Island. She wouldn't say whose yacht, but she implied that she was going to have way more fun than anyone else in Ingrid's house. No boring concert on the green for her.

Molly had been annoyed, dismissive, and secretly a bit jealous of Mardi's date, since Tris seemed to have disappeared for the holiday and she was stuck on a boring picnic with Cheeseboy. But as it hit her now that Mardi might be in real danger, her irritation vanished in a desperate surge of fear and love.

"Mardi!" she screamed, her voice carrying across the water with a force that put the local opera singers to shame. "Mardi, where are you?"

"Please, Molly," Marshall tried to reason with her, "if your sister is in any trouble, the coast guard will rescue her. They can do much more than we can."

Ignoring him, she rushed to join Ingrid and Freya, who were pushing through the crowd toward her. As the three witches fell into an embrace, they sang out Mardi's name in unison. It was an incantation. They had no doubt that Mardi would now know that they were coming for her.

Marshall looked on, soaked and bewildered but unwilling to abandon Molly.

"We need a coast guard boat!" Freya shrieked. With that, she turned and led the others to the docks, running as fast as her heels would allow. Molly assumed they would lose Marshall at this point, but, amazingly, he kept up, his eyes pulsing the brightest blue through the storm, as though he had somehow been touched by their magic.

Molly watched in admiration as a shivering Freya ordered a member of the coast guard to hand over the keys to his boat. Although he had been ready to spring into action, he simply stepped aside and allowed the three drenched women and their gangly sidekick to commandeer his motorboat.

"Look, I have to go," she said to Marshall. "Stay here. Please."

Marshall shook his head. "I won't leave you!" he said bravely.

But Molly couldn't risk his life as well, and she mouthed a spell to send him to safety.

He ran back to shore, and she joined Freya and Ingrid on the boat.

All three of them honed their perceptions on Mardi's aura. They sensed distress, but they also sensed a strong life force. Without bothering to turn the key, they revved their boat's engine. They didn't steer or even seem to get their bearings as they maneuvered at supernatural speed, unperturbed by the giant swells and echoing cries for help all around. In a flash, they were at the side of a large sailboat floundering between the bridge and the firework barge. Its name, *Dragon*, was written in red script across the hull.

Molly had a flash of recognition. Wasn't that the name of the Gardiner brother's boat? Had Tris mentioned it? Had she heard it somewhere else? Why would Mardi be on the Gardiners' boat? But this line of suspicious questioning was quickly subsumed by the urgency of finding Mardi.

A huge wave washed over their commandeered boat. The witches withstood it like pillars of stone. They scanned the black storm for Mardi's even blacker hair and dark eyes.

Freya stood, spread her arms, flew onto the *Dragon*, and disappeared belowdecks, only to resurface a moment later and cry out, "No one's left on the boat." She leapt back among them. "She's either on a lifeboat or she's swimming for shore."

The raging sea was dotted with orange lifeboats, tossing every which way. Coast guard boats were trying to tow them, while stopping constantly to pull people from the water. It would be a miracle if no one drowned on what had been, less than an hour ago, the most promising night of the summer to date.

Molly secretly began to bargain with fate to get her sister back. She swore under her breath to appreciate Mardi more, to share her best clothes after they had passed their prime instead of consigning them. She also promised to work closely with Mardi to solve the mystery that was plaguing them. If only she could have her sister stay in this world now, they could prove their innocence together. No power could deny them that. "Please!" she cried. "Please!"

In silent accord, like hunting dogs on a scent, Molly, Ingrid, and Freya began to sense Mardi's energy in the water nearby. They scanned the foam swirling around the *Dragon* as they slowly moved their little boat in the direction of her aura. Their impression grew progressively stronger as they headed toward the bridge. She had to be swimming, or drifting on a lifeboat, in the direction of Gardiners Island, where Fair Haven was now lit up from every window to provide a beacon of light in the tempest.

As they were searching the foaming water, Freya screamed, "A boy! Floating over there in a life jacket!" The boat veered in the direction of the bright yellow splash of color. Sure enough, there was a small boy, floating limp and lifeless, his hair splayed around him as if it were turning to weeds.

Molly burst into tears as Freya pulled the drowned child on board. The boy looked about six. Jo's age.

Ingrid raised her arms to the angry sky. "Mother! If you can hear us, you have to help us now. He's only been gone a few minutes. His soul is still lingering in this world. Mother, please! Send him back!"

From nowhere, Freya produced a lantern that she shone onto the boy's chalk-white face. They all held their breath. Nothing. No sign of life returning. If anything, his jaw appeared to clamp into an even tighter mask of death.

Molly knew enough about resurrection to know it was a dangerous proposition. You could only bring people back if they hadn't crossed to the other side yet.

Muttering spells in unison, Ingrid and Freya acted as one. Molly watched with astonishment. She and Mardi had never worked their magic together except to play tricks on people. She stared at the child's pale, lifeless face. So this was what death looked like. This was what had happened to Parker and Sam. It was horrible.

Ingrid and Freya's voices grew louder against the howling wind. But despite their spells, the boy remained limp in their arms. His face in the lantern light turned to marble. His childish lips went pure white.

"Please, Mother," Freya whispered.

Then, from out from the heart of the storm shot a bolt of lightning. It hit their boat, electrifying it in a bright and terrifying flash. Molly screamed, but Ingrid and Freya continued their chanting unbroken, staring at the boy, allowing themselves to smile as a dusky color returned to his cheeks and he began to cough up seawater, gasping his way back into the life he would never know he had lost.

Molly was awestruck. So this was what witchcraft was all about.

As Molly, Ingrid, and Freya all leaned in to comfort the confused and terrified little boy, they were stunned by the sound of Mardi's voice.

"Finally! I thought you'd never get here," she said as she hoisted herself onto the boat.

Molly wrapped her sister in a tight embrace. "Mardi! We've been so scared. *I've* been so scared. What happened to you?"

Mardi looked over at the *Dragon*. "I'm not totally sure," she said. The fact that they could hear her clearly, even though she was speaking in a normal voice, made them suddenly aware that the storm was dying down as quickly as it had appeared. Within moments, the sky was clear and the tempest was fading to a dream. The *Dragon* bobbed peacefully on a glossy sea.

"We thought we were going to capsize." Mardi seemed to be straining to remember. "Trent put me on a lifeboat. I thought he was going to jump into the lifeboat with me, but once he saw that I was safe, he disappeared."

Molly wanted to ask who Trent was, but she didn't want to interrupt the flow of Mardi's story. She told herself he must be the captain the Gardiners had hired for their boat. There really wasn't any other possibility, was there?

"I figured," Mardi continued, her eyes glittering with the intensity of what she had just lived, "that he had gone to rescue people in the water. There was no way I was going to sit there like some pathetic girl when I can swim as fast as he can. So I went after him, and I found him helping with the coast guard, dragging people to their boats. We worked side by side for a while. Then we were separated by an enormous wave. I've been treading water, looking for him, for a while now. I'm exhausted. If you all hadn't come . . ." Her voice cracked, and she lost her veneer of toughness. "Thank you," she said. The three women embraced her.

Everything was going to be fine. The stars were not only visible again but twinkling happily. The whole upheaval had lasted barely an hour.

"I hope Trent is okay," Mardi said to no one in particular. "He's so strong, though. I'm sure he made it home."

And where was home? Molly burned to ask, but for once she held back so as not to start a stupid fight. She might never be this happy to see her sister again. It was a moment to savor.

Molly took Mardi's hands in hers and said nothing. She could not help but notice that her sister's fingers and neck were bare. The ring they had shared since before they could remember, their only heirloom from their vanished mother, their magical ring, was truly gone. Worse, Molly knew she was the one who had lost it.

* 19 *

SHELTER FROM THE STORM

$\mathcal{M}$iraculously, no one had drowned in the freak storm on the Fourth of July, and there had been no severe damage to the docks or beaches, no flooding or erosion. It was as though the sudden gale had been a threat, a warning, or a test. But in the days that followed, as calm was restored to the town of North Hampton, a characteristic forgetfulness set in among its inhabitants. Since it left no visible traces and had not touched any other part of East End except for the little town, the storm quickly faded from conversation and from conscious memory.

Despite the general amnesia, there were a few in North Hampton for whom the events of July Fourth remained starkly clear and menacing.

Freya and Ingrid had summoned Mardi and Molly to another memory session with Jean-Baptiste in Freya's living room to talk about the storm and its possible connection to what was happening back in New York, to try to stimulate their memories again. The session was to take place at eleven P.M., which was around the same time that Mardi and Molly became vague about the sequence of events at Bret's party. Jean-Baptiste felt that holding their session at the corresponding time of night might be a way to harness some power of suggestion. Only the twins were late.

Ingrid, Freya, and Jean-Baptiste had gone ahead to the lobster dinner Freya had cooked to raise everyone's spirits. But at the last minute, Mardi and Molly had to babysit the kids until Matt, who was working late on a case, could get back from the precinct.

It was close to midnight when they began their drive out to the isolated stretch of beach where Freya's unexpectedly sleek house nestled in the dunes. As Mardi sped along the empty roads, past dark farms and shadowy dwellings, she knew Molly was probably freaking out. Molly was clenching her teeth, but she wasn't screaming, as she usually did, about how she didn't want to be decapitated in her prime. Ever since the rescue at sea, the sisters had been holding back from lashing out at each other. In fact, they were being almost pleasant.

Whereas normally they would have spent the entire drive bickering and insulting each other, with Molly yelling that Mardi should have her license revoked and her ridiculous car impounded, while Mardi called Molly a lame princess, they were now chatting amiably, even giggling together about the makeshift dinner they had just pulled off for Henry and Jo.

They'd never made pasta before. They hardly even knew how to boil water. And yet somehow they had managed linguine with pesto sauce this evening.

Jo had explained to them that you salted the water and didn't put the pasta in until it was boiling. She showed them the big pot, the colander, and the pesto sauce in the freezer that her mom made every year with basil from their garden. Mardi had left a plastic lid on the first batch in an attempt to defrost it in the microwave. That hadn't gone so well, much to the kids' delight. But she'd nailed the second batch, and everyone had been cheerful. The linguine had even come out al dente.

After dinner, as instructed, they had put on an episode of *Little House on the Prairie* for the kids. Mardi was immediately sucked into some drama involving stolen candy at Mr. Oleson's General Store. She would have been embarrassed in front of Molly if she hadn't seen that Molly was also glued to the screen. It had taken them a while to notice that Henry had wandered off.

They found him sitting on the kitchen island. He had built a pyramid out of steak knives. Before they could stop him, he slammed a rolling pin into the heart of his creation and sent the blades flying all around his little body. Molly screamed, but he remained unscathed, and unperturbed, as the blades stuck into the wooden countertop, surrounding him in a jagged circle.

Mardi and Molly laughed about it now, as they drove through the warm night, top down, their long dark hair flying. "Either that kid is a budding warlock or he's a total klutz," Mardi said.

"What do you mean, he's a klutz? He never gets a scratch."

"I mean that maybe he's such a spaz that Ingrid has covered his little diapered ass with the most powerful protection spell out there. Hasn't that occurred to you?" Mardi asked.

"I guess that's the kind of thing mothers do?"

"I guess. . . . Not that *we* would know."

They drove on in companionable silence. Mardi even slowed down a little.

It had been several days now since the storm, and Mardi caught herself wondering how long this cease-fire with Molly could possibly hold out. She was stealing a glance at her gorgeous sister as she pulled into Freya's driveway when her phone beeped from beside the gearbox.

It must be Trent again. They had been texting one another, trying to set another date to go out in the boat and make up for their disastrous attempt to see the fireworks together. As Mardi had guessed, Trent, sensing that Mardi was safe, had made it to shore that awful night, after making several rescues.

Even though they had barely touched, the two of them had an understanding now. She slid her tongue stud back and forth over the roof of her mouth in anticipation.

But the text wasn't from Trent. It was from a blocked

number. She lifted her glowing phone to her face as she killed the motor.

I know what you and your sister did. You're not fooling anyone.

Mardi's first impulse was to share this freaky message with her sister. How bizarre that it was coming through at the very moment they had arrived to begin their memory session in order to recover more details of the night of the murders. She began, "Molly, you're never going to believe this—"

But as she was handing over the phone, she was stopped by a continuation of the message, scrolling before her in real time.

If you share this message with anyone, especially her, something terrible will happen to your twin. I'm warning you.

Mardi snatched the phone back and held it close. Molly, her curiosity piqued, lunged for it.

"Come on, show me! What is it?" Molly's tone was playful at first, but once she saw that Mardi wasn't joking and really wasn't going to show her the phone, Molly's whole face darkened.

Mardi recognized a tantrum brewing and tried to stave it off. "Look, I'm sorry, Moll," she said. "It was a mistake. It was nothing."

"If it's nothing, why won't you show me?"

"Look, I can't, okay? You have to trust me."

"Trust you?" Molly hissed. "How do you expect me to trust you if you're keeping secrets all the time?"

Mardi found herself in the absurd position of having

to protect her raging sister from an unknown enemy. She was sorely tempted to hurl the phone at her. But Mardi held strong, jumped out of the Ferrari, and made for Freya's front door, with Molly screaming up the walkway behind her.

"You know I saved your life in the storm! You are so ungrateful!"

"Look I can't show you what's on my phone 'cause I'm only trying to protect you!" Mardi screamed.

That gave Molly pause. "From what?"

"I can't say, okay?"

"No, not okay!"

"Be careful," Mardi taunted. "If you keep gritting your teeth like that you're going to have to start wearing a mouth guard. Not a good look."

"I should have let you drown!"

The door to the house swung open, releasing a delicious odor of lobster broth. Freya, Ingrid, and Jean-Baptiste looked out in alarm at the battling twins.

"Girls," said Jean-Baptiste, "I'm afraid you are not displaying the spirit of harmony required for our important task tonight."

Mardi and Molly glared at each other, then said in unison, "It's her fault."

"Let's leave notions of fault behind," he urged, ushering them inside. "It's time for you to come together, Mooi and Magdi. We all know the storm on July Fourth was no accident."

Mardi was startled into a feeling of gravity by the

sound of her given name, Magdi. She snuck a glance at Molly and saw that she too was suddenly struck by a sense of urgency at hearing herself called by her ancient appellation, Mooi. They were made from their father's spirit; when they were born, Thor had given up some of his powers and instilled them in his daughters.

Quietly now, the twins followed the god of memory into Freya's living room and took their places on the Le Corbusier sofa looking through the giant window out onto the moonlit sea, while he sat in the Eames chair facing them.

"Before we begin," said Mardi, "can you tell us, Jean-Baptiste, if you think the storm was a warning from the White Council?"

"I am convinced it was not," he answered.

All four women stared at him in surprise.

"The White Council does not need to act in such underhanded ways. They are a legitimate body, not a terrorist group. That storm was an act of rogue black magic. The same black magic, I fear, that the White Council fears you girls are releasing into the world."

"Wait!" Mardi jumped up from her seat. "You're saying that, according to the White Council, *we made the storm*? That's insanity. We had nothing to do with it."

"You did not intend for the storm to happen. Nor did you know of it beforehand. But"—he sighed—"I'm afraid that does not mean you had nothing to do with it."

"Girls." Freya spoke soothingly as Molly sank back into the sofa. "I think we can all agree that the only way to figure out what is really going on here is for you to clear up your amnesia. The answers lie on that night back in April."

Freya and Ingrid looked on as Jean-Baptiste quietly spoke. "Please, let's begin. Can you tell me anything you recall about the victims on the night of the party? How they looked? What they wore? What they did?"

The twins squinted inside, homing in on a visual of Sam and Parker.

Sam was überthin in that rich New York way, with bony wrists and a silken curtain of white-blond hair swinging breezily across her pointy, lightly freckled face. She had such a conservative, preppy style that pretty much anything she wore in warm weather could be mistaken for a tennis dress of some kind, and anything she sported in cold weather looked like Vermont après-ski. With some prompting from Jean-Baptiste, Mardi and Molly could recall that on the night of Bret's party, Sam had been wearing a navy-and-white sleeveless jersey dress with navy flats and a rather sweet cropped cream-colored Burberry jacket with a plaid lining and had been carrying a truly unfortunate floral Lilly Pulitzer tote.

Meanwhile, her boyfriend, Parker, had been experimenting with the Brooklyn hipster aesthetic. The results were mixed. He was tall and well built enough to carry off the plaid flannel shirt and suspenders that the look required. The work boots were borderline cool. But the facial hair was an unqualified disaster. Molly could picture him in Bret's living room, rolling his own cigarette, probably from tobacco grown on someone's roof in Red Hook. His beard, such as it was, fell dramatically short of the Brooklyn boy ideal. It grew in soft patchy wisps on his otherwise baby-smooth chin.

But besides noticing the details of their appearance, the twins couldn't say anything about them. They weren't sure how long they had been dating. They assumed they both lived on the Upper East Side, but it was possible that Parker hailed from downtown, or even perhaps from Brooklyn itself. The twins really had no idea.

"Honestly, we didn't know them enough to like them or not like them," Mardi said. "I don't mean to be insensitive, because it's terrible what happened to them. But they were totally random."

"Did Bret know them well?" asked Jean-Baptiste.

"I don't think so," Molly answered. "In fact, now that you mention it, something else is coming back to me. Bret did make noise at some point about how there were a bunch of crashers at his party. But he didn't seem that annoyed. It was more a way for him to show off, saying there were all kinds of kids who wanted to be at his pad, under his ridiculous giant spider sculpture, swimming naked in his indoor pool. I mean, Bret is a super-pretentious guy."

"Maybe that's why you liked him," Mardi chimed in.

"Why *I* liked him? *You're* the one who practically straddled him against one of those disgusting million-dollar tarantula legs."

"Girls, let us stay on track, so to speak." Jean-Baptiste was firm and calm. "You say that this young couple was not particularly meaningful to you or to your host. Would it be fair to say that they were expendable?"

"Harsh!" the twins exclaimed in unison.

After that they saw no more. Their minds were blocked.

The storm of retribution was blowing all right. But from where?

✳ 20 ✳

COME TOGETHER

$\mathscr{T}$he next night, after a busy day at the Cheesemonger, Molly was about to head home to Ingrid's for yet another stultifying family dinner when she got long-awaited word from Tris.

Sorry to be MIA. I was out of town surfing in Montauk for a few days. I missed you. Still do. Any chance you could come over for dinner tonight?

She was reminded of how much she loved the long-form, old-fashioned nature of his texts. Normally, she would have nothing to do with a guy who made her wait this long for a sign of life, especially after they'd hooked up. She was Molly Overbrook, after all, one of the very hottest tickets in New York City, if not the hottest. She needed no one. Yet somehow he was reeling her in. She told herself it was only a summer fling, that there was nothing else going on in North Hampton. So she might as well have her fun.

Besides, she absolutely had to go to Fair Haven to search for the ring in the library. Mardi still hadn't noticed that it had gone missing, and Molly had to find it before her sister realized and completely freaked out.

Molly waved good-bye to Marshall as she pedaled off in the direction of the bridge to Gardiners Island.

Luckily, she was wearing a silvery shift that moved perfectly from day into night. Her wedged espadrilles in black patent leather also segued beautifully. She smiled a self-satisfied smile. Somehow she must have known, as she was getting dressed earlier, that she had a reason to look good this evening. Despite her banishment, she hadn't lost her groove on the East End. She hadn't succumbed to rubber flip-flops, Top-Siders, or, God forbid, fleece.

As she started across the bridge, a crescent moon rose, filling her with a sense of possibility. She tingled with anticipation.

"Harsh," Molly whispered to herself, recalling the end of last night's session as she leaned her bike against a dune on the other side of the bridge. "Expendable? Sam and Parker weren't, like, the most gripping, beautiful people in school. But, expendable?" She shook her head.

The whole mystery was a drag. Molly decided that there was no point in driving herself crazy with it. She wanted to block it out of her mind and have a totally oblivious and irresponsible good time with Tris right now.

As if reading her mind, Tris appeared at the base of the garden path carrying two bottles of beer.

Tris's deep, sparkling eyes were as powerful as she recalled. Damn, that boy was sexy. As he leaned in for a kiss, she melted.

Slowly, he pulled away in order to hand her a bottle. "This is exactly what you need right now."

"And how would you happen to know exactly what I need?"

"We're in the same place, remember? I'm right here with you, doing time in the world's most boring town because I refuse to be who they want me to be. Doesn't that sound familiar?"

As they walked arm in arm toward the magnificent house, Molly decided on a whim to find out more about the story of this place that Freya had begun to tell her about the other day in the Cheesemonger.

"So, is it really true," she asked, "that Fair Haven is built on a seam between Midgard and the Underworld? Are we walking through the gloaming right now? Is that why it's so misty even though the sky is clear?" Although she kept her tone light, she realized as she spoke that she really did want to know the answers to her questions.

But Tris seemed completely nonchalant about the history of his ancestral home. "I don't know. I'm a prisoner here, remember? The only thing that I find engaging about Fair Haven at the moment is that you're here."

Inside the vast, low-lit house, Tris guided her gently

back to the library, which was one of the few rooms small enough to feel intimate when there were only the two of them.

"It feels especially empty inside Fair Haven tonight," she said.

"Most of the staff doesn't live in the house. I think the housekeeper might be down in the kitchen. But otherwise it's just us." He winked. "And, of course, the madwoman in the attic."

"You mean your stepmother?"

"Bingo." He laughed. "Ask Freya. Mother doesn't think anyone's good enough for a Gardiner boy."

She raised her eyebrows as they sank into the club chair that had become their particular haven of softness and comfort amid the grandeur of the mansion. The caress of the worn leather was as exciting and warm as his skin. "You really think she wouldn't approve of even me?"

"Do I look like I care, Molly?" he whispered, leaning down and pressing against her. As his tongue caressed hers, Molly felt that she had never existed so fully in a moment. She did not step outside herself to wonder what she looked like, nor did her mind wander, as it usually did, to the next conquest she planned to make.

She had no idea how long they had been entangled when he nibbled her earlobe and tickled her every sense with his voice. "You're making me hungry," he said, and pulled away.

She leaned back, expecting him to start unbuttoning her shirt.

Except he meant it literally.

Tris nodded toward the kitchen. "You want anything? I'll make us something. Stay here."

She had the fleeting sensation that he did not want her to leave the library. Was he hiding her from his stepmother? She supposed she didn't really mind. When in doubt, being served was always the best option. She stretched catlike as he released her from his embrace. Her entire body was flushed.

As soon as he left, though, a current of alarm ran through her. She remembered the missing ring. This room was the only place it could possibly be. It had to have fallen off the last time she was here. That was the only answer. Maybe Tris had unhooked the clasp of her gold chain, sometime around the moment that he had unhooked her bra. Or maybe the chain had slipped over her head. It was all a blur. She scoured her memory for some detail, the clink of metal hitting the floor, the feel of it sliding down her body. But there was nothing. Logic told her the ring had to be here, yet she had no sensual impression of losing it.

She felt several times in the cracks of the chair. To no avail. She moved every piece on the ivory backgammon board. Nothing. She checked along all the mahogany bookshelves in case a maid had found the ring and decided to put it up in a safe place where it could easily be spotted. No such luck. She ran her eyes and fingers over every surface, the side tables, the windowsills, the elaborate bar cart. Then one by one, she took the cushions off the antique sofa and checked underneath them.

Her heart was beginning to pound. Anxiously listening for Tris's footfall, since he had been gone a while now, she got down on her knees to check under each piece of furniture. She did not spot anything, not even a speck of dust. The once cozy little library was yawning with emptiness because it did not seem to contain the one thing she needed.

The only place left to try was the oriental rug. Its rich silken fibers gleamed in the room's low lamplight. Suddenly her searching gaze caught on a shiny gold band. She lunged for it, practically splaying herself on the floor. But the sparkle proved to be a mirage, the mere illusion of a ring in the rug's intricate Persian pattern. Molly sighed and kept looking, more determined than ever, her eyes inches from the ground.

"What the— What are you doing on the floor?"

Tris loomed above Molly in his crisp whites, carrying a silver tray. His expression as he stared down at her was inscrutable. Was he suspicious? Amused? Angry? As he put the tray down on a low table, she saw that it bore two cold lobsters, an heirloom tomato salad, a baguette, two crystal wineglasses, and a bottle of white Burgundy in a slender ice bucket. This was a far cry from the usual late-night fare of fast food and beers that most guys under twenty-five, even the sophisticated, jet-setting ones, would proudly produce. Tris was something else.

And she may have just totally blown it with him.

She started to get up.

"Don't," he commanded softly.

"Don't?"

"Don't move. Whatever you are doing down there on the floor, I like it. You look so hot right now lying on the rug. You have no idea."

Oh, but she did. She had a very good idea.

As he lay down beside her, she met his wicked smile with her own.

✳ 21 ✳

THE TEXTING SONG

𝒯he texts were freaking Mardi out. Since receiving the creepy note right before the memory session with Jean-Baptiste, she had gotten three more. Each one implied that the texter knew something incriminating about "that night." Then whoever it was threatened to hurt, or even kill, Molly if Mardi said anything to anyone.

I saw the evil you allowed to take place that night. . . . It was your power that killed them. . . . It will soon become clear that you are the guilty ones.

If you tell anyone about me, especially her, she will be . . . destroyed . . . cast down . . . forever lost to you.

Could this be some kind of warning from the White Council?

No, of course not. The Council did not traffic in blackmail. It was someone who knew their secret—the only problem was that Mardi herself had no idea what their secret was.

She was tempted to turn her phone off, but she was also secretly hoping to glean some information from whoever was torturing her. She tried answering the texts with Who are you? How can I help you? But there was no reply.

For once in her life, Mardi craved advice from an adult. But who to turn to? And how to get help without giving too much away and putting her sister in potential danger? Of course, this so-called stalker could just be some lame-o. But there was no way to be sure. And as much as Molly could drive her crazy, Mardi didn't want to live out eternity knowing she had sent her own twin sister to the Underworld.

Dad was *so* not a good candidate for someone to talk to. He would panic, and he would press her for specifics. If she mentioned her dilemma to Jean-Baptiste, he might put her into one of his involuntary memory trances and get too much information out of her. This pretty much left Ingrid and Freya.

It was about nine in the morning. Mardi rolled out of bed and went to splash some cold water on her face. She remarked to herself that it had been a while since she had had the ring. The rose gold band should pass any moment now from Molly to her. It was time.

Should she turn to Ingrid or Freya for her problems?

As she weighed the two options, she craned her neck in order to see her snaking rainbow tattoo from various angles. The colorful reflection glistened as it undulated. It seemed to have a life, and will, of its own.

As she stared into the mirror, it dawned on her that

the bridge tattooed on her shoulder no longer existed. This was the bridge that had collapsed centuries ago, stranding several hundred gods and goddesses in Midgard, including their father. The rainbow bridge etched into her skin was a powerful symbol of a lost time.

Mardi looked deep into the reflection of her own dark eyes. She saw a sixteen-year-old witch with symbols of ancient history engraved on her body. She wasn't just some stupid club kid with a random tattoo and a tongue stud. Mardi Overbrook was the real deal. And it was time for her to step up.

In that instant, she realized that she didn't have to decide between Ingrid and Freya. This wasn't a competitive twin thing where one sister got to win out over the other. Mardi had to stop thinking like a kid. She decided that she would speak to them both, to gather as much wisdom as she could. She would start with Ingrid, because Ingrid was downstairs.

Mardi came upon Ingrid in a rare moment of stillness. She was sitting barefoot at the kitchen island, still wearing her simple white cotton bathrobe, her blond hair pulled back into a ponytail, exposing her delicate features and translucent skin. In front of her was a steaming cup of coffee, a china plate with a blueberry muffin from a batch she had baked yesterday with Jo and Henry, and a dog-eared paperback of her favorite novel, *To Kill a Mockingbird*.

No one else was visible in the big, bright, open family living space. Molly was probably still asleep. And

Matt must have taken the kids outside to give Ingrid some peace. But Ingrid did not look peaceful. She looked drawn and worried. In this unguarded instant, she had let down her perfect posture and had allowed her expression of motherly kindness to fade away. She was frowning. There was a sad droop to her shoulders. She hadn't touched her muffin. The book on the counter was closed.

"Good morning, Ingrid," Mardi said softly, so as not to startle her.

"Mardi, dear, good morning. I didn't see you." Ingrid turned and forced a smile. "Let me pour you some coffee. You take it black, right? And here, have a blueberry muffin before the rest of the gang gets here and they vanish. You know, we picked these blueberries ourselves on the farm down the road."

Ingrid, Mardi understood as she watched her fussing over the coffee and then carefully placing the muffin on a pretty floral plate, was a compulsive nurturer. She put a perfect pat of salted butter next to the muffin, because she knew that Mardi only liked her butter salted. That was how attentive she was.

But even though Ingrid was doing her usual bustling in order to take care of someone other than herself, her movements were distracted. It was as though she were on autopilot. Something was wrong.

Mardi sat down beside her at the island counter, trying to figure out how to approach the subject of her mysterious texts without directly mentioning them. She had no idea where to begin.

"Ingrid, is something wrong? You look upset."

"I'm worried. You know, part of my work at the library is counseling women with health issues or psychological stress. And there has been a rash of domestic violence in town. I don't like it all."

"You think it might connect to the other weird stuff that has been going on here?"

"I'm certainly starting to think that whoever, or whatever, is causing these disturbances has it in for women in particular."

"You don't think it's random at all, do you?"

"I'm afraid I don't."

At a loss for what to say next, Mardi took a bite of blueberry muffin with a dab of butter.

"Wow, Ingrid," she said. "This is delicious. Thanks."

"Can you taste the lemon?" Ingrid asked, suddenly very intense, like her mind had shifted to a distant place where lemons were somehow really important.

Mardi took another bite. "I think so. Did you squeeze in some lemon juice or something?"

"It's lemon rind," Ingrid said sadly. "It's was my mother's recipe. She always took such care grating the lemon rind because she said it brought out the flavor of the blueberries like nothing else . . . You'll see, Mardi, if you ever lose someone, it's the details that will haunt you, all the tiny ways they expressed their love," she said, her voice hoarse. "Joanna has been gone ten years, but the grief never ends. You just get used to it."

Tentatively, Mardi put a hand on Ingrid's thin shoulder. She wasn't in the habit of comforting other people, but this gesture felt right.

"How did your parents get stuck in the Underworld?" Mardi asked.

"They sacrificed themselves in order to save Freya. It's a long story." Ingrid sighed. "They had watched both of us hang once, during the Salem witch trials, and they couldn't face the sight again . . . "

Ingrid seemed to lose her train of thought. Mardi did not prompt her, but stayed very still, waiting while Ingrid stared at the pattern on her plate without really seeing it.

Mardi shuddered. The White Council's threats to damn the sisters forever if they were found guilty of murder were starting to seem a lot less abstract.

"My mother's gift as a witch was bringing souls back from the dead. That's why I called on her to help me save the little drowned boy during the storm on the Fourth of July."

"You mean, the kid on the boat with you?"

"Yes, he was technically dead when we pulled him out of the water. But we were able to intervene. It's very, very rare to be able to pull off a resurrection. Even for us with our direct connection. We were incredibly fortunate that our spells were heard." Ingrid paused to gather her thoughts. "I don't mean to be preachy,

Mardi, but the situation you and Molly have gotten us in with the Council puts all this in danger. If we couldn't practice magic anymore, we would have had absolutely no chance of saving that boy."

"I get it, okay!" Mardi recoiled defensively.

"I think maybe you finally do get it," Ingrid said softly. "Anyway, my mother's sister, Helda, lords over the Underworld. And my mother knows every twist and turn of the path a soul takes to get there. She knows all the rules. And one of those rules, Mardi, is 'a soul for a soul.' The little boy we rescued the other day from drowning, his soul was still in the mortal world, his name was not yet written in the Book of the Dead, so we were able to snatch him back without sacrificing anyone . . . But, when Freya was hung in Salem, she was lost. My mother and father decided to drown themselves in the deep water you see through these very windows, to exchange themselves for their daughter so that she could come home."

"But wait, why did your dad have to go too?"

"He didn't. He chose to."

"Why?"

"Because my mother is his eternal mate. They had just reconciled after a centuries-long separation. They were madly in love again. He was going to die with her. No one ever found their bodies, of course. But they share a headstone in the town cemetery."

Gently, Mardi patted her shoulder. "Is it hard for you with Matt? Because he's, like, your soul mate, only he's not going to be around forever? He's a really great guy. And a great dad. I can see why you chose him. But, well, it must be really sad sometimes to think about all the time you're going to have to spend apart."

Ingrid nodded. "I think about it constantly but I try not to ruin the time we have together by mourning his death. Live in the present, Mardi."

Speaking of, the door to the deck clamored open and Matt and the kids spilled into the room laughing and shedding sand everywhere as they dove into the muffins.

Mardi's window of opportunity to tell Ingrid about the weird texts had closed. But she had learned something. She'd learned just how important it was, for the whole ecosystem of her people, that she and Molly get out of the mess they were in. If only they knew what exactly they had done so that they could actually defend themselves.

Seeing as she hadn't had a chance to talk to Ingrid about those weird texts, Mardi decided to go and lose herself in heavy lifting on the docks, to tackle a big shipment of equipment coming in for the new restaurant. Then, after work she would go to the North Inn to talk to Freya and see if she could get somewhere.

"I'm heading out! I'll see you guys later!"

The little family managed to return her good-bye through mouthfuls of breakfast. Ingrid gave her a wink.

She hopped into her convertible and put the key

in the ignition. Before she could turn it, though, her phone vibrated inside her favorite vintage bag. The bag's brown suede fringe trembled against her bare arm. She instantly knew what this was. She wished she didn't feel compelled to pull out her phone and look at the screen, but she had no choice.

Meet me tonight at ten in the dunes by the bridge on Gardiners Island. Or else.

22

A SKY FULL OF STARS

Although she was infatuated with Tris, Molly felt a little tug at her heart as she left Marshall behind after a charm-filled afternoon with him at the Cheesemonger. Cheeseboy was growing on her like a fine mold.

Today she had been complaining that she was addicted to the New England clam chowder he wouldn't stop making. (Her doubts about the people of North Hampton being ready to embrace a chowder other than their signature Manhattan had been way off—they were lining up for the stuff.) She told him how fattening it was and teased him about being a soup dealer who ought to be arrested for peddling the stuff to poor teenage girls with no willpower.

"You have more willpower than I've ever seen!" he'd said, interrupting her.

"What do you mean? I just told you I can't stop eating your creamy, starchy, potato-filled soup. Not to mention your brownies."

"I mean that you have willpower because you take

what you need. You don't look like a girl who starves herself to be beautiful. You look like a girl who gets what she wants, which makes you beautiful."

"If you say so." She shrugged. But she was secretly pleased. Marshall might not have a chance against Tris, but he sure knew how to appreciate her like she deserved to be appreciated.

So it was with a twinge of something like regret that she said, "Later, Cheesepal," as she rode off to do a quick change for her evening among the dunes with Tris. He had told her to meet him that evening on the other side of the bridge, and to dress for a night under the stars.

All day, she had been thinking through her outfit. She had settled on a light gray cashmere hoodie over a whisper-soft black tank top, cropped white jeans, and flat snakeskin sandals. Underneath it all, a creamy lace ensemble.

Once she was ready, she went downstairs to ask Ingrid and Matt if she could borrow their car. She didn't feel like biking all the way to Fair Haven in the dark and then pedaling home at sunrise. She was starting to get circles under her eyes from her late nights with Tris, and it was impossible to find decent concealer in this lame excuse for a town.

"You look nice," Ingrid said as Molly appeared. "I'm sure you're on your way out, but would you like a glass of wine with us first? We're celebrating getting the kids down."

She and Matt smiled at one another over the wide rims of their Burgundy glasses.

"Hey, guys, can I borrow the car tonight?" she asked.

"I'm not so sure that's a good idea," Matt said, furrowing his brow.

What? Was he actually getting precious about the family Subaru wagon all of a sudden?

Molly was tempted to hex him so that he would pour his wine into his ear and get over himself, but she felt Ingrid's eyes on her and reined herself in.

"May I ask why it might not be a good idea, Matt?"

"You haven't heard?"

Molly shook her pretty head.

"There's been a rash of traffic light outages today all over town. It looks like vandalism, but it's pretty strange because the power goes in and out randomly in isolated sets of lights, without warning, for only a few minutes at a time. It's like someone who has no real plan of action is playing with the power grid. There've been four car accidents so far, and strangely, all of them involve girls your age. No one has been seriously hurt, although one teenage girl is in the hospital for some broken ribs . . . I'm not so sure it's safe to drive until we know what's going on."

"Don't you think it's just a coincidence? I mean, there's no way whoever is doing this can see who is driving the cars, is there?" Although Ingrid directed her questions at Matt, she gave Molly a significant look.

"Well, the outages certainly aren't systematic, if

that's what you mean. Something is short-circuiting in the grid. Or else someone is messing around with our power—and putting innocent people in danger. But you're right that they couldn't target specific cars, though."

Molly's head started to spin as she sank into a chair with her wine. Innocent people . . . random accidents . . . The parallel hit her hard.

Or was she reading too much into things? Seeing symbolism where there was none? Was she falling victim to Daddy's and Ingrid's paranoia?

Through the static of her thoughts, she heard Matt and Ingrid tell her to go ahead and take the car, but to be really careful. They even made a lame joke about her being in the "unlucky demographic."

"Thanks," she said, jumping up before they could change their minds. "Don't wait up for me!"

She grabbed the keys from a hook by the front door and raced off, trying not to freak out about the connections between random traffic accidents and random subway deaths. Or about her growing suspicion that her missing ring might have something to do with both of them. Whatever. She had a date.

As she neared the end of the bridge, she saw Tris outlined in her high beams, glowing like a bronze Adonis. He was wearing jeans and a soft brown sweatshirt. But nothing could take away from the overall impression of elegance that he radiated, an elegance which Molly felt was uniquely worthy of her own.

He raised his hand, and she slowed down to kiss him through her open window. She slid into the passenger seat and let him take the wheel. For the short ride to Fair Haven's sandy parking areas, his strong, graceful movements transformed the lowly maroon station wagon into a timelessly cool vehicle.

Once they had parked in the garage of one of the estate's outbuildings, he told her to close her eyes. He then blindfolded her with a silk scarf and led her through the dunes for what felt like ten minutes. As he brought her to a stop, the insides of her eyelids were suffused with orange light and her body was filled with warmth. She had to be standing in front of a fire.

Gently, he untied her blindfold to reveal a bonfire encircled in beautiful carpets like a Bedouin encampment. There were cashmere blankets and piles of Moroccan pillows in all sizes. High wooden posts bearing large osprey nests gave the scene the aura of a sacred temple guarded by rare and magical birds. The stars twinkled above.

A golden bowl heaped with caviar caught the firelight. Two bottles of champagne were nestled in an antique silver ice bucket, radiant in the starlight and the glow of the flames.

"Wow," she said. "And I'm not easily impressed."

"I knew you wouldn't be," he whispered, threading his strong arms around her and pulling her toward him, his blue eyes glinting orange, gold, and hypnotic. "That's why I tried so hard."

They fell into each other, rolling among the blankets and pillows in the gorgeous shadows created by the flames. Every once in a while, they would come up for air. He would feed her some Beluga from a pearl spoon and they would swig champagne straight from the bottle. She could feel herself giving in to him. There was something deep and eternal about their connection. But he also gave her the thrill of the unknown.

As she was unbuckling his belt, slowly, savoring the moment, he suddenly leapt to his feet in a single athletic bound, with all the speed and grace of a startled deer.

"Molly, I'm so sorry. I'll be right back."

She couldn't help but be a little taken aback by his sudden exit. What was that all about? Things were just getting fun. She tucked her knees into her chest, stared into the bonfire, sipped some champagne, and listened to the sound of the sea lapping the beach, feeling a little frustrated.

She began to wonder where he was. How long could it possibly take a guy to pee? Molly looked at her watch. It was close to ten o'clock. She took another drink, spaced out into the starry sky, and tried not to check the time again. When she finally gave in and looked at the face of her Rolex again, she saw that almost ten more minutes had elapsed.

Where was he? Had he ditched her? She felt her eyes begin to shoot angry sparks. Her ancestral rage rose up with the swiftness and fury of a tidal wave. She toyed with the idea of collapsing the osprey nest platforms into the bonfire. But it didn't seem right to make a bunch of endangered birds suffer for his rudeness.

He was always doing this—disappearing for no reason. What was up with that?

She felt around in the soft, luxurious mass of fabrics for her sandals. Once she had slipped them on, she stood and brushed off the sand, making sure to get some in the caviar.

Then she heard footsteps approaching.

So he *was* coming back, after all. He'd better have a great excuse. It was going to take a lot for him to explain himself.

As she was composing her face into her signature unreadable and hard-to-get expression, she heard the footsteps grow fainter. Was he walking away from her now? Was he toying with her?

And then he started walking toward her again, running even. It was as if he had forgotten exactly where he had made their love nest and had circled around before finally spotting the smoke from the fire and orienting himself in the right direction. But this made no sense because he knew these dunes inside and out.

What was going on?

As Tris came around the side of the dune toward the bonfire, she thought she heard him humming a familiar tune. What was this song again?

She turned to confront him. She was going to let him

have it. By the time she was through, he would be a puddle of tidewater, because nobody, no matter how rich or how beautiful he was, kept Molly Overbrook waiting this long.

Only it wasn't him. The person who stepped into the firelight was not Tris Gardiner at all.

23

GIRLS JUST WANNA HAVE FUN

$\mathcal{M}$ardi and Trent had been working side by side all day, unloading kitchen hardware and cases of wine, stocking the cellar of the restaurant, which the owner, Joshua Goose, had decided to call Goose's Landing. Her body was electric with Trent's presence. The space between them was charged with everything they dreamed of doing together.

When they finally kicked back for a beer after a job well done, with Luis and Mario, the brothers who were helping out with the construction, Molly sat next to Trent on the dock so that their knees touched and their bare shoulders rubbed. He was shirtless, and she was wearing a lime green halter-top that Molly liked to tease her was straight out of a '90s Spice Girls video. Their dad had had a fling with Posh—or was it Scary?—in the '90s, and they were never going to let him live it down.

The brush of Trent's skin made Mardi tremble. She wanted him. And yet she was the one who kept making excuses to avoid intimacy. She could not overcome her defensive and off-putting nature. Precisely because she was so attracted to Trent, she always had a reason why they couldn't be together. On July Fourth, she had finally been ready to let go, but the crazy storm had spectacularly ruined their moment. Since then, the time had never been right again for her to lose control.

She took a long, deep sip of beer and decided that she would finally make something happen this evening before she took off to her rendezvous in the dunes with her stalker. Maybe she would ask Trent to come to Freya's bar with her. She pictured him pressing her into one of those wooden booths to the sound of blaring '70s rock, and she glowed inside.

As though he could read her thoughts, he flashed her a big open grin. If they had been alone, she would have kissed him. But they never seemed to be alone at the right time.

"Another round of Brooklyn Lagers?" Trent asked.

But before anyone could answer, there was a violent crashing sound from inside the restaurant, the clang of smashing glass.

Trent, Mardi, Luis, and Mario leapt up and ran inside to find that several beams had collapsed in the cellar, breaking hundreds of bottles and flooding the basement in a bloodred river of wine.

"How the Hell did this happen?" Trent's face went dark.

"Those beams were very secure," said Luis, utterly baffled.

"The engineer signed off on them yesterday," Mario backed his brother up. "We do good work! Someone else has been down here."

"Is there someone who doesn't want this place to open?" asked Mardi.

"Not that we know of," said Trent. "Right, guys?" He focused his piercing blue eyes straight on the brothers.

Mario and Luis shook their heads. Then they looked at each other questioningly, their eyes full of discomfort.

Trent practically leapt at them. "What's going on here? What are you not telling us? This is serious."

"Whoa," said Mardi, touching his hard, tensed arm. "Relax. Don't be such a bully." She had never seen him so revved up.

"Relax? Mardi, it's dumb luck that one of us wasn't down there just now when the ceiling caved. We could have been killed." Then he turned again to Luis and Mario. "Sorry, guys. I'm not accusing you of anything. You do good work. But if you know of anything that could help us figure this out, you should say something.

"It's weird, this collapse," Mario said. "Like that accident yesterday in the farmhouse where we have been working out on Anemone Road."

"What accident?" Trent couldn't control the alarm in his voice.

"It makes us look bad, but really we're very careful," Luis jumped in. "It's like someone is trying to make it look like we don't do our job. But this accident at the farmhouse, it couldn't have been our fault."

"I can explain what happened," Mario interjected, seeing that Trent was about to explode with impatience. "We redid the baby's room in the attic. But we didn't touch the structure. We built some shelves and painted and fixed some wiring. So it couldn't have been our work that made the roof fall in yesterday."

"Was the baby okay?" asked Mardi as Trent squeezed her hand.

"Yes, thank God, the baby wasn't in there sleeping. The beam that fell from the ceiling split and drove a stake through her crib." Mario gave Trent and Mardi a searching look as if to ask whether they really believed him. "We are very sorry, but it wasn't our fault."

"We trust you. But we need to find out what the Hell is going on," said Trent with a quiet yet strong anger that sent a thrill through Mardi's body. She was furious on these guys' behalf too. As she squeezed his palm, she felt a searing heat pass between them.

"Mario, Luis. Don't worry," Trent continued. "We'll get to the bottom of this. My guess is that it has nothing to do with you at all."

"You think it's random? Like the messed-up traffic lights?" asked Mardi.

Trent released her hand and squinted into the horizon, as though the sunset might hold some explanation. "It's random . . . and it's also not at all random," he said. He was silent for a while.

Mardi sensed his profound confusion—and she also saw the fierce intelligence with which he was fighting that confusion. In that moment, she felt she embodied the very same struggle that he was caught in.

"There is something evil in the air," he said, looking her straight in the eye.

She met his blue gaze. "You mean like black magic?"

"I think you know what I mean."

"You're just like me, aren't you, Trent?" Made of myth and magic.

Slowly, he nodded.

"Trent," she turned his face gently toward hers, "let's go get a drink at Freya's bar and talk this over." Now that they had told each other who they really were, she wanted to talk to him about what had happened back in the city and explain how she was trapped in it. Maybe he would be able to help her figure out how it was all connected? Maybe the same evil force that had murdered those kids in New York was now tracking Molly and Mardi down here on the East End? There were so many questions.

And Trent was the only soul she wanted to open up to right now.

But before she could speak any of these thoughts, he was turning away from her. "Guys," he said to Mario and Luis, "don't worry about cleaning up the restaurant yet. It might be dangerous down there. Just leave it for now, okay?"

The brothers nodded.

"Mardi, I've gotta go." He took her hands in his and scrutinized them for a few seconds, then looked up and met her dark eyes. "There's something I have to do."

"What is it?" She was stunned. Hadn't they just made a deep connection? Where the Hell was he going?

But he wouldn't say.

Instead of going to the North Inn to talk to Freya, Mardi sped aimlessly in and around town, killing time until her rendezvous with her stalker. She was trying to temper her anger at Trent's bizarre brush-off. She wasn't the only one who pulled back every time something was about to happen. They were acting like repellent magnets. The closer they almost got, the harder they pushed each other away.

The streets were empty, probably because of the traffic light scare. North Hampton felt even more dead than usual. She wanted out of here so badly, she could scream. She knew Freya and Ingrid kept brooms hidden in the house. Maybe it was time to fly this coop.

But she couldn't fly now. She was trapped by this stupid feeling of responsibility creeping in on her from all sides. It was so unfair. How did a teenage prankster like her end up at the heart of some big, life-threatening power struggle that she wanted nothing to do with? Why couldn't she have the fun of being a witch without the heaviness of being a goddess? Why was she wasting a gorgeous hot summer night going to meet some psycho in the deserted sand dunes?

She supposed it would be worth it if the psycho could at least tell her what she and Molly had done to deserve all this. But still it was a good thing she was alone in the Ferrari, because the angry magic sparking from her every pore would have hexed any mortal within spitting distance.

At a few minutes before ten, Mardi set off across the Gardiners Island Bridge. She hadn't been there since the party on the night of her arrival. Unlike that evening in late June, Fair Haven was not ablaze now with festive torchlight and gleaming chandeliers. The house glimmered so faintly that it might be an illusion. The wind in her hair became icy, and she had to suppress the urge to turn back. What if the stalker was violent? After all, he or she had threatened to hurt Molly. Not that Mardi couldn't handle anything that came her way. But still . . . She steeled herself and pressed harder on the gas. The urge to know what was going on was a lot more powerful than any fear.

Just off the bridge, she pulled over on the side of the road, got out of the car, and waited at the edge of the dunes. She noticed that there was another car parked in the distance and wondered who else might be there.

After a few minutes, she called out a soft "hello."

No response.

She decided to start looking around, to show who-ever was messing with her that she was not afraid.

As she began to wander into the dunes, she smelled smoke. Her animal instincts came alive. She looked up to see gray wisps floating skyward about a hundred yards away. She went straight toward the smoke only to find herself blocked by a large mass of sand. She could hear rustling and the popping of dry wood in flames. Whoever had summoned her had built a fire under the stars.

Mardi did not try to tread lightly. In fact, she stomped, making sure to show that she wasn't the one sneaking around here. She had nothing to hide.

She followed the smoky odor and the faint sounds until she found herself up against a large dune. The fire had to be on the other side, along with her stalker. Humming to keep her spirits up, she went around the mass of sand. At first, she was hardly aware of the tune she was channeling. But after a few bars, she realized it was "Wannabe," the Spice Girls song she and Molly used to play at full volume in order to torture Dad and tease him about his series of one-night stands with the '90s ingénues. It was one of the few truly joyful memo-ries that she and Molly shared. She wondered why it had popped into her head at this bizarre moment.

As she came around the dune, she caught her breath. There was a fire here, all right. A bonfire surrounded by fancy oriental rugs and huge silk pillows, blankets, champagne bottles, the remains of a caviar feast now covered in sand. It looked like the aftermath of some exotic orgy. And right in the heart of it sat her sister, looking a little disheveled and totally shocked.

"What are *you* doing here?" Molly jumped up and tried to smooth out her clothes.

"I could ask you the same question." Mardi tried to keep her voice steady. "Did you ask me to come? Is this your idea of a sick joke?"

"Of course not. Why would I invite *you* to Fair Haven? This is my territory."

Instinctively, Mardi believed her. Molly had not summoned her here. She could always tell when her twin was lying. But what did she mean that Fair Haven was hers?

Molly looked into the night, beyond Mardi, as though she was waiting for someone else to appear.

"So, who were you here with?" asked Mardi. "Who built you this fire?"

"How do you know I didn't build it?"

"Come on, Molly. Campfires are so *not* in your skill set. Just tell me, who's the lucky guy?" Mardi gestured to the dregs of the Dom Pérignon.

"Flattery will get you nowhere. And it is totally none of your business who I happen to be seeing."

Mardi couldn't take the suspense any longer. It couldn't be Trent, it just couldn't . . . He wouldn't do this to her. But she had to clear this up. "His last name doesn't happen to be Gardiner, does it?"

"I told you, it's none of your business."

If only Molly would come out and say yes or no, Mardi would be able to tell where the truth lay. And Molly knew this, which was why she was torturing her with evasion.

"Fair enough," said Mardi. After all, she hadn't told Molly much about Trent. Not that there was anything to tell.

"But I *will* say that the lucky guy, as you call him, might actually be something of a disappointment." Molly dug her perfectly pedicured toes into the sand.

"I can relate to that." Mardi sighed, thinking back to Trent's abrupt and chilly departure from the docks earlier this evening. "Guys aren't necessarily worth it."

Nodding her head in agreement, Molly asked, "So how did you end up here tonight, anyway?"

"I was exploring, okay?"

"No, that's not true. A minute ago, you said that someone asked you to come."

"Okay, you've got me. Believe me, I want to tell you who it is. But I can't."

"Wait, but if you know who told you to come here, then why did you just ask if it was me? You're not making any sense, Mardi."

Molly sounded more worried than angry. Perhaps she too was beginning to sense that something was really amiss tonight.

"Can we call it a premonition and leave it at that, for now?"

As Molly squinted at her, Mardi wondered nervously if her sister was going to buy this incoherent explanation. She was also trying to figure out how to convince her to get the Hell out of here, because she was beginning to suspect that this whole setup was some kind of trap.

"Whatever you want to call it." Molly shrugged, obviously not up for a fight. "By the way, were you really humming the Spice Girls just now when you found me? Or did I imagine that?"

"I think I was. Maybe it was my way of reaching out to you. I mean, it's kind of our song."

"Wait a second." Molly laughed. "You're even wearing the Scary Spice green tube top. This is cosmic." She started to hum the tune herself.

"Molly," Mardi interrupted her, "let's get out of here."

As Mardi spoke, the massive bonfire doubled in size, its flames appearing to lick the stars. Both girls jumped away from the scorching heat and ran as the carpets and blankets all caught fire and the air filled with smoke.

Together, the twins raced through the dunes toward the entrance to the bridge where Mardi had left the Ferrari. They arrived panting at the car to find a message scrawled bright red across the windshield: *Bitches burn in Hell.*

"Do you think this means us?" asked Molly.

They could hear the fire crackling and raging. The

moon and stars were hidden by a thick curtain of black smoke.

"Wait a second. Do you remember? 'You bitches are gonna burn in Hell'?"

"You know about that night . . . " Molly's voice trailed off into the fiery night.

Mardi looked at her twin. "Molly," she said, "where is our ring?"

✳ 24 ✳

WAKE ME UP WHEN IT'S ALL OVER

The next morning, Molly awoke in a funk. Her eyes were puffier than ever from too much alcohol and not enough sleep. She was down to her last stick of concealer with the awesome brush applicator, and it was only the first day of August. She was going to have to stretch the concealer through Labor Day, when she would finally return to civilization, a prospect she would have greeted with pure joy and utter relief if it weren't for the fact that she was a suspect in an ongoing police investigation.

Although it was hard to believe that anything terrible would actually happen to her and Mardi, it was no longer an impossible scenario. Especially not after last night's conflagration and freaky misogynist message. The thought that Daddy might be right about the trouble they were in was now gnawing at her insides. Why had Tris deserted her last night, leaving her to the mercy of some psycho spirit? Where had the ring gone, and why did it seem to matter so much? She hated the feeling, which she had all the time lately, that there was a lot going on that she didn't understand. Molly was so not used to being in the dark.

Downstairs, Ingrid's happy little family was cooing over their homemade granola. It was more cheer than Molly could take right now. She felt like making a twister out of the stuff and causing it to spiral out to sea while the children cried inconsolably. Seeing Mardi slumped over her coffee cup desperately trying to ignore the self-congratulatory granola fest, Molly understood that at least her sister felt the same way she did.

Get us out of here. Now. We don't want your life. We like takeout! And we miss our dad.

"Who would like to try some of our granola?" Ingrid practically sang. "We made it with organic oats and locally foraged honey."

"Tell them about the raisins, Mommy!" cried Jo.

"Raisins!" Henry echoed from his grubby high chair. Molly shuddered, remembering what had happened to her shirt earlier in the summer.

"Oh, the raisins! We dried them ourselves in the sun, from grapes grown at Duck Walk Vineyards down the road. Can I give you girls some? With yogurt or with milk?"

"Midnight likes hers with milk!" Jo squealed, pointing to the cat who was lapping at a bowl on the floor.

"I'm not hungry," the twins groaned in unison.

"I'm sorry, but I can't let you two leave the house

without breakfast. It's the most important meal of the day."

"You're not our mother, Ingrid!" Molly snapped, immediately regretting her words when she saw Ingrid's face fall. She attempted some damage control. "It's just that we aren't used to having a mother. Daddy somehow gets cereal and milk into the house, and we manage just fine on our own. We're not really used to this whole domestic thing."

"What you call 'this whole domestic thing' is what we call life," said Matt, putting his arm around his wife.

"That's great for you," said Molly. "But I'm really not hungry."

"Just a tiny bit, please?" begged little Jo. "We made it for you guys."

Wow. Who knew cooking and guilt were so intricately bound together? Molly supposed this was one of the things a mother would have taught her.

Jo leaned into her and whispered, "I did a doubling spell on the brown sugar while Mommy wasn't looking. It's so much sweeter than she thinks it is. Shhh."

"Okay." Molly gave up. "I'll try some. With milk."

"Me too," said Mardi. "With yogurt, please."

Begrudgingly, Molly admitted to herself that this granola was even better than the stuff she always ordered at Balthazar back in the city. Much to the general delight of the family, she and Mardi each had two helpings, heaping with fresh-picked berries, before getting ready to face the day.

As Molly left the house to head to work, Mardi followed her outside toward her bike.

"Um, Molly," she said tentatively.

Before her sister spoke, Molly knew what it was about. "Look, Mardi, I should have told you the ring was gone, okay? I thought I could find it myself before you noticed."

"What the Hell? Why didn't you tell me right away? Where did you have it last?"

"I'm not exactly sure." Technically, this was true. "Look, I've had enough drama for now after last night. Can I just please go have a normal day at work, and we'll talk about this later?"

"Molly, it's our mother's ring. It's all we have of her. *And* it turns out it may have some kind of power that we don't even understand. I think that guy in the pool wanted our ring. Remember?"

Molly's mind started to reel. The creepy dude. The ring. The story from that opera Marshall was telling her. Somehow it all clicked. She had to go talk to Marshall. Even if he had no clue what was going on in her life, he might unwittingly hold a key.

"We'll get it back, okay? I have to go."

"We really need to talk about this, Molly!" Mardi's voice carried after her as she pedaled off toward town.

At the Cheesemonger, everything about Marshall seemed particularly sweet today. In contrast to Tris, he was open and funny. He had no idea about the White Council and the murders and threats of the Underworld. He was simply happy to run his mother's little store in this mellow town, where the biggest thing going was outdoor opera, and the biggest risk you could take was making New England clam chowder instead of Manhattan. He was so cute and didn't seem to notice a lot of girls patronized the shop just so they could flirt with him.

In the lull after the lunch rush, she sat down on a stool quite close to where he was chopping celery and decided to open up a little about some of what was weighing on her, without, of course, venturing into forbidden territory. She was craving sympathy, and Cheeseboy was pretty much a font of the stuff. And she also wanted to know more about the legend of the ring.

"Cheeseboy," she began, "I've had this weird thing happen. Remember the gold ring I had, the one that I started wearing on the chain around my neck?"

"Sort of," he said. He sounded attentive, but he couldn't look at her because he had to keep his eyes on his chopping knife.

"I lost it."

"Do you ever take it off to do prep work? I don't think I've seen it lying around, and I'm pretty observant about that kind of thing in the shop. I'll keep an eye out, though. I'm sure you'll find it. Stuff like that is usually under your nose. You're so used to seeing it all the time that sometimes it's hard to actually notice." He sounded considerate and concerned, not belittling her anxiety, but also not stressed out, because his general vibe was one of mellow optimism. She appreciated him so much right now.

Suddenly, he started to sing a rousing tune that sounded like an air from the Wagner opera she wanted to ask him about. It was as though he anticipated her every need. Cheerfully, he was hitting his cleaver into the chopping block in time to the music so that the pieces of diced celery hopped and skipped onto the counter.

"That's from the Ring opera, right?" She smiled.

"Yes, it's 'The March of the Valkyries.' Your ring dilemma has inspired me. As you've probably noticed by now, I take all my musical cues from life."

"So, I've been wondering something." She grabbed a celery stalk and pensively bit into it. "On July Fourth, before the thunder and lightning started, you were telling me the plot of the opera. About the ring. It started out with these three enormous mermaids swimming around in a plastic pool."

"Rhinemaidens," he corrected her with an impish wink. "They are Rhinemaidens. And they were being chased by Alberich. He wants their love, but since they won't give it to him, he steals their magical gold. Whoever makes a ring from their gold has ultimate power. So, the ring is pretty much the most desirable object in the world."

"So, Alberich wants to take over the world?"

"What he really wants is to use the ring to subjugate and punish the maidens who have humiliated him. And if the world gets in the way, then, sure, he'll take it over and destroy as much as he has to. That's the way he rolls."

Molly grew quiet, thoughtful. In his geeky enthusiasm for an opera based on what he assumed was myth, Marshall night have unwittingly guided her to a clue about that fateful night in April. Someone had been wielding unnatural power over events. Someone who hated women had been threatening Molly and Mardi. She sensed that the threat had something to do with the ring. It was clear now that the ring had powers she and her twin had not fathomed. Had it fallen into the wrong hands?

She couldn't, of course, mention any of this to Marshall, but she could express her gratitude to him for giving her some insight into her nightmare. He may have just gotten her closer to the moment when she could finally wake up and live her life again. Gratitude was not a familiar emotion for Molly. She tried to imagine what would make him happy.

It wasn't very hard. She took his chin in the palm of her hand and lifted his sweet face to hers. Then she kissed him.

He reeled backward, so amazed at his luck that he had no idea how to react.

"Marshall, you're the best. If you were a cheese, you'd be the Brillat-Savarin!"

"The cheese of the gods?" He laughed, blushing to the roots of his sandy hair.

"Exactly."

✳ 25 ✳

I KNEW YOU WERE TROUBLE, PART TWO

*A*fter the feel-good granolafest, Mardi put on her black racing suit and silver goggles. Then she took off for a long swim in the bay. She needed it. She had a lot to process. As she pulled her body fluidly through the water, stretching her arms, rotating her core, kicking, awakening her every muscle, she was able to align her thoughts and questions.

How had Molly lost the ring? Why did she race off just now instead of talking about it? It was almost like she had an idea and had to act on it right away.

Mardi now knew from the memory sessions with Jean-Baptiste that the ring was way more than a keepsake from their mother, whoever she was. They had always assumed it was a benevolent, private symbol between them. But Mardi was sure now that it harbored powers, and that those powers could be terrifying.

With Mardi and Molly, the ring was safe. In the

wrong hands, it was a mortal threat. Someone else had it now, and that someone was testing out its powers on this poor unsuspecting town, targeting its women most of all.

The weirdo in the pool had wanted their ring, seemingly to punish the twins. He hated them. But why? Granted, she and Molly were obnoxious, but they didn't deserve the flames of Hell. Did he despise all women, or "bitches," as he called them? Or was it personal?

Was he the stalker?

Although she swam and swam, Mardi came no closer to any answers.

She moved on to her next dilemma: Trent. Why had he ripped himself away from her yesterday, acting like he had important business that she couldn't come along on, right after they had officially recognized each other? She hated being pushed aside. She had offered to have a drink with him, and instead of letting her in, he had pulled a typical lone-male-wolf act. If he hadn't been a warlock himself, she would have turned him into a wolf cub for a few hours just to show him what an idiot he was being.

Could he have been racing off to meet her sister on Gardiners Island? That would qualify him as a psychopath, and she so didn't want to go there. But every time she tried to figure out who else Molly could have been seeing in her Bedouin love den in the dunes, she came up blank. It was infuriating.

All this anger was causing her to swim so fast that

she was out of breath. She forced herself to stop and float on her back for a couple of minutes to reassess. She felt a wave of appreciation for this beautiful sea and this quiet, leafy town, a town that seemed so sleepy and peaceful and yet was full of magic and mystery. She certainly couldn't complain that her life was boring here. Even if it was stressful.

She tried to slow down and think more rationally about Trent. Assuming he wasn't messing around with her sister, she should write Trent off for acting like such a jerk on the docks last night. But she didn't want to, and not just because she was so attracted to him. There was more to it than that. There was something deep going on with him, but he wouldn't share it with her. Did he think she was stupid? Immature? Selfish?

Mardi sighed across the glassy sea. Slowly, methodically, the bulk of her anger spent for the time being, she made her way back to shore and a shower before going down to Goose's Landing to help with the cleanup.

She put on an old Black Flag cutoff T-shirt for the occasion, with frayed denim shorts and black Doc Martens. And she wore a spiky dog collar and black lipstick.

"Wow, Mardi," said Freya, who had stopped by for a cup of coffee with Ingrid on her way to set up the bar. "Are you trying to look scary for anyone in particular? Who's the lucky guy?"

"Not scary," Mardi snapped. "Just totally unavailable." And before either Freya or Ingrid could respond from behind the steam of her fresh-brewed latte, she was out the door.

She found Trent alone on the dock outside the restaurant, picking up their beer cans from the evening before. He was frowning, and there were dark shadows under his eyes.

"Hey," she said.

At the sound of her voice, he smiled instantly, but when he looked up and saw how severe she had made herself look, he seemed to remember how things stood, and his happy expression disappeared.

"Hey," he finally managed. "I'm glad you showed up today. It's gonna be a tough one. It's a nightmare down in that cellar."

"Yep." She wasn't going to give him an inch. "Should we get started?"

"We can't go down there quite yet. We have to wait for the fire department to give us the go-ahead. They should be here in a few minutes. Want to go hang out on the *Dragon* until they come? I got this new sandwich press I want to try out. Do you like panini?"

"What is with you, man? Last night, you're all doom and gloom, and you won't even tell me what's going through your head. And when I show up today, you want to talk about panini? I'm not going to pretend like nothing's happening just because you don't feel like dealing with it. Either tell me what went down last night or tell me you're not going to tell me. But quit messing around."

"I'm just trying to be friendly. I could tell I pissed you off last night, and I thought I'd see if I could lighten the mood."

"Bad idea."

"So I see."

"I'll come hang out on the *Dragon*, but I don't want some stupid sandwich. I want answers."

"Okay." He looked straight at her. "I promise. Answers. No sandwich. Let's go."

They walked silently through the noonday sun to the boat and climbed aboard. She could see salt crystals dazzling in the soft hair on his arms. He must have taken a swim this morning too, but he hadn't showered yet. He often worked through the day with the sheen of the ocean on his skin. This was one of the things she used to think she liked about him.

As soon as they climbed onto the deck of the boat, he went into the cabin and returned with his panini press on the end of an extension cord, along with a cutting board, a knife, some focaccia and ham, cheese, and basil.

"I don't want there to be any more misunderstandings. I'm not offering you a panini," he said matter-of-factly. "I'm making one for myself. I'm starving."

Looking at the food, smelling the basil and fresh bread, Molly realized that she was starving too. But there was no way she was going to admit it.

"I owe you an apology," he continued.

"I don't care about apologies. I want an explanation. I want to understand what's happening."

"I wish I knew. But what I can say for sure is that someone with unnatural powers is messing with this town. I don't think it's the White Council trying to show disapproval. I think it's someone else, someone playing with a great power they can't necessarily control. It's an ancient power of some kind. I needed to talk to Jean-Baptiste last night, to see if he had any notion of what I should do."

"You sure you weren't at Fair Haven last night?" she hissed.

"What?" He looked genuinely confused.

"With a girl who looks identical to me, only more Fifth Avenue and less Williamsburg."

"Are you talking about your sister, Molly?"

"That's the only sister I have."

"Mardi, I have no idea what you are talking about. Why would you think that? I was with Jean-Baptiste last night. And I swear he looks nothing like you. Although he is very Fifth Avenue. You gotta give him that."

In spite of herself, she cracked a smile.

"Okay, so you were with Jean-Baptiste. And?"

"And there is something else, but the problem is that I can't tell you any more or someone may get hurt. It's not that I want to be secretive. I'm in a bind, Mardi. Please believe me. Haven't you ever been in a bind before?"

"I guess so." She found herself wanting to tell him about the blocked texts from someone claiming to have incriminating information about Molly and her, threatening her sister if she told . . . *anyone.* She realized she couldn't even explain the cause of her suspicions without risking her twin's life. She too was in a bind. "Yeah, I have a potential source of information too. Maybe. It's either a real source or a totally sick joke. But there's a threat if I reveal too much that someone might get hurt."

"So, it seems like, for now, we can only tell each other without telling each other."

"I guess that's right," she admitted, deeply grateful for the fact that he wasn't pushing her to talk.

"Is that going to be okay with you, at least for now?" he asked, constructing a sandwich on two thin slices of golden bread.

"I guess it has to be." She shrugged.

He nodded, closing the hot press so that the cheese began to sizzle. "You sure you don't want one?"

"I might have changed my mind," she admitted.

He lifted the perfectly grilled sandwich and handed it to her in a blue cloth napkin. "Here." He smiled. "All yours. No strings attached and no questions asked."

✷ 26 ✷

LOVE ME TWO TIMES

The North Inn, like the neighborhood dive it was, often smelled like spilled beer, but because it had a witch for a bartender, it also smelled like the fresh herbs and fruit juices that went into Freya's potent cocktails. The wooden booths were beaten up and carved with countless sets of initials and messages that had completely lost their meaning over the years. It shook to the rhythm of rock and roll, beating time with the slap of glasses and dollar bills on the counter. Even Molly, through her crinkled little snub nose, was able, on some level, to appreciate its undying energy.

Freya was known for her ability to cure heartbreak, for dispensing magic that kept many relationships alive. Somehow, the people of North Hampton never noticed that she did not grow old alongside them, but stayed timelessly gorgeous with her lush mane of hair, tiny waist, and breathtaking cleavage.

When Molly came in on a hot Friday evening, having just kissed poor Marshall and left him beaming and wordless, the North Inn was heaving. It was karaoke night, and even though it wasn't even nine o'clock yet, the microphone was starting to get some play. A mousy young woman, whom Molly recognized as one of Ingrid's fellow librarians, was crooning Beyoncé's "Halo" to her boyish, smooth-chinned fisherman boyfriend, who, Molly noticed, was still wearing his waders. Beaming up at his librarian, Fishboy sipped a pink cocktail from a wide-rimmed glass. Whenever there was a musical interlude that gave her a break from singing, he passed the glass to her.

"Want an Infatuation like that happy couple?" asked Freya, leaning over the bar toward Molly.

"What is it?"

"Hibiscus, rosewater, and English gin. Or maybe you'd care for a Forever, like the mayor and his husband?"

Molly looked over at two trim men in their early forties, dressed in striped button-downs. While they waited for their turn, they looked intently through the karaoke songbook, discussing the possibilities with much animation.

"Is it good?"

"Champagne fortified with fresh daisy petals is always good."

Molly smiled at Freya's ingenuity. Having taken the only available stool at the bar, she was surrounded on all sides by locals. From working in the shop, she recognized many faces. But she realized now that she knew no one beyond smiling distance. For a second, she felt sad that she had made almost no inroads in North Hampton. In just over a month, apart from having won over and then broken two hearts, she would leave the East End without a trace . . . Although maybe she would come back next summer? She was taken aback by the thought. Was this tacky, disorienting place actually growing on her?

"So what'll it be?" asked Freya.

"Do you have a drink called Clarity? I'm so confused right now."

"Let me guess." Freya smiled, reaching for an unlabeled bottle of honey-colored liquor. "Too many men in your orbit?"

"Not exactly," Molly began to fidget with her beaded clutch. "I'm used to having a lot of boys circling around. But this time, I sort of like two guys at the same time. Like, I'm being pulled in two directions. I don't know how to choose."

"Who says you have to choose?" Winking, Freya poured a shot of the golden liquid from her mystery bottle into a shaker and added some sort of green cordial.

"I don't know why I have to choose, but it feels like I do."

"It sounds to me like you don't need to ask that question because the answer is already blazing inside you." Freya laughed kindly. "Molly, you seem like you could handle it all."

"How do you know?"

"Because I've been there. I thought I had to choose between two guys, and it almost destroyed me." Freya paused to muddle some blackberries with several kinds of herbs that she snipped from bunches in tall glasses on their own dedicated shelf behind the bar. When she was satisfied with her mixture, she added it to the shaker.

"So what did you do?"

Freya smiled mysteriously as she gave her cocktail a couple of hard shakes, then poured the glistening concoction into a rocks glass over ice and handed it to Molly. "I'm still working it out. Things are always evolving between the three of us. We'll see what happens." She winked. "I like to live in the moment. So should you."

Molly raised her glass in Freya's direction and took a sip of her cocktail. She had no idea what it was. There were traces of fruit along with vaguely medicinal notes and a deep, rolling, satisfying flavor whose name was just outside her grasp.

"This is awesome," she said, "better than anything I've tasted in any pretentious mixology place in the city. What is it?"

"It's called Embrace. But it's not a regular menu item. I just invented it for you. And you, Molly, are the only person I will ever mix it for."

"I'm flattered. What's in it?"

"If I tell you, it will lose its potency. I have to watch my secrets around fellow witches," Freya teased.

"What do you mean, potency? What's it going to do to me?" Molly was intrigued. After one swallow, she was already starting to picture kissing Tris and Marshall at the same time. She felt her face flush, just thinking about it.

Molly drained her glass and pulled Freya out from behind the bar toward the karaoke machine. Too impatient to bother with flipping through the index of the songbook, she muttered a little incantation causing it to open to the page she wanted.

Freya threw an arm around Molly. "Now, this is my kind of music! I love the Doors!"

"So does Daddy," Molly yelled over the intro, grooving to the fact that she and Freya were both wearing short, fitted white dresses. Freya's was flared and retro, while Molly's was a slinky number from the latest designer collection. Yet despite the differences, they both wore their dresses so well that it looked like they could have planned their outfits specifically for their star turn at the North Inn.

As they launched into the song, the entire bar fell under their spell. Conversations came to abrupt ends. Drinks sat untouched. At first, everyone appeared to be in a trance. Then Freya moved her hands in a come-hither gesture that got people singing along, one by one, until the whole Friday-night crowd was belting out Jim Morrison's lyrics.

Molly had never done anything this fun and silly.

North Hampton was beginning to grow on her, lyric by lyric.

But just as effortlessly as she had drawn them into the song, Molly silenced everyone with a simple finger to her lips. Not a soul could disobey her. The room went silent except for the two gorgeous white-clad witches finishing out their anthem.

There was rapturous applause, whistling, and many rounds of drinks were offered and bought. But Molly couldn't manage to take another sip. She felt the effects of Freya's cocktail growing stronger and stronger, and was soon barely able to fend off the random guys who wanted to do shots with her. The room was starting to spin.

"Are you okay?" Freya asked as she busily attended to the rush their song had created behind the bar.

"Not really," Molly admitted. "I'm not usually such a lightweight. But I think I might get sick."

"I'm so sorry, sweetie. My potions can be pretty strong. Why don't you go outside and get some fresh air? I'll be out in a few. And don't you dare get on your bike. I'll call you a cab."

Stumbling out into the parking lot, Molly kicked off her heels and stood barefoot, head in hands, trying not to puke. So, this was the underside of the Embrace. The effects of the drink were showing no signs of wearing off. But instead of keeping her on top of the world, with heady visions of boys submitting to her will, her buzz was going sour.

Her head was filling with the recollection of the one boy back home she had never been able to control. Bret. She hated to pronounce his name, even if it was only in her head. And she hated the memory of his chiseled face from the night of the party in his Upper East Side penthouse. For as long into the evening as she could remember, he had toyed with her and Mardi alternately, never committing to one, driving them both crazy with jealous rage. They had never liked the same boy before, and it was awful.

What a bullshit artist that boy was. A rich bullshit artist with bleached blond hair. Why was she thinking about him now? Was it the potion? Was Freya's handiwork causing her to see all the boys she wanted to be with? Did she want to be with Bret?

No, no, she told herself. Absolutely not. But even as she insisted inside that she had never wanted him, a new recollection surfaced to contradict her.

It started out like that vision she and Mardi had had during Jean-Baptiste's first memory session, the one where they were naked in a black swimming pool and being chased by some weirdo. As they slithered and swam away, the three of them were trapped in a dreamlike loop.

The vision rose up again inside her, vivid and terrifying. Had Freya meant to do this with her cocktail? Molly heard powerful strains of opera blaring in surround sound from the black marble walls. She saw the guy with her and Mardi in Bret's penthouse swimming pool. He was saying something, something hostile. It sounded like "bitches burn in Hell . . ." Feeling sicker and sicker, Molly strained her senses through time and space to catch his words. *Bitches burn . . .*

Deep in a trance, she could finally hear him hissing through the steam of his overheated pool. The weirdo didn't just look like Bret. He *was* Bret. She was sure of it now, as sure as she had ever been of anything. They were the same person—or the same creature.

"Don't touch us!" Mardi screamed.

"You stupid witch. I have no interest in you or your sister. I hate you both. I hate all you bitches! It's your gold I want! Give me the gold!"

"Not our ring! Never!" Molly found herself yelling hysterically out into the emptiness of the North Inn parking lot. The sound of her own voice roused her from her nightmare.

Now Freya was holding her, pressing a cool, wet washcloth to her forehead.

"Whoa, relax, relax. Molly? Earth to Molly. Are you with me?"

"I think so." Molly thought she was speaking out loud, but she was so disoriented that she couldn't be certain.

"This is all my fault. I'm afraid I went a little too heavy on the absinthe. What were you screaming just now about a ring?"

"I—I don't really know," Molly stammered. She was shaking, scanning the road for her cab. Ingrid's house was only a ten-minute ride from here. She had never wanted so desperately to be in her bed. "Can—can I sit down?"

"Sure," Freya said, leading Molly toward the three stairs to the North Inn's door.

But just as Molly let herself collapse onto the bottom step, a pair of headlights pulled into the lot, followed by a Subaru wagon with Matt behind the wheel.

"Your chariot has arrived." Freya couldn't completely repress a smile.

"Evening, ladies," Matt said pleasantly through his open window. He was wearing his detective uniform— a nondescript sport coat and tie. "Ingrid sent me to pick her up; she had a premonition she'd need a ride home," he said.

Molly frowned and glared at Freya. "If I throw up in his car, I'm never speaking to you again."

27

RED, RED WINE

So, my sister was so drunk when she got home last night that she told me Freya is basically seeing both of your brothers, and that supposedly Freya and Killian used to shack up right here in this cabin. Is it true?"

"Which part?" asked Trent with a smile.

"Any of it?"

"I don't know what's going on between the three of them, and it's none of my business. But this is Killian's boat . . . my brother, the lady-killer," He gestured with mock grandeur to the cherrywood and leather interior that was his home here on the East End. Then he put on a silly Dracula accent. "So prepare to be seduced."

They had repaired to the *Dragon* after mopping out the flooded wine cellar of Goose's Landing. When no one was looking, they had resorted to a little magic to undo some of the more alarming red stains. Mario and Luis were going to start repairing the structural damage tomorrow morning.

Trent told her he'd swiped a really good bottle of

Bordeaux from the cellar at Fair Haven. As he uncorked it, he hummed the old reggae tune "Red, Red Wine."

"What else did your sister say about my family?" Trent asked.

"Not much. She was pretty incoherent. Freya gave her one of her cocktails. But it was one she'd never mixed before, and it got a little out of hand. Poor Molly. I usually think she deserves what she gets, but no one deserves to be that sick. She spent half the night curled up on the bathroom floor throwing up. It was really a bummer."

"Is she okay this morning?"

"She's fine. Ingrid gave her a pretty radical hangover potion. I'm going to have to steal the formula from her. I've been thinking that if Molly and I ever have to go underground we could always support ourselves by selling the stuff on the black market. Seriously, it works wonders. Molly looks like she slept ten hours last night. She's so happy that she's not even a tiny bit bloated. It's like Christmas!"

"How come I haven't met her yet? I guess I've been hanging at the docks too much. I hear she's quite a stunner," he said, his eyes twinkling.

Mardi curled her lip. "Don't worry. She's not your type."

"Aren't you guys really identical?" he teased as he handed her a full glass of dark wine, his eyes twinkling blue as a sun-kissed sea.

She ignored him. "Yeah, but you wouldn't be able to stand her for five minutes."

"And I can stand you for at least five minutes?" His eyes were definitely shining.

"Besides, she has a boyfriend." Mardi couldn't help but feel jealous at Trent's interest in Molly.

"Oh, yeah?"

"She's been hanging out at Fair Haven. That's why I thought—"

"I think we've established it's not me. So, then, who?" Although he was trying to keep his tone light, she could tell this was an important question.

"No idea." Mardi was suddenly concerned. Who *could* Molly be seeing? She'd never stoop to dating an employee of the house. Was there yet another brother lurking at Fair Haven? A stepchild? Some relative Trent didn't want to acknowledge? Could she really trust Trent? She wanted to. More than anything.

"So, cheers to cleaning up gallons of this stuff!" Mardi touched her wineglass to his and took a big sip. As if it fortified her courage, she put the glass down and stood up next to him. "This is great, but you know what could be better?" she asked huskily.

He raised his eyebrows and put down his glass. "I think I do."

She leaned toward him but he was faster, and he pulled her into his arms. She closed her eyes and their lips met, slowly at first, then harder, and faster, more urgent, until they had knocked the wine off the table in a hurry to fall into bed, so that the red wine bloomed like a cut on the carpet.

* 28 *

PERFECT DAY

$\mathcal{M}$olly needed to appear innocent while delivering a message that could, potentially, make her seem pretty guilty. She had to look her best. She thumbed through the possibilities on the rolling clothes rack she had swiped from Freya's enormous attic wardrobe. She hadn't wanted her beautiful stuff to get all mussed in Ingrid and Matt's small minimalist guest room closet.

She looked over the hangers out onto the beach and the sparkling bay. It was gorgeous outside. She had texted Marshall that she needed to take the day off for "personal reasons." Velvet Underground was playing in the background, Lou Reed crooning about a perfect day, just like the one she was about to have.

She toyed with the idea of a cap-sleeved orange sundress, but decided it would be a mistake. Yet the baby blue romper was too babyish. On the other end of the spectrum was a fitted navy button-down dress she had bought for a funeral. She tried it on with a pair of beige pumps and checked herself out in the full-length mirror that she had also borrowed from Freya's stash. It was all right for a funeral, she thought, laughing to herself.

There had to be a happy medium. She went back to her rack. Her solution jumped out at her in the form of a lightweight Chanel suit. Freya had had the hemline taken up, but not too much. The jacket was cropped, but she had a great silk tank that would cover her belly button. And she could finish it with some cork wedges that were fun yet discreet.

As she put the final touches on her hair and makeup, she smiled at herself in the bathroom mirror. "Perfect for a perfect day," she whispered.

Molly's mission was a delicate one. She had decided to seek out Jean-Baptiste and tell him about the vision she'd had of Bret chasing her and Mardi around because he wanted their ring. She was starting to think that the scene she had relived in her absinthe delirium in the parking lot of the North Inn wasn't a simply a paranoid vision, but a memory. Hazy as it was, it had a feel of truth to it.

Slowly, painfully, the night of the accident was coming into focus. And she had a feeling that the ring, missing now, had also briefly gone missing that night.

Molly realized that she could potentially incriminate herself—and her twin—by telling Jean-Baptiste that she had recalled events leading her to believe that her and Mardi's ring was a factor in the killings. Maybe this would make her look guilty. But maybe she was?

No way. They were being framed—she was sure of it. Someone knew that they were considered trouble-makers at Headingley and in bars and clubs all around the city, that they were constantly on the verge of being expelled but always managed to charm their way out of trouble at the eleventh hour. And this same someone was well aware that the White Council wouldn't mind having an excuse to put the Overbrook sisters out of harm's way for a few thousand years.

Could it actually be Bret who was trying to banish them to the Underworld? That phrase, "bitches burn in Hell," pursued her and Mardi like an echo through time. First the night of the party. Then on the wind-shield of the Ferrari while a freak fire raged in the night. Could it all be Bret? Who was Bret, anyway? The sisters had always guessed he was paranormal. But how? And why would he have it in for Mardi and her? What had they ever done to him?

If she could get Jean-Baptiste to see through her eyes, perhaps he could shed some light on this thicket of images and impressions. Perhaps he could help her to remember a little bit more, and more clearly, so that together they could unravel the facts, clear the Overbrook name—find out what really happened that night and what was going on right now in North Hampton.

• • •

Briskly and purposefully, Molly knocked on the pale pink door of Rose Cottage, the bed and breakfast where Jean-Baptiste was spending his East End summer.

In seconds, as though she had been lying in wait for a visitor, Mrs. Ashley Green, a pleasantly plump woman in her late fifties, wearing a flowing lavender-and-white batik dress, opened the door with a gracious smile.

"Well, don't you look lovely," she said. "I believe I recognize you from the Cheesemonger. I buy all of my scones from you for my guests. I used to bake them myself, but yours are so much more divine than anything I could produce. My favorites are the apricot currant. Do you have a favorite?"

"Um, I really like—"

"You also do wonderful soups. At first I was skeptical, like everyone else in town, of the New England chowder, but I have to say that I'm now a convert. An absolute convert!"

"Yes, it was a big risk, but it paid—"

"It paid off. Why, yes it did! Come in dear. What can I get you?"

"Actually—"

"No, don't say it. I can read it in your eyes. Such pretty dark eyes. And what lovely dark hair you have. I can see exactly what you want. I have a gift for reading people you know. I can say beyond a shadow of a doubt that you would absolutely kill for some lemonade and shortbread right now."

"Excuse me, but—"

"This way. Come this way."

Before she could object, Molly was led through a fever dream of chintz and Victorian antiques into a kitchen whose walls were covered in mounted floral china plates. She was seated at a table and presented with a tall glass of lemonade and a plate of shortbread.

"This is really lovely of you, Mrs. Green, but I'm not—"

"Now, don't you try to be polite. I'm sure your mother taught you never to act hungry in a stranger's home, but I'm no stranger to anyone in this town."

At the mention of a mother, Molly's heart sank a little. No one, except a couple of unfortunate and short-lived nannies, had ever attempted to teach either of the twins manners of any kind.

She suddenly grew impatient with the aggressively friendly Mrs. Green and whispered a spell that stuck the dowdy woman's lips together long enough that she could get a word in edgewise.

"Listen, I'm not hungry, and I don't eat cookies that are pure butter anyway, and I need to see one of your guests. A Mr. Mésomier."

Frightened and confused, Mrs. Green stared bug-eyed at Molly, as if from underwater, making the faint guttural sounds of the gagged and the drowning.

Molly released the poor woman, who immediately went off on a tangent about how the strangest thing had just happened, and had Molly noticed that her mouth wouldn't move for a few minutes there?

Just as Molly was ready to turn Mrs. Green into a gingerbread woman, take a bite out of her, and put her remains on the hideous china plate next to her vile shortbread, Jean-Baptiste stuck his elegant head into the kitchen.

"Why, Molly, how wonderful to see you," he purred, not appearing remotely surprised. Within moments, he had dispatched his annoying hostess and was seated across from Molly, shrink-style, on a brown velvet settee, while she was perched nervously in a toile-upholstered window seat.

"You look smashing," he opened.

"So do you," she replied. She meant it. He was wearing an impeccable canary yellow linen suit. And his pocket square today was kelly green. "Do you always do solid-color pocket squares?" she asked, genuinely curious.

"I do," he answered. "If you ever see a man who looks like me but is wearing a patterned pocket square, you can be sure he's an imposter."

"Good to know." She smiled.

"But I don't think you came here to ask about my sartorial preferences. To what do I owe this pleasure?"

With that, it all came pouring out of her. The images of the pool, the ominous sounds of the opera overhead, the bitches burning in Hell. The shared ring that Bret had been after, which she thought went missing briefly that night; the fact that it was now missing again; all the intertwining themes and variations.

She tried to describe the wall of secrecy that was coming up between her and her twin. The two of them had always butted heads, but they had never been such bitter rivals as on the night of the party. And every time they tried to get close here in North Hampton, they inevitably started to argue.

"It's weird. I don't know what's going on with us. I mean, we've always fought, but we've also always known what's up with each other. I feel like someone's using our competitiveness to keep us apart. Is that weird?"

Jean-Baptiste nodded. "Yes, you and your sister must make every effort to unite your powers. The two of you must tell each another everything that you recall, even if it feels like nothing more than a dream. I believe that the ring may hold the answers we are seeking, although truly it is the power of your memories that will ultimately uncover the fates of those poor murdered children and prove your innocence.

"Whoever is behind these crimes is trying to divide the two of you—and I have to say you are easy targets for discord—so that you will not combine your recollections and come to the solution. You are being kept in the dark by your own inability to work together. If you and Mardi can find the strength to work together, you will be able to remember exactly what happened that night."

"And do you think that remembering what happened will help us understand what is going on here, now? All the random acts of evil and hate?"

"I'm afraid they aren't so random, Molly."

"There *is* a pattern. Whoever is behind this craves power. And hates women."

"Yes, Molly." He closed his eyes to concentrate. "You are beginning to see clearly now. I believe that, united, you and Mardi have enough clarity to combat this evil."

With Jean-Baptiste's wise words ringing in her ears and heart, Molly rushed from Rose Cottage, leapt onto her shiny red bicycle, and began to ride toward the docks, where she hoped to find Mardi and come clean. But she had only pedaled for a block when she heard her phone beep.

A text. Could it be Tris? Was he finally going to tell her why he had vanished from the dunes the other night? Although she knew she should be furious, she wanted more than anything to give him the benefit of the doubt, to join him again among the cashmere blankets. And maybe even to confide in him about all the crazy stuff that was going on in her life. He was, after all, her kind.

She pulled out her phone. OMG! It *was* him. And he was saying all the right things.

I'm so sorry. I can explain everything. Meet me as soon as you possibly can inside the greenhouse on the west side of Fair Haven.

Without hesitating, Molly changed direction and began to speed toward the Gardiners Island Bridge. It wasn't that she had changed her mind about bonding with Mardi. She had every intention of doing so. She knew it was important.

But first, she had an urgent booty call to answer.

✳ 29 ✳

BAD BOYFRIEND

$\mathcal{P}$lease, Mardi, don't go. Spend the night with me on the *Dragon*." Trent's voice was at once silky and rugged.

"Believe me, I don't want to go." It was true. She felt amazing. As the sun began to dip, bathing the boat's deck in soft pink light, every nerve in her body tingled with pleasure. She stretched, long and feline, within the comfort of his muscular embrace. "But I promised Ingrid and Matt I would be home by seven to babysit."

This was true. But it wasn't the only reason she gave herself for wrenching her body from his. You always wanted to leave a fresh situation with a boy on a high note, with a lingering sense of possibility. There was no point in exhausting your options right after the first kisses. Mardi was a sucker for the exquisite torture of the long, drawn-out conquest. August was going to be an eventful month.

He waved sweetly as she climbed off the boat. And

she was sure she could feel his melancholy gaze caressing her sinewy back as she walked along the dock toward shore. But when she turned for a last look from the harbor, he was gone.

Sinking dreamily into the driver's seat of the Ferrari, she felt the vibration of her phone in her back pocket. It was probably Ingrid reminding her that she and Matt were going on a date tonight and that Mardi needed to be home soon or else telling Mardi what she had prepared for her and the kids for dinner (Ingrid loved to discuss dinner).

But of course it wasn't Ingrid.

Meet me at greenhouse at Fair Haven ASAP. You know where it is.

Buzzkill.

Psycho stalker.

Mardi kicked one of her tires, then texted Ingrid that she was sorry she was going to be late. Something had come up at work.

Ingrid immediately messaged back that this was *disappointing*. She and Matt were now probably going to lose their table at the coveted Bistro Margaux and possibly even miss their movie.

I have come to expect more from you, Mardi.

Mardi wished she could tell Ingrid what was going on.

Her wonderful mood shattered now, Mardi gunned it across the bridge to Fair Haven. *You know where it is,* the stalker had written, which meant whoever was texting her knew Mardi was familiar with the greenhouse. They had been spying on her while she ate dinner there, among the potted palms and ferns, with Trent on the night of the party. She had a mental flash of the Venus flytrap snapping its green lips around a live worm.

As she was parking the Ferrari, her eye caught on a flash of red against one of the dunes. It was a bicycle. *Ingrid's* bicycle. The one that Molly rode everywhere. Why was her sister here now? Shouldn't she be at the Cheesemonger finishing up her shift?

Molly was here again? Like the last time Mardi was summoned? It had to be more than coincidence.

Mardi glanced at the massive house, which looked deserted at first, all of its windows shuttered and draped—although on closer examination, there was one parted curtain on the top floor. She felt as if she was being watched as she crossed the vast green lawn of the estate toward the western side of the house to the beautiful wrought-iron and glass structure where she had first gotten to know Trent. So much had happened already this summer that the June evening of the party seemed distant and rosy, from a different time.

In order to show whoever was observing her that she was not afraid, she took strong purposeful strides.

As she approached the greenhouse, she saw that there was a figure pressed against the glass. It appeared to waver slightly among the fronds and branches, as though it were flickering, only half real. Maybe it was a trick of the light, a tree with a vaguely humanoid shape that struck her nervous imagination. But, from a closer vantage point, Mardi saw clearly that this was no tree. And it was not one, but two people, two people writhing as one.

What she finally witnessed was so bizarre that at first she could not process it. The guy and the girl pawing one another in the greenhouse were none other than Molly and . . .

Trent?

Trent? Her Trent?

He had the same dark hair, the same expression on his face . . . the same one he'd made when he'd kissed *her* earlier that day.

Mardi watched, her heart falling into her stomach, and felt as if she might vomit. Her most far-fetched suspicions were actually true. This was a nightmare.

Molly had her back pressed into the glass wall, her skirt hiked to her waist, and her legs wrapped around Trent's hips.

Trent was holding her up against the glass, his face buried in her neck.

So this was what her stalker wanted her to know.

Mardi had never felt so betrayed—or so stupid. Only a few hours ago, she had finally let herself trust Trent, and he had been playing her all along. *How come I've never met your sister . . . I hear she's quite a stunner . . . Aren't you guys really identical?*

Mardi couldn't move. Not even when he began to unbutton the front of Molly's dress, not even when Molly pulled off his polo shirt.

Mardi felt sick. How could she have ever touched him? How could she have been so completely wrong about him? If the world was confusing before, now it had stopped making any sense at all.

She and Molly never liked the same guy. They had sort of fought over Bret, but they were sort of repulsed by him too. It wasn't the same. This was different. There was a *code*. No matter what happened—no matter how much she and Molly bickered and fought, they were *sisters*. Twin sisters.

If Trent liked Molly better, then there was nothing Mardi could do about it. She would step aside.

She was about to leave when Trent looked up and caught her eye.

She froze.

But he only smiled.

A malicious, terrifying grin.

A shit-eating grin.

One that confirmed all her fears. He'd *wanted* her to

see this. He had sent her all those texts! He'd wanted her to know he was toying with her all along. Toying with them. Two-for-one special. Maybe it ran in the family, what with the weird triangle of his older brothers and Freya Beauchamp.

For the first time in her life, Mardi Overbrook was too hurt to fight. She had no rage left in her. She turned away and ran.

✳ 30 ✳

FOUND OUT ABOUT YOU

$\mathcal{I}$t was four A.M. Molly opened the front door quietly. Her head was still swirling with African violets, pink and white water lilies in a trickling fountain, lacy ferns, exotic herbs, and that awesomely weird Venus flytrap that Tris had fed from a stash of writhing worms. He had told her that he was taking care of the plant for his brother Killian.

She had never felt so jazzed by a boy in this life—maybe ever. Of course, Cheeseboy was a wonderful side dish, and there was no reason not to keep him warm, but for now, she was going to focus on the young heir to Fair Haven.

Tris had explained his disappearance from the dunes. His stepmother, Mrs. Gardiner, was not only chilly, judgmental, and overly fond of gin. She was also mentally unstable and sometimes self-destructive in her cries for help. She had been acting strange all that day, saying dramatic good-byes to Tris and the staff for no particular reason, since she wasn't going anywhere they knew of. And she would not take off her fur-collared "traveling coat," even though it was the first week of August.

While Tris had been with Molly in front of the fire that night, he'd had a sudden, strong premonition that Mrs. G had done something awful. He'd rushed off to go check. Sure enough, there was an empty bottle of sleeping pills by her bed and she was turning blue. He'd had to call 911 immediately.

"That's weird," Molly said. "I didn't hear an ambulance."

"They always come by boat. It's faster. And more discreet."

"Got it." She nodded. "I'm really sorry. Do you think she'll be okay?"

"Depends on your definition of okay. But I don't want to think about it anymore now."

He kissed her.

The kisses had led to so much more, she thought dreamily, remembering their hot make-out session. Tris had wanted to go all the way, but Molly had stopped him. He had taken off his shirt and she was half undressed, but that was as far as she had allowed him to go.

She wanted to tease it out.

"No," she'd said. "Not yet."

"But I want to," he'd begged. "I want you so much. I've wanted you for so long."

"I do too," she'd told him. "But good things come to those who wait."

She smiled, recalling the musky scent of his cologne and the intensity of his touch, as she closed the front door softly behind her, took off her shoes so as not to make noise on the wooden floors, and tiptoed into the dark living room.

"Where have you been?" Mardi's angry whisper hit her out of nowhere.

Molly steeled herself. She wasn't going to let a fight with her sister wreck a perfect night. She was going to keep things under control.

"I saw you."

As her eyes adjusted to the darkness, Molly saw Mardi as a long shape coiled on the sofa like a snake preparing to strike. Midnight was nestled in the crook of her knees.

"And what exactly did you see me doing, perv?" Molly knew she shouldn't engage, but the urge was stronger than ever. She couldn't let Mardi have the last word.

"You were in the greenhouse at Fair Haven, making out with Trent."

"Trent? Who's Trent?"

"Trystan Gardiner. My boyfriend. Everyone calls him Trent."

"Mardi, you're delirious." Molly moved toward the couch. "Trystan Gardiner is *my* boyfriend. And he doesn't go by Trent, everyone calls him Tris, including me."

"He's Trent, you idiot."

"Nuh-uh. His name is Tris! Trystan, get it? Tris!"

"Trent!"

"Tris!"

They were still whispering viciously, their faces now just inches apart so that to each one the other's features looked distorted and gray in the darkness. Midnight was looking from one to the other. The kitten's wide copper eyes flashed between them.

"Wait—there's only one Gardiner brother in town this summer, isn't there?" Molly asked suddenly.

"Duh! Haven't you heard a word I said?"

"Then that means your Trent and my Tris are the same guy?"

Mardi rolled her eyes. "What do you think?"

"So you didn't know you were with my guy?"

"Of course I didn't know," Molly snapped, deeply offended. "Did *you* know?"

"Of course not."

"So why did you ask if I knew? Tris or Trent, or whoever he is, the guy has been playing both of us."

Molly was devastated. "But Tris is so not your type."

"Trent is so not yours. I met him first at the party at Fair Haven."

"No, *I* met him first at the party at Fair Haven!"

As they glared at each other, the kitten arched her back and hissed. But they paid no attention.

Molly decided she had to leave. She had never been this humiliated before. In fact, she had *never* been humiliated. She couldn't stand it. And her sister, whom she was supposed to be bonding with, was driving her even more insane. As much as she hated Tris now, she hated the idea of Mardi having him even more.

She had almost . . . and her sister . . . what had she done?

"Ew! Did you sleep with him?" Molly demanded.

"No! Did you?" Mardi asked.

"No!"

But even if Mardi hadn't slept with him, it still didn't make it okay. They had kissed, that was for sure, and that was enough for Molly.

She hated this house. She hated this town. She hated everything. She didn't know where she wanted to go. But she knew she wanted out of this hellhole. Now.

She ran upstairs, threw a few clothes and a toothbrush and makeup bag into her Hermès tote, and, without so much as a good-bye to Mardi, who might still be stewing on the couch for all she cared, Molly stormed off into the breaking day, with Midnight's eyes shining after her in the dawning light.

PART THREE

Summer Loving!
Had me
a blast
Summer Loving!
Happened
so fast

31

I WILL SURVIVE

$\mathcal{M}$ardi was still lying on the sofa, staring at the living room ceiling, when Ingrid came down in her simple white cotton bathrobe, looking fresh and wholesome, to grind the coffee.

"Good morning," said Ingrid. "Did you sleep well?"

Mardi hadn't slept at all. What had just happened? She and her sister had been seeing the same Gardiner brother. It was unbelievable. And to think she had actually liked him—Trent or Tris or Trystan, whatever his name was. And he had liked her too—just as much as he'd liked her sister, that was clear.

It was so gross and so awful.

"Coffee?" Ingrid chirped as she poured fresh grounds into her elaborate coffee machine.

Mardi grunted.

"Hang in there. The java is percolating. Help is on the way." Ingrid appeared to have forgiven her for never showing up to babysit last night.

But apparently Jo and Henry, who came bounding

downstairs at the sound of her voice, were not so understanding. They both jumped on her and started hitting her with their stuffed animals. "Where were you? We were supposed to have a dance party with Mini and George. You promised!"

"Party!" Henry echoed.

Mini and George were a toy mouse and a monkey puppet. Whenever Ingrid and Matt were safely out of the picture, Mardi and Jo animated them, making them sing, dance, and fly all over the house, much to Henry's delight.

"I'm sorry guys." Mardi rolled over to escape their soft blows. "Something came up."

She put her face in her hands and pressed her fingers into her forehead, trying to fight the grogginess invading her body. And then she felt it. The ring. That tiny, deeply familiar weight on her right hand. Her eyes widened as she pulled her hands from her face to examine it. She completely forgot that she was supposed to be upset. Lovingly, she twisted the ring around and around, marveling at its simple carved diamond design. How long had it been here?

Her first instinct was to find Molly and tell her. Then she remembered she was in a huge fight with Molly. Then she remembered why, and she was overcome by a wave of sadness and anger so strong she grabbed the suede fringe bag she had dumped on the floor next to her and bolted from the couch for the front door. She didn't need Ingrid's organic fair trade coffee. She didn't even need to brush her teeth or wash her face. What she needed was to make Trystan Gardiner pay. Now.

"Mardi!" Ingrid ran to stop her. "What's this all about? Is there something you need to tell me?"

"No."

"Where's Molly?"

"I don't know."

"You don't have any idea where she is?"

Mardi shrugged and made for the door again.

Ingrid frowned. "Listen," she said, "I'm responsible for you two here this summer. Your dad is an age-old friend of mine. I promised him to keep an eye on you. And I promised to help you get to the bottom of that accident in New York so that we wouldn't all suffer for your carelessness. Now, if something serious is going on, you owe it to me and to Freya and Jean-Baptiste to let us in."

"Oh, my God, Ingrid, this has nothing to do with the White Council or the investigation. If you must know, it's about a guy. It's kind of a rude awakening, but it's not life threatening, except maybe to him when I get a hold of him."

"What did he do?"

"He was playing both of us."

"Playing both of you? You don't mean . . . ?" Ingrid softened her tone.

Mardi nodded, her eyes filling with tears.

"Oh! How awful! Who is he?"

"Trystan Gardiner."

"Trystan Gardiner?" Ingrid said, taken aback. "Are you sure?"

"I think I know who we were both dating, Ingrid."

"But it doesn't sound like him. I *know* Trystan . . . He's a bit rough around the edges, but he's got a good heart."

"A heart that's big enough for two, clearly." Mardi cracked a bitter smile. "Can I go now?"

"Are you sure you don't want any coffee?"

"No thanks, Ingrid. I'm pumped up enough as it is."

"Okay, I know I'm not your mother. I'm sorry about Trystan, but it's hard to believe he would do such a thing." She gave a sad little smile. "Do you mind keeping an eye on the kids for me for a minute before you go? I need to get some zucchini from the garden."

"Yeah, whatever."

Once Ingrid was out the door, Jo came up to Mardi with her hands behind her back and a wildly happy expression on her little face. Henry was trailing her, meowing like a cat.

"We have a surprise for you!" Jo was trembling with excitement.

Mardi tried to pretend she cared. After all, these kids weren't to blame for the fact that she was miserable. She mustered as much sham enthusiasm as she could. "No way! You guys are the best! What could it be?"

"Look!" From behind her back, Jo produced a small, purring Siamese cat.

"Killer?" Mardi experienced a wave of the purest

delight. "Killer, it's you!" The cat leapt into Mardi's arms, nestled in the crook of her neck, and gazed up adoringly into her face. Midnight looked on with a gentle curiosity.

"I thought you might miss your familiars. It seemed so unfair that your daddy made you leave them behind. So I transported them for you. It was the hardest spell I've ever done."

"This is amazing, Jo. You are one talented little witch." She scratched Killer gently under the chin, loving the familiar feeling of her short fur. Never had she been so happy to see her constant companion. "But what do you mean by 'familiars'? I only have one familiar. It's just me and Killer. Killer and me."

"Oh, but I rescued Molly's familiar too!"

"You mean Fury is here?"

"Yes. She's in Molly's bed right now. She's a really funny-looking doggy, right?"

Mardi had to laugh. "Miracles never cease."

Jo and Henry stood beaming at her.

After a few minutes of bonding and reconnecting with the beautiful creature, she handed Killer back to Jo. "I need you to take care of her for me for a few hours, okay? I'll be home soon. And try to make sure she and Fury don't see each other. They tend to fight a lot."

"Sort of like you and Molly?"

"Something like that."

* 32 *

THE BEST DAY OF MY LIFE

$\mathcal{M}$olly knew that there was one person in this town whom she could count on to help her no matter what, without judgment and without asking anything in return. And he would do it with a smile and a sense of humor.

Marshall would be at the store by now, baking muffins and scones, prepping for the day, singing some goofy song. She would ask him to help her get out of here for a few days, to lend her his car and hook her up with a hotel recommendation somewhere on East End, anywhere that wasn't here. Better yet, she would have him drive her out of town so that she wouldn't have to deal with crossing that weird misty force field that surrounded North Hampton all by herself. Maybe she should have been with Marshall all along.

She still couldn't believe what had happened.

Tris had ingratiated himself so smoothly, pretending to be banished to North Hampton just like her, giving her the sense that he was uniquely qualified to understand her. But what infuriated her even more than the emotional betrayal was the physical one. She had practically begged him to touch her. She had craved his kisses, the feel of his tongue and hands all over her body. Even now that she despised him, she could not help but feel turned on when she pictured herself with him. Physical attraction, she was learning, was a cruel, cruel thing.

She got it now—"Tris" and "Trent"—he thought he was so clever! Why not just call himself "Tryst"? That was probably the most appropriate name for him. She realized that in order to exact the true punishment he so richly deserved, she was going to have to ally herself with Mardi. United in fury, they were a terrifying force. And she knew she also had to ally herself with Mardi in order to solve the mystery of the disappearing ring and get to the bottom of the murders. The summer would be over soon, and if they didn't clear things up before then, the White Council would lay down the law and Daddy would freak. But for right now, she simply couldn't deal. All this anger and responsibility was giving her a migraine. Her skin was a mess. She needed a break.

Having applied her lip gloss and checked her hair in her compact mirror, she tapped on the glass door of the Cheesemonger. As she expected, Marshall lit up like a puppy the moment he saw her. He came running to open the door for her.

"Molly! What's up? Why are you here? You're not

supposed to be working today." He moved to hug her, but then stopped himself, obviously not sure where he stood, despite the kiss she had bestowed on him the other day.

She got straight to the point. "Marshall, I need your help. I can't really get into it, but things are incredibly rough at Ingrid's, and with my dad and our New York legal problems, and with other stuff here in town. I have to get out of here for a few days, or I'm going to explode."

"Gee, I'm sorry to hear that."

"Do you think you can get me out of here? To Shelter Island or Montauk or anywhere reasonably close by that isn't *here*? I've never been to either Shelter or Montauk. I hear they both have some cool new boutique hotels. Sunset Beach sounds like heaven right now."

"I'd love to go away with you, Molly," he said. "But I don't know if I can leave the shop. No one else can run it."

"What about your mom? Won't she cut you a break? Where *is* your mother anyway? Why is she leaving all the work to you? When is she coming back?"

"I'm not exactly sure where she is." He winced down at his shoes as though the subject was painful for him. "Somewhere in South America, I think. And she may never actually come back."

"If it makes you feel any better, my mother is totally MIA too. I don't even know her name. The only thing Daddy has ever said about her is that she was a . . . "

Molly almost said *giantess*, which was in fact what Daddy had let slip once when he was very drunk, but she caught herself in time and improvised: "A lot to handle."

He nodded.

"Maternal love is overrated. Case in point: we've both turned out just fine without it. Let's stop feeling sorry for ourselves and blow this Popsicle stand. I can't take another minute of it. If we hurry, we can be gone before you're supposed to open the shop. Then no one will be able to stop us."

He began to waver. "Yeah, who needs mothers anyway?" he whispered. She could see that he was unable to resist her charms. Who could?

"I guess we could check out Montauk for a few days." He gave a shy smile. "I've been wanting to eat at this new place for ages. It's called the Crow's Nest. Apparently, they do a beautiful mezze plate. And we can stay there. It's one of those trendy repurposed motels."

"Don't say 'trendy.' It sounds terrible. Like the exact opposite of what you want it to mean." Molly was relieved to find that, even in the throes of fury and exhaustion, she had not lost her critical faculties.

"Sorry," he said. "I get really goofy when I'm excited. And this idea is growing on me fast. You're so right that we should take a vacation. We deserve it! It'll make our customers miss us. They'll end up appreciating us more because we're not always at their beck and call.

Right? I hate being taken for granted. More than anything."

"That's the spirit! Let's go!"

"Okay. I guess I just need to pack and take care of a couple of things at home first. Do you want to wait for me here? There are plenty of breakfast treats! I made the blueberry scones you like." He laughed, half nervous and half triumphant. This was probably the best day of his life.

He was such a spaz. But Molly had to love him.

"So we're good?" she confirmed. "You'll be back soon?"

"Golden."

✳ 33 ✳

RING OF FIRE

$\mathcal{M}$ardi found Trent or Tris or Trystan, or whoever the Hell he was, climbing off the *Dragon*. He gave her a big open smile that implied he was ready to pick up where they had left off yesterday. What kind of idiot did he take her for?

"Hey, beautiful, I missed you last night. You should have stayed," he said with a slow, sexy grin.

She put her hands on her narrow hips and glared at him with the full force of her dark, dark eyes.

He returned her cruel stare with a confused look. How had she ever been drawn to those blue eyes? She saw them now for what they really were: watery, shifty, weak.

"Mardi, is there something wrong?"

"You are scum, and the only reason I'm stooping to talk to you right now is to tell you that I'm never going to speak to you again. Oh, and also that I'm quitting my job. In case that isn't obvious."

"What are you talking about?" He looked and

sounded genuinely baffled. But she knew now what a skilled player he was. To assume such divergent parts as to be able to seduce both Overbrook sisters at once, in alternating moments, you had to be more than a brilliant actor; you had to have a split personality.

"Give it up will you?" She seethed. "Dude, I think you're a psychopath. If I cared about you even one little bit, I'd consider having you committed. But I wouldn't lift a finger to help you now. I saw you with her yesterday. In the greenhouse at Fair Haven."

"With who? I wasn't at Fair Haven yesterday, Mardi. I was here, with you."

"Are you really going to make me spell it out?"

He looked at her expectantly.

"Fine, Trystan Gardiner. Here is how it went down. After we hung out on your boat yesterday afternoon, I got a text telling me to go to the greenhouse in Fair Haven. I assume it was from you, since you obviously enjoy messing with people's heads. I went because you've been threatening to hurt my sister if I don't do everything you say. But you know that, of course."

The color drained from his face.

Mercilessly, she continued. "And when I got to the greenhouse, what do you think I saw? I saw you sucking face with my twin sister, yeah . . . we're identical . . . whom apparently you've been leading on whenever you aren't busy trying to get in *my* pants."

"Mardi, wait. I think I might know what's going—"

"I know what's going on—you're sick!"

"Mardi," he thundered, taking a step toward her, his face red with frustration, "listen, will you? Whoever that guy was, it wasn't me."

"Oh, right. As if there are two of you—"

"I was here with you. I was here all night. I wish you'd stayed with me. I've never met your sister before. Listen to me."

"I saw you!" Hadn't she? Hadn't she gotten a good look at him as Molly pulled his pastel polo off over his head.

Pastel polo?

When did Trent ever wear polo shirts?

Not to mention Bermuda shorts.

But it was definitely Trent, wasn't it?

The doubt must have showed on her face, because Trent began to talk again. "Look, I think I know what's happening here. I think I know who's been sending you those messages and who was with your sister. And if I'm right, he's very dangerous. We have to make sure your sister isn't with him. Do you know where Molly is right now?"

"Nice try," she sneered, turning to go.

He tried to hold her back by the shoulder. As she turned around to punch him, he blocked her, grabbing her wrist.

"Get your hands off me!"

"Mardi, please listen." He let go of her wrist.

"To what? More lies?"

"Look down at your right hand," he said.

"Why?" she asked. Yet even as the question escaped her lips, she knew the answer. It was on her middle finger.

Her ring.

"I slipped that ring back on you yesterday. I needed to get it on your body without you knowing in order for you to assume its power again. That's the way the curse works. If you demand the ring, it assumes its destructive power. If you receive it, it becomes pacified. And that's why I haven't been able to be open with you until now. I had to wait until the ring was restored. And for that to happen, I had to find it."

"Where? What?"

"I stole it back for you, Mardi. It was taken from your sister in an unconscious moment, and I retrieved it. Whoever possesses that ring has massive power. All those accidents, those near deaths in town over the past week, those beaten women, were the ring bearer's experiments with his newfound domination. If I hadn't gotten it back to you, anything could have happened. Hold on to it, please. Don't let anyone take it from you until we figure out what to do."

Although she was beginning to believe him, Mardi was still on guard. "So if that wasn't you in the greenhouse with Molly, who is the guy who looks *exactly* like you except for the clean-cut clothes?"

"I think his name is Alberich. He's a shape-shifter

who's long been in disfavor with our kind. He's been after your ring for centuries, while your mother and her sisters shared it."

My mother and her sisters?

The maidens in the pool.

Rhinemaidens.

Thor had said their mother was a hottie, and more importantly, that the twins carried part of their parents' spirits and memories with them.

"Okay, so let me get this straight. You stole our ring back from a creep who passes himself off as you."

"Well, not exactly. When the wine cellar caved in, and I realized I hadn't seen the ring on your finger in a while, I went to talk to Jean-Baptiste. He had noticed that neither you or Molly had it in your last session with him, and he was very concerned. I couldn't tell you directly, and neither could he, because if you yourself had gone after the ring, knowing what it could do, its power could have turned on you. It's cursed, Mardi. You dominate it while it is on your person, but as soon as it leaves the warmth of your—or Molly's—flesh, it becomes incredibly, irrationally dangerous. Alberich thinks he can harness its power for himself, but he has no real control over it, not the way you guys do. He wants to use it to take revenge on the women of the world, to subjugate them and make them suffer, because he has felt humiliated for centuries by their rejection. He wants to enslave them. To see them burned by the state as witches. He wants to unleash the kind of wave of lawless paranoia that the world hasn't seen since the Salem witch trials."

"So you're saying he made himself look like you in order to convince Molly that he was Trystan Gardiner and seduce her to get ahold of our ring? So he could punish us for being powerful female witches?"

"Something like that. As I said, he's a shape-shifter. So he could take my form, but he could also take others. He could have looked like almost anyone in town when he got the ring off her body. The only feature he can't change is the color of his eyes, which, if you look closely, are a much lighter, colder blue than mine. That's how you could have told us apart if you'd gotten closer."

She stared at him, at his warm blue eyes that shone with affection.

"I'm telling you the truth," he said. "Please believe me."

She looked into his eyes, and somehow she knew he wasn't lying. Ingrid herself had said she couldn't believe Trystan would do something so awful.

"The eyes aren't the only difference," she finally said.

"Thanks. That means a lot." He took her hand. "The reason Alberich became Tris was to keep a constant eye on Molly once he had taken the ring. He's a maniac. He's experimenting right now in order to harness the ring's power for his master plan. In the meantime, he doesn't care who gets in the way."

She gasped.

"What?"

"Those kids who died in the subway accident in New York. The ones we're accused of killing or brainwashing or whatever. We've been trying to figure out why they were targeted. But now I see they *weren't* targeted! They were anonymous victims, collateral damage. Alberich stole our ring and was going after us, trying to get us accused and punished." Mardi was shaking. "They just happened to be in the wrong place at the wrong time."

"I'm sorry," said Trent.

"Bret! He's Alberich!"

"Who's Bret?"

"The host of the party. It was his penthouse. He must have drugged us, stolen our ring, and entertained himself by sacrificing two of his party crashers on the tracks of the 6 train, then he framed us for the murders. And now he's morphed into Trystan Gardiner . . . Wait, I can't believe I haven't asked you—how'd you find the ring?"

"He's a Nibelung from the shadow world. He likes to burrow. I knew he would bury it. And his arrogance would push him to bury it somewhere symbolic."

"But how did you know it was the greenhouse?"

"I didn't. I got really lucky. I was feeding Killian's flytrap, and I noticed the dirt under the box of worms was loose. I had a premonition, and I started to dig."

She looked at him admiringly. "I think someone

guided you to the ring. Someone powerful and benevolent. I think someone is watching over us."

"Listen, we have to find your sister before she tries to
get to Tris and give him Hell like you gave me. That
wouldn't end well. Alberich does not respond posi-
tively to criticism."

"I can try texting her, but she'll probably blow me
off."

"Tell her it's an emergency."

"I have a better idea."

* 34 *

LEAVING HERE

$\mathcal{M}$arshall should have been back by now. Molly had made herself two cappuccinos, eaten a morning glory muffin and a blueberry scone, bemoaned eating so much, and rearranged the cracker shelf in the store so that it moved from lightest to darkest packaging. If he didn't get there soon, she was going to start messing with the geography of his cheese case, switching the French chèvre with the Italian capra. She had never been so anxious to get moving in her life.

Her phone vibrated, and she pulled it from her tote, hoping it was him. No such luck. Just a message from Mardi. Great. She didn't even want to read it.

Technically, what had happened with Trystan wasn't Mardi's fault. It was Trystan who was the total socio-path, just like the rest of those Gardiner brothers. Rationally, Molly knew this, and deep down she knew that her sister was as hurt and humiliated as she was.

The only reason they'd had a fight was that they were both mortified, and neither one could handle seeing her mirror image reflected in the other. They liked to think they were so different. And yet they had been fooled by the same guy.

She didn't read Mardi's text, because she didn't feel like answering it just yet.

Still, Molly figured that once she'd had a bit of time to simmer down, she would return to town and ally herself with Mardi, and together they would take the sleazebag down. *Hard.* Even if he was a warlock like he claimed, he would be no match for the two of them in full fury mode. He'd better be taking his vitamins right now. In a few days, his sick joke was going to turn on him.

But right now, she wasn't ready to do anything except run away and forget. Marshall, she realized, was what she had wanted all along. He was kind and funny and creative, and he made her feel like she was all these things too. He believed there was sweetness in her. And the force of his belief made her feel as good as she ever had.

She knew now that Marshall was a great guy. But what was taking him so long? If he didn't drive up soon, customers were going to show up and ruin everything.

She fiddled with the window display. Maybe she should read her sister's text. It might be important. Okay, she would read it, but she certainly wouldn't let Mardi know her whereabouts or her plans. She had to retain at least some dignity in this disaster.

Molly flicked on her screen and gasped. Mardi had sent a photo of their ring, on the middle finger of her right hand.

Look familiar? It's back. Where r u? Need to talk.

She typed back: I'll tell u, but only if u promise to give it to me.

Even as she finished typing, she was surprised by her reaction. She'd never been covetous of the ring before. It had always been the one thing that escaped the realm of their competition, like a free radical hopping between them. But something had changed since she discovered they were kissing the same guy.

Seeing the ring on her screen had made her sick to her stomach. She wanted it back, and she didn't want Mardi to have it. Couldn't she have one thing that was hers alone? She and Mardi shared everything—the same lustrous dark hair, the same blue-black eyes, the same nose, the same dimple on the right cheek!

She was tired of sharing everything.

A thought occurred to her that made her suddenly furious. What if Mardi had actually been hiding the ring from her this whole time? She knew it was irrational, but stranger things were happening these days.

Molly got so mad at her hypothesis that she burst all the jars on the pickle shelf. When that didn't quite satisfy her rage, she glared at the bottles of homemade organic ketchup until, one by one, they smashed, dribbling a reddish brown glop down the glass of the counter. It looked like a crime scene.

There. She felt better.

Marshall finally pulled up at the curb in the old yellow pickup truck he used to gather local produce. Only now she wasn't quite ready to go with him.

Mardi had texted back: OK. You can have it. Just come back will you?

Molly smiled triumphantly. At shop. Meet me here.

"Ready to go?" Marshall called through his open window with a touch of nervous impatience.

"Actually, not quite."

"Do you need me to come in and help you carry anything?"

"No, I'm fine." The last thing she needed was for him to see the havoc she had caused with her little tantrum just now. He'd never be able to leave his controlling mom's precious shop in that state. They'd be stuck here cleaning for days. If they left now, it would be easy to blame on vandals when they got back. After all, there had been such a rash of seemingly random destruction in town. Her mess would fit right into the pattern. And someone else, as always, would clean it up.

She just had to stall him long enough for Mardi to arrive. She might have to resort to magic if her sister didn't show soon. There was no way she was leaving that ring behind.

"Molly, we really should get a move on. It's getting late."

"Hold your horses. I'm waiting to say good-bye to my sister, okay? She's on her way."

"What? Why?" he asked, sounding uncharacteristically annoyed.

Before Marshall could protest further, the Ferrari came screeching around the corner of Main Street. It stopped right in front of Molly. Mardi rolled down the window, and Molly was instantly mesmerized by the ring glowing on her hand.

"Mine," she said.

"Fine, Molly. But we need to be careful." Mardi slipped the ring off and handed it to Molly. "Please get in the car."

"Give me a minute to close up the shop," Molly hedged. She looked back at Marshall in the cab of his truck, but couldn't see him.

She ran into the quaint little wallpapered bathroom at the back of the shop, unhooked a thin gold chain around her neck, slipped the ring around it, fastened it carefully, and checked her reflection in the mirror over the washbasin. The ring was much shinier than she recalled. The diamond etchings in the band seemed more pronounced now, and the metal was radiant. It was as though she had never really looked at the ring before and was finally seeing it for the treasure it had always been.

Feeling stronger and steadier now that she had it back, she rushed outside and was startled to see her sister standing right at the door with a serious look on her face.

"I get it," Molly said, preempting the lecture Mardi

was sure to deliver. "We have a lot to talk about. But right now—" She froze midsentence. There was Tris himself, running up behind Mardi. And Mardi was turning to him as if he was a close friend.

"Mardi, have you completely lost your mind? What is going on? Do you remember what this guy did to us?"

"We can explain," Mardi said, her face hopeful and pleading.

"Uh-huh!" Molly said. "It's all falling into place now. You've been in on this all along, haven't you? That whole act back at Ingrid's about how shocked you were to see me kissing Trystan in the greenhouse was a total scam. The two of you have been playing a joke on me!"

"Molly, come on. Please don't be so paranoid! I would *never* do that to you. And I wouldn't be able to stand you kissing a boyfriend of mine even if it was the best joke in the world. You're not being logical."

But now that she understood the magnitude of the deceit all around her, Molly couldn't bear to listen to her sister pretending to reason with her. Not for another second. It was simply too offensive. She turned to Tris. "I don't know who or what you are, but get out of my way."

But Tris didn't move. Instead, he attempted yet another one of his tricks. "Molly, I'm not Tris, and I never have been. I've never met you till today. I go by Trent. Everyone in town knows me by that name. There's never been anyone named Tris Gardiner."

"What are you talking about?"

"Please let me try to explain," he said, actually sounding sincere.

"Come on, Molly," Mardi pleaded. She was truly an excellent actress. "Hear us out."

Did they take her for an utter moron? "No way. You guys are the people I least want to hear from right now."

With that, she ran to the truck, opened the door, and said, "Okay. I'm ready."

"Great," Marshall said with a broad smile, gunning it out onto the road.

"If my sister thinks I'll listen to anything they have to say, she has another thing coming. I'm never setting foot in North Hampton again."

They drove in silence for a while. Not until they were on the outskirts of town among the fields of potatoes and corn, where the old farmhouses were acres apart, did Molly begin to exhale. She fingered the ring she wore around her neck. "We never really learned the Cookie Monster lesson," she said, touching it gently.

"It's all right," he said. Then, still driving fast, he reached over with his right hand to carefully take the ring between his thumb and forefinger. "Pretty." His fingers were sort of grimy, she noticed.

"Thanks," she said, then pulled it away, uncomfortable at the thought of anyone else touching it right then. It was hers.

The ring was finally hers alone.

✳ 35 ✳

YOUR LYIN' EYES

$\mathcal{M}$ardi watched with a sinking feeling as Marshall's yellow pickup disappeared down the lane. Did Molly really believe Mardi was capable of playing such a horrid prank deliberately? It was an awful blow to realize how estranged they were. Sure, they bickered and scratched at each other, but in the end, they were sisters . . . twin sisters. They only had each other, really.

"I can see why she doesn't believe us," Mardi sighed. "You and me showing up together when she still thinks you're the one who totally screwed her over and made her look foolish. Looking foolish might be Molly's worst nightmare. And as far as she's concerned, that nightmare has come true. I know, because I felt the same way she does until only an hour ago. I just wish I could have convinced her to let me explain."

Trent put his arm around her. "It's not your fault. Give her a day or two to calm down, and then you'll be able to reach her. As long as she doesn't have the ring, she's safe. But for now, you and I need to figure out what to do with that toxic thing."

"What do you mean?" Panic rising, Mardi looked at her bare hand.

"You gave her the ring?"

"She's my sister—we share it! She asked for it back."

"And you gave it to her?"

"Yes! That's the way we operate. It's both of ours! It's our only bond. I had to give it to her, especially now. I thought it would make her trust me. Also I sort of felt like the ring wanted to go to her. I don't know, maybe I'm imagining it. It's hard to tell anything for sure right now, when we're all in such high gear. But I wanted it off my finger. The urge was stronger than I am."

"Nothing is stronger than you, Mardi," he said.

His words flooded her with a new sense of purpose. He was so beautiful, his skin golden in the morning sun, his muscles taut in anticipation of the challenge ahead. She wanted to pull him back into the Ferrari and have her way with him in the passenger seat, but this was no time to let herself be distracted.

"We have to think . . . Molly is in danger from Alberich as long as she's got the ring. And she has no idea that Tris is really Alberich. So if he finds her . . ."

Trent scratched his nose. "You saw the way she reacted to me just now, when she thought I was Tris. She's not going to let Tris anywhere near her, except maybe to try to blow his head off. And I'm sure Alberich knows that. He's going to try to get to her as someone else."

"Yeah, thankfully, I don't think she'd be all that delighted to let Bret into her personal space right now either."

"No one she trusts?"

"Well, there's Cheeseboy, but he doesn't cou—" Her heart leapt into her mouth. She had a sudden vision of Marshall's blue eyes twinkling. The image superimposed in her mind with that of Bret's baby blues lit up under the body of his giant bronze spider.

Her memory was kicking back in. The haze of forgetfulness was clearing. She knew with absolute certainty that Marshall's eyes were Bret's eyes. They both had the same long tapering fingers, so appealing at first and ultimately so menacing. "Trent, that guy who just drove her away in his pickup—that's him! Bret! I mean Alberich!"

"Wait—what—who?"

"The guy—in the pickup truck—he owns the cheese store?"

"What guy?"

"Marshall Brighton—he grew up here with his mom. He runs the store for her while she globe-trots or something. He said it's been here for ages."

"His mom?" Trent frowned and his eyes were cloudy and confused. "No. That's wrong. That place popped up a few weeks before you two arrived."

"He seemed like such a great guy. He was always trying to show Molly and me how to forget our differences and bond."

"Sound familiar?"

"What are you saying?"

"Think about the nature of the ring itself. For as long as you can remember, it's masqueraded as a sisterly bond between you. For years, it's been hiding its destructive power. Evil can lurk for a long time in the sweetest of guises."

"Well, we have to get it back! And we have to get my sister back!" They ran back to the car and slammed the doors. Mardi hit the gas and floored the pedal, but even as they drove quickly through town, she knew they could be anywhere by now. Even the Ferrari wasn't fast enough to cover every possible hideaway on the East End before it would be too late.

"I can't believe I let her leave with him!" she cried.

"It's not you. It's the ring. It's Alberich. It's fate. But we can turn it around. There has to be a way."

"Jean-Baptiste! He can help! Maybe he'll have some guidance or know some way to visualize their whereabouts."

"Good idea."

They drove to Rose Cottage, where Mrs. Green told them that Mr. Mésomier had gone out earlier.

"Did he say when he would be back?"

"No, I'm sorry, he didn't. Would you like to come in and wait? I have delicious coffee and fresh-squeezed orange juice and a basket of scones from that lovely Cheesemonger shop. I'd be so delighted to entertain you until Mr. Mésomier returns. I'm so very fond of you young people."

As fast as they could, Mardi and Trent begged off and jumped back into the car.

"Where to now?" she asked, agitated.

"If only we could find a way of scanning the landscape for that yellow truck. We need a bird's-eye view . . . I've got it! There's an airport in East Hampton! We can charter a plane! How fast can this old girl get us to East Hampton?"

"The Ferrari isn't old—she's experienced! There's a big difference." She couldn't believe she was arguing this point right now. Like anything mattered except finding her sister. But somehow it seemed important to keep perspective.

Perspective. A bird's-eye view. When in her life had she ever really had perspective?

Then it hit her. The answer.

"We're not going to East Hampton. We don't need a plane." Without another word, she turned on her ignition, shifted into gear, and drove like lightning, tearing through the sleepy streets of North Hampton, heading to the only recourse she knew.

* 36 *

MONTAUK

*M*olly sat across from Marshall at the breezy outdoor restaurant of the Crow's Nest, atop a gentle hill sloping down to the shore of Lake Montauk, about a mile outside the groovy surfer town. She was trying to relax, but she was still angry at Trystan as well as the whole confusing mess in New York, angry at Daddy for sending her to East End in the first place. Worst idea ever. But her fiercest fury was reserved for her sister. Mardi was dead to her. And yet Molly couldn't get Mardi out of her mind.

"This will help," said Marshall as their waiter uncorked and poured a French Provençal rosé.

"Yeah," she said, trying to muster some enthusiasm. "Daddy always says there's nothing like a little wine at lunch to make you feel like you're on vacation. Which basically means that he's been on vacation every day of his life."

The waiter placed a dish of grilled octopus on a bed of spiced yogurt in between them along with two small share plates. Delicately, Marshall cut the octopus in half. She admired the precise motions of his long graceful hands, which were almost clean now. He'd obviously scrubbed them since they arrived at the hotel, although there was still a trace of dirt beneath his fingernails. She noticed for the first time that his spidery fingers were not unlike Tris's, a weird coincidence that made her stomach twist. She had to get ahold of herself.

"Look, whatever happened between you guys, it's over. And whoever he is, he never deserved you. We're out of North Hampton now. If you don't want to go back, we never have to."

"What do you mean, never go back? What about your mom's shop?"

He shrugged.

Was he proposing or something? All the other tables around them were laughing and lighthearted. She wasn't up for some big declaration of undying love right now. She was here to forget, not to fend off crazy propositions.

"Or if you'd like, we could talk about the weather, or the flight path of those ducks down there on the lake, or something really pleasant and meaningless."

Sarcasm? From sweet Cheeseboy? The last thing she felt like dealing with was his adolescent petulance right now. She decided to ignore it. "Anyway, cheers, and thanks for bringing me here." She lifted her rosé glass to his.

He looked down at his plate and batted around a

piece of octopus. He seemed to be groping for the right words to say. Finally, he said, his blue eyes blazing, "Everything I've done is for you."

His intensity was making her uncomfortable. She put down the fork she had been about to raise to her mouth and began to fidget with the neckline of her dress. There was something odd here that she couldn't place, something deeply amiss. Maybe it hadn't been such a good idea to bolt from reality after all. Maybe she should have stayed in North Hampton and faced the music. Maybe she was missing her last chance to solve the enigma of what happened in New York. What if her leaving with the ring meant that Jean-Baptiste could no longer help the others? He had been quite clear when she had gone to consult him: the ring was key.

As she reached to touch it where it dangled in her cleavage, Marshall grabbed her hand and caressed it with surprising skill. A totally unexpected jolt of excitement passed through her body. She felt herself give him an electric smile almost against her will.

"Is everything to your liking?" the waiter asked, interrupting.

Molly nodded, even if she couldn't keep her eyes off Marshall's blue ones as the waiter refilled their glasses and cleared their appetizer plates. "Your main courses will be out in just a minute."

She barely heard the waiter. "What were you saying before? About how everything was for me?"

"Everything I did this summer was for you," he whispered.

She knew he was cute, but had she ever noticed just how cute?

He strengthened his hold on her. "What do you say we skip dessert—"

Just then, the waiter chimed in. "I would wait to make that decision until the time comes if I were you. We have a pretty tempting dessert menu. I would personally recommend the peach and basil crumble and the wild blueberry crème brûlée, but if you are chocolate lovers, the mousse is incredible."

Molly had no idea what this guy was talking about. And, judging from Marshall's rapt expression, he wasn't paying any attention to the dessert options either.

She took a long cool drink. "I'm not hungry all of a sudden. Do you think we should just skip lunch entirely?" She was churning with desire. How had this happened so fast? One minute she was annoyed with him, and the next, she wanted nothing more than to hook up. How had it never happened before during all those hours working side by side at the shop? Had her infatuation with Tris blinded her to this awesome guy who was right under her nose?

"What are you suggesting?" he asked, a sexy resonance to his sweetness that she had never noticed before.

"It's like what you said that time I was looking for my ring in the shop. Sometimes you're so used to seeing something—or someone—all the time that it's hard to actually notice what's awesome about him."

At her mention of the ring, she reached for it instinctively, and again he seized the moment to take her hand.

"I never thought I'd hear you say anything like that." He was practically trembling. "I've—I've been infatuated with you, Molly. And not just because you are the most bewitchingly beautiful girl I've ever seen. Your potential is enormous. Together, we could be fantastic."

Although she wasn't sure what he meant, she was swept away by the grandeur of his language and the racing of her own pulse. Nothing mattered in this magical moment except for the here and now, in Montauk, with him. Not the looming trial in New York. Not the White Council. Not Daddy freaking out. Not her treacherous sister. And certainly not Trystan Gardiner.

Somehow they managed to finish their lunch and stave off the waiter's enthusiasm for dessert and coffee. Marshall signed the bill to his room number, and they set out arm in arm, hip to hip.

The minute they were outside the restaurant, he pulled her in for a deep kiss.

"What do you say we share a room tonight?" she sighed, whispering in his ear.

"I want that more than anything, believe me. I've waited so long."

37

LEARNING TO FLY

$\mathcal{M}$ardi and Trent burst into Ingrid's house to find Ingrid, Freya, and Jean-Baptiste in a cluster around the coffee table. For once, there was no food or drink in sight. All three looked tired and defeated. The kids' toys lay scattered on the floor, but the kids themselves were nowhere to be seen. Midnight meowed aimlessly through a picture window onto the empty front yard, a living barometer of the family stress.

Briefly, Mardi wondered where Killer was and how Killer and Midnight were getting along. But this was no time to ask about cats.

Barely registering the presence of Trent, Ingrid looked up at Mardi. She didn't even say hello. "Your father called about an hour ago. It seems there's fresh evidence against you. Apparently there are several witnesses willing to testify to the fact that you and Molly threatened that young couple who died. You told them you were going to mess with their minds. You actually came out and bragged to them that you were witches!"

"No, we didn't! Even if we did, we weren't ourselves. Listen, we know what happened now. But we need your help to make it right."

Jean-Baptiste let out a tired sigh. "I'm afraid it's too late, Mardi. We did our best. But evil has been unleashed and you are blamed. Now your fate—our fate—is at the mercy of the mortal realm."

"Yeah," said Freya bitterly. "And we know how well that turned out for us last time." She drew a deadly finger across her throat.

"Well, I don't know about you guys," Mardi persisted, "but I'm not giving up."

"And I'm right behind her," said Trent.

"Trystan!" Ingrid said. "What a surprise. Mardi, what's going on?"

"Look, there's no time to go into details right now. You were right about Trystan—I mean Trent. But um, we need your brooms. Immediately."

Ingrid went crimson. "If you think, young lady, that after all the trouble you've caused, I'm going to open up my broom closet just because you've asked—"

"Ingrid, please!" Jean-Baptiste interjected as Freya took Ingrid's arm.

Ingrid shook Freya off. "You and your sister have put our whole community at risk! Everything we've worked for! We are refugees here! We should be sticking together, taking care of each other. And you've broken that covenant!"

"I know." Mardi wasn't backing down, but she was

crying tears of regret—and tears of determination. "And I'm going to do something about it. If you really care, Ingrid, then listen."

"You should hear her out," said Jean-Baptiste.

"Come on, Ingrid," Freya pleaded. "Give them a chance."

Ingrid raised an eyebrow. "Fine. I'm listening."

Mardi stumbled over herself to get her story out, with Trent interjecting here and there to clarify where he could.

They explained that the ring that Molly and Mardi had been wearing on their right hands was a legendary ring. A cursed object of intense desire that possessed such power that, in the wrong hands, it could unleash terrible violence and cause great suffering.

Everyone wanted it.

And no one should have it.

They told them about Alberich transforming himself. In his New York incarnation as Bret Farley, he had murdered Parker Fales and Samantha Hill to test the power of the ring he had borrowed from the unsuspecting twins and to frame them so that they would literally be sent to Hell. He had used his newfound strength to cloud their memories, but had not been able to resist the temptation of torturing them by leaving them with certain vivid mental scraps from his triumphant night. That was why they had retained such striking images and impressions of the bronze spider, the black pool, the blaring Wagner.

He wanted to lord his power over the beautiful twins who were the talk of all New York. To take his revenge on the daughters of the Rhinemaidens who had taunted him centuries ago, and on all their kind, mortal and immortal.

Here in North Hampton, Alberich had taken on two alternating shapes. He was Tris Gardiner, and he was Marshall Brighton. The seducer and the sweetheart. He had managed to steal the ring from Molly yet again, which explained the series of accidents and near accidents plaguing the town. Alberich was playing puppeteer. And women were his primary victims. He hated women. Ever since his rejection by the Rhinemaidens, he had dreamed of growing powerful enough to subjugate and humiliate them for all time. That was why, now that he had the ring again, so many women were being threatened and hurt.

The ring had the power to unleash vast evil. For years Molly and Mardi had unconsciously kept this evil at bay. But in Alberich's hands, its gold was beginning to burn with a bright malice. While he was experimenting with it and learning to control it, Alberich had kept the ring buried in the greenhouse at Fair Haven, where Trent, who knew the ancient legend, had found it.

That morning, Trent had given Mardi the ring, but Mardi, desperate to earn her sister's trust, had passed the ring back to Molly. And Molly had immediately run off with it. By now, she could be anywhere on the East

End. She was with Marshall, but she had no idea he was really Alberich. If Marshall got ahold of the ring again, there was no telling what he would do to Molly this time. They had to save Molly. And they had to get the ring away from Alberich before he not only ruined the twins' lives but found all sorts of hideous outlets for his raging misogyny. If he realized his dream, powerful women were going to burn as witches again.

"And the only way to find them fast enough," said Mardi breathlessly, "is on your and Freya's brooms. We know you have them, Ingrid. Hiding in the attic. Jo showed them to us the other day."

Ingrid couldn't suppress a slight smile.

"Freya, Ingrid," Jean-Baptiste began with gentle authority, "I think you should give these two a chance. They've shown great ingenuity and a true desire to plumb their memories for the truth. If we don't empower them now, we give in to the forces that are out to destroy our way of life."

Freya didn't hesitate. "You're welcome to my broom!"

Mardi flew to embrace her and was consumed for a moment in Freya's sweet musky scent. "Thank you, Freya."

"All right." Ingrid was starting to give. "But we have to cast a very powerful concealment spell. The last thing we need is for the White Council to get wind of UFO sightings on the East End that look suspiciously like witches on broomsticks. We won't be able to give you full visibility, you know. It's going to be tricky." She was suddenly struck by a fresh doubt. "You *have* flown before?"

Neither Mardi nor Trent answered.

"Mardi?" Ingrid wasn't going to let this slide.

Mardi looked pleadingly at Jean-Baptiste.

He nodded with encouragement.

"Only a few times in the Caribbean with Dad," she admitted. "He taught Molly and me during our spring breaks, in empty skies. Kind of like driving in a parking lot, I guess. He told us that if he ever caught us flying in a populated area, we'd be grounded until the end of time . . . But I do know how to steer and stuff. And I'm super coordinated." Mardi realized she wasn't painting the ultimate picture of responsibility, all raccoon-eyed in yesterday's rumpled clothes. But she'd come too far to give up now.

"What about you, Trystan?" Ingrid asked.

Trent squirmed. "Ingrid, please call me Trent."

"Maybe I should call you by your real name, Tyr, the god of war? I can't help but think you are a little bit to blame for what has happened to these girls this summer."

He nodded. "But this time I'm on your side, Ingrid. It's why I came back to North Hampton. To help stop the spread of violence that Alberich and his ring have started. I've been practicing my tolerance for adversity and uncertainty. This is my calling. At the same time"—here he looked straight at Mardi—"I'm falling in love for the first time."

Mardi could only blush deeply to the roots of her dark hair.

"All right, I'll get the brooms," Ingrid said. "On one condition. Freya flies with Mardi. There's no way I'm calling Troy to tell him one daughter has been kidnapped and the other has wiped out against a telephone pole. Let's go, Freya."

Freya and Ingrid ran upstairs, with Midnight at their heels, to get their brooms from the hidden closet behind Freya's amazing array of clothes and shoes.

Jean-Baptiste closed his eyes and began to murmur a series of ancient protective spells. Mardi reached over to take Trent's hands.

"Hey, Tyr," she whispered.

"Hey, Magdi."

God of war. Goddess of rage. They belonged together.

When Jean-Baptiste opened an enquiring eye on them, they both giggled. "It always stuns me," he said, straightening the silver gray pocket square in his plaid jacket, "how quickly you young people can lose your gravitas even in the most dire situations."

"Sorry!" they said sheepishly.

"Oh, my goodness, don't be sorry. It's a gift you have, a wonderful gift. If we all felt the weight of the world in every single moment, we would be in a very sorry state. Please, keep laughing."

Ingrid and Freya, still shadowed by Midnight, appeared at the bottom of the stairs, broomsticks in hand. Mardi was struck by how ordinary looking the broomsticks were. Simple wood and straw. And yet they were the means by which she was about to save her sister, and hopefully save her family, such as it was, while at the same time squelching a force of evil that threatened the women of both the human and the witching worlds. These brooms looked like such a low-tech solution to a massive problem that for a moment she doubted everything.

Soon she was outside, high in the afternoon sky, the land and water rolling out below in a glorious patch-work. For a few moments, she could still make out Ingrid's watchful figure, the little black cat perched on her shoulder, taking it all in.

The Earth was beautiful from above. She was sitting behind Freya. Beside her, Trent looped and circled. She had never felt closer to people she loved. Except one of them was missing and in grave danger. *Molly Moll, where are you?*

As the magical rescue team broke through the misty barrier enshrouding North Haven, a protective layer created centuries ago by Joanna Beauchamp and main-tained now by her dutiful daughters, the East End opened up before them, a narrow strip of bright green-ery and golden sand jutting out into the bright sea.

Mardi felt something move in the suede bag she wore over her shoulder. She reached to adjust it and touched the top of a soft, familiar head poking playfully out from under the flap. But it wasn't her cat. She looked down to meet Fury's sorrowful gaze. Molly's familiar wanted his mistress back. "I know how you feel. We'll get her back, buddy—don't worry. I'm glad you came along for the ride."

* 38 *

I SHALL BE RELEASED

𝑀olly's room at the Crow's Nest was the ultimate in beach chic, with white clapboard walls, blond floors, driftwood mirrors, a blue-and-white batik bedspread, and soft sheer curtains billowing with a late-afternoon breeze. It was like making out inside the pages of the Calypso Home catalog.

Marshall was an amazing kisser, and his wiry arms were proving strong and almost comforting. She felt lulled by his touch and was drifting softly into a beautiful oblivion.

So when she finally realized that Marshall was whispering the word *mine*, over and over again between kisses, she had no idea how long this had been going on and no grasp at all on what it might mean, although she felt a wave of nausea from hearing the word.

"What's mine?" she asked, trying to sound flirtatious.

"Why, Molly," he said, his tone suddenly cold and imperious as he looked down at her, and she realized she was almost naked and felt vulnerable beneath his steady gaze. "You're mine."

"Oh . . . right," she said, wondering why she suddenly felt scared instead of excited.

"But believe it or not, it's not you or your delectable body I really want, although I will take them as my due, but the Rhinegold you wear around your neck. Because the Rhinegold will let me keep you forever. All of you."

Molly pushed him off of her. "Rhinegold." She groped after the memory of that word, mustering all her remaining strength to pierce the fog clouding her mind, and she forced herself to look at him, really look at him.

"Who are you?"

He smiled and for a moment she thought she saw Tris Gardiner's handsome face. Then it changed again, and he was someone else entirely.

"No!" she screamed through a sharp pain in her throat. "Bret! You're Bret!"

Marshall was no longer Marshall. He had grown smaller, and his arm muscles had thickened. His face had morphed into that of the boy from the black pool in Bret's penthouse. Only the ice-blue eyes were unchanged. From his right hand he dangled the rose gold ring from her broken chain.

"I may not be a witch like you, but my sleight of hand is excellent." He cackled. "I ripped it from your neck without you even noticing."

She clawed at the empty space around her throat.

"Cheeseboy is in charge now. As I said, Molly, you're mine now. Along with this ring. And everything it can bring to me."

She tried to protest but discovered she couldn't, and Marshall was the reason why. For the first time in her life, she was on the wrong side of a serious hex. It was a profound lesson in how the other half lived.

But her fighting instincts had not abandoned her. She would bide her time like a reptile in the shade and wait for her moment to strike. She lay back on the bed, pretending to give up, and raised her arms above her head in a seductive pose.

"That's my girl. You looked just like this that night," he said. "Want to see?"

She nodded, thinking it was what he wanted to hear. He pulled her up to the head of the bed and propped her up against a mass of large decorative pillows. She found that her limbs had stiffened and her hands no longer moved at all. Her entire body, except for her eyes and ears, was in the process of shutting down.

"Now you know how it feels to be powerless." He laughed. "Get used to it, Goddess No More."

Instantly, the room darkened as the television screen on the dresser lit up to show a close-up image of Molly's own face. She appeared dazed, drugged even, her pupils dilated and her stare fixed. She looked almost exactly like she felt right now: terrified, yet somehow determined to pierce the veil of her enchantment. Next on the screen, there was an image of Mardi, similarly out of it, but biting her lip in an effort to remain connected to her inner strength. Seeing her sister so vulnerable yet so resolute, Molly wanted to reach out to her through time and space and tell her how sorry she was and how much she loved her.

But it was too late.

Mardi and Trent, she knew with sudden certainty, had been telling the truth that afternoon. She had been too angry to hear it. The curse of discord had been too strong.

Was there time left to fight it?

The screen went blurry, and when it focused again, it showed a shot of the two sisters side by side. They were sitting on a bench in the neon light of a subway platform, wearing their outfits from the night of Bret's party. Molly instantly recognized the red dress and the nude snakeskin pumps she'd bought that same afternoon. Mardi was wearing a skintight silver jumpsuit that she had found at a consignment shop called A Star Is Worn, where stars sold their old clothing and the proceeds were donated to charity. The jumpsuit had belonged to Cher, God knew how many years ago. Molly had made cruel fun of it that night, but seeing it pop out now in this grainy screen image, in all its shiny boldness, she was flooded with a new appreciation for

Mardi's quirks. What if she never saw all those wacky vintage clothes again?

The focus left the twins and started to dart and swerve around the station, finally settling on another pair of figures, whom Molly instantly recognized as Parker and Samantha.

Samantha was clutching her big floral bag. Parker was swaying from foot to foot in his Brooklyn-inspired faux work boots. They were biding their time, waiting for a late-night 6 train, craning their necks to look down the dark tunnel in search of the first glimmer of oncoming headlights. Molly hadn't taken many subways in her life, but from her few experiences, she recognized their gestures of vague impatience.

The camera image started to weave back and forth between the human couple on the edge of the tracks and the pair of dazed witches on the bench.

"You'll have to excuse the handheld look." Bret laughed. "I shot this on my phone."

Slowly, a deep rumble became audible beneath the images. Molly's heart started going wild. Then Bret's voice sounded, crackling through time. "Girls, this is your cue. Get to it!"

What was he talking about? What was he commanding them to do? Molly had a suspicion, but it was too awful to contemplate.

The phone camera zoomed shakily onto Molly and Mardi, who were slowly standing and starting to walk, zombie-like—in the direction of the doomed couple.

Molly's eyes widened in horror as she watched her former self, shot from the back. She was advancing in her high heels toward the unsuspecting mortal pair. Beside her, Mardi strutted, but not with her natural sultry gait. It was a stylized walk, like that of a robotic chorus girl.

Were they really about to push Parker and Samantha to their deaths? What had the poor kids done to deserve such a brutal end to their short lives? Crashed the wrong party? Been in the wrong place at the wrong time? How could she and her sister have forgotten everything about this night?

The answer to these questions flashed suddenly before Molly in the form of the ring, which Bret now held up right in front of the phone camera. It was in such close-up that the diamond pattern looked enormous. For the first time, this pattern struck Molly for what it really was: the motif on the back of a rattlesnake. She couldn't believe that she and her sister had been sharing it for so long. What did that mean, then—that they were evil in nature? Molly was ashamed of herself, ashamed of the two of them.

"The power is mine now!" the on-screen Bret howled with delight.

Even if they had been hypnotized, she and Mardi *were* guilty. And she was about to witness their crime.

As the sound of the oncoming subway train grew louder, Molly wished she could close her eyes to spare herself the sight of what she was about to do. However, not only was she now fully paralyzed on the bed, but her eyes were stuck wide open. With no control or dignity left, she was forced to be a spectator to her own horrific actions.

On-screen, Molly and Mardi approached the unsuspecting couple while Bret whispered triumphantly into his phone. "That's it, girls. A little bit closer, and then you can shove. Make sure you time it right. I think we have about thirty seconds to go." Then he started counting down. "Thirty, twenty-nine, twenty-eight . . ."

When he reached twenty-seven, an incredible thing happened. Molly and Mardi stopped in their tracks. Trembling with an otherworldly resolve, they turned toward Bret, grasped each other's hands, and cried out in unison, "No!"

"No? You cannot defy me! Obey the ring!" Bret's triumphant tone devolved into one of desperate fury.

But the twins were somehow standing firm.

Their eyes blazed as they held hands.

They were the twin goddesses of rage and strength. Thor's daughters, Magdi and Mooi, daughters of thunder, children of lightning, and together they embodied the spirit of their father's powerful hammer.

A hammer that was falling on the pathetic creature.

The image on the screen began to shake. Bret was getting angry and desperate. As the train lights came into view on the tracks, he suddenly screeched. "You! You, over there! Do it!" And seemingly out of nowhere, an older man with a briefcase appeared, sailing across the platform, barely touching the ground with his wing-tip shoes. He must have been a banker or a lawyer waiting for a late-night train home from some lonely weekend work at the office, but he had been of no interest to Bret and so had not appeared in his video until now.

It was only in the last seconds, since Mardi and Molly had somehow found it within themselves to resist, that this unwitting bystander was pulled in to commit murder so that the twins could be framed. With supernatural speed, he rushed at the doomed couple. Before they even had time to yell, they were shoved onto the tracks. The man turned to leave the station, oblivious to what he had just done.

Then the most extraordinary thing happened.

Molly's memory kicked back in full force. With every fiber of her being, she felt what happened next as it unfolded before her on the television screen.

Still holding hands, she and Mardi had flown into the air and onto the tracks after Parker and Sam.

Witches to the rescue!

Molly saw Mardi grab an astonished and uncomprehending Parker. She herself held Sam in her arms. The girl's face was frozen in a silent scream. And just before anyone hit the rails, the four of them began to soar upward out of harm's way.

Only they were a fraction of a second too late.

Before they were high enough to clear it, the train, its horn blaring wildly, barreled into them.

The last thing Molly saw was the golden ring sailing down after them, flashing into the void. Bret had hurled it at them.

The four of them were killed instantly.

As the screen went dark, Molly's memory went blank again along with it.

"Such useless valiance, such senseless courage," Bret lectured, caressing her motionless thigh. "You and your sister made a pathetic, ridiculous attempt to save those expendable mortals. You had the brazen stupidity to try to combat the power of my ring, but you were obviously no match for it. You will soon learn to obey."

No match for it? But how had they gotten from the horrifying moment under the 6 train to the following day, when she and Mardi had awoken a few minutes past noon, both of them in their beds, feeling a little hungover but not especially worse for wear?

"As you can imagine," Bret droned on, "you goddesses have a connection or two in the Underworld. That's how it always is with you people. You take care of your own. The rest of us, of course, aren't so blessed. Someone called in a favor for you, and you two beauties were returned to the present in the blink of an eye. You never even knew what hit you. Those mortals, not so much. They're not summering on the East End right now, are they? More like being devoured by worms."

Molly's first thought was that Daddy must have gone into overdrive to fix everything, and fast, that very night, to rescue his girls from the jaws of Hell. Then she realized it couldn't have been him, because he didn't know what had happened. If he had had this kind of proof, he would have taken it to the White Council long ago.

So, if not Daddy, then who?

And there was another unanswered question. Why, Molly burned to know, had Bret cast off the ring he was so obsessed with, so that it reappeared the next day on Mardi's right middle finger, as though nothing had happened?

With frightening insight, Bret answered her silent query. "The reason I threw the ring back to you bitches is this: I didn't want you—or anyone else—to link the ring to what had just happened. Now that I had learned how to use it, I wanted to bide my time until I was ready to harness its power to establish a pure world order, with women in their place. I knew I could get it back from you again quite easily when the time was right. Thanks to your vanity, you've been an easy target all along. Like all women, you live to manipulate and are blinded by your childish pride. You've proven quite susceptible to my charms, Molly Overbrook. You've fallen for me behind three different masks now. I've gotta hand it to myself, and you have to admit, you find me irresistible."

She realized now just when he had stolen the ring from her. He hadn't taken it when they'd hooked up at the Fair Haven library, when she assumed it had fallen off in the heat of passion. Instead, he'd taken it at the Cheesemonger, after she had fainted. He had probably caused her to her faint so that he could come to her rescue, so that he could charm her and rob her blind in one fell swoop. Even though she despised him, she couldn't help but recall how tenderly she had felt toward him in that moment. She glared at him now from among the pillows. If she could have moved, she would have scratched his eyes out.

"So, Molly, what you've just seen in my little homespun video was my test run, so to speak." He dangled the ring in her face. "Now we are on to bigger and better things. Too bad you won't be joining me in my glory. You would have made a stunning, if spoiled, queen. But the paralysis you are feeling right now is only going to get worse. By nightfall, your heart will stop. It's a potent spider venom. I distilled it myself and sprinkled it into your rosé. I've always been able to count on your appreciation of the finer things, haven't I? And, besides, I have a great fondness for spiders, in case you haven't noticed. In fact, I adore them. *Maman*, my glorious bronze tarantula, whom I believe your sister admired greatly in my penthouse, is my favorite object on Earth."

Although her nerves were filled with poison, Molly had not entirely lost hope of escape and victory. She might be stuck here on this bed right now, but her twin wasn't.

Although it was irrational for her to expect Mardi to burst into her hotel room at the Crow's Nest Hotel in the wilds of Montauk, when it happened, Molly was not at all surprised.

What took you so long?

✳ 39 ✳

SISTERS ARE DOING IT FOR THEMSELVES

𝓜ardi was standing in the open doorway, her mouth agape.

She, Trent, and Freya had found the yellow pickup truck parked outside the Crow's Nest and had asked about the young couple, casting a spell on the receptionist to learn where Molly and Marshall were staying. Marshall's room had been empty, so when they found Molly's door, Mardi kicked it down even though it wasn't locked.

The three of them found Molly lying on the bed while that vile boy lay next to her. His features morphed back into Trent's handsome ones, and she recoiled.

"Molly!" Mardi yelled. "You beast, get off her!"

What was wrong with Molly? She was just staring at them speechless. No matter—she, Trent, and Freya tackled Alberich and wrestled him to the ground. She grabbed the ring from his fingers.

Fury jumped out of Freya's bag and started to bark angrily and nip at Alberich's ankles.

Alberich was no match for the four of them. Without the ring in hand, his shrieking threats were empty.

Freya and Trent tied him up with the curtain sashes.

"Give it your best shot," he sneered. "You're just as weak as your sister."

"Freya, may I?" Mardi asked.

"Do it," Freya urged.

Mardi punched him unconscious with her bare fists, and then, for good measure, hit him with a catatonic spell. Then she turned to her sister, whom Trent had covered with a blanket.

Her stomach twisted in jealousy a little at that, but she tried to push it aside. "Molly, what's wrong?"

Her sister was utterly still and stone-faced. Fury was nuzzling her neck to no avail.

"There's something wrong with her!" Mardi yelled, taking her sister's hand in hers and noting her dwindling pulse. "I think she's paralyzed!"

"Poisoned, more like it," said Freya, who was an expert. She found a sewing kit in the hotel bathroom, took out a needle, pricked Molly's left index finger, squeezed out three drops of blood onto her own thumb, licked them thoughtfully, and pronounced, "It's a neurotoxic spider venom. He must have transformed it so that it could be given orally. I know the antidote by heart. But I don't have the herbs here that I need to prepare it. We're going to have to get her home, and I'm going to have to rush to the greenhouse for my ingredients. We have to act fast. Mardi, gather her stuff."

"What about Alberich?" Mardi asked, looking at him bound and unconscious on the floor. "Even if we kill him, there's no guarantee he won't claw his way back somehow."

"You all go ahead and take care of Molly," said Trent. "I'll stay here. I've got him covered."

"But what are you going to do with him? I don't understand. How are we going to contain him?" Mardi asked, throwing Molly's clothes haphazardly into her Hermès tote, not even bothering to fold them. She knew Molly would be screaming at her now about being such a slob— if she could. She'd never thought she would want Molly to be able to scream. But she did. More than anything.

"I was thinking about calling the North Hampton police to take him back to town and arrest him," said Trent. "But I've changed my mind. Matt's strong, but I don't imagine he's any match for Alberich's evil charms. And I'm afraid that Matt doesn't know the way to Limbo, which is where he belongs. So I've called upon the Valkyries. They know the way. And they owe me many a favor. The Valkyries and I, we go way back. They'll be here soon, and we'll be rid of Alberich for the foreseeable future. Sound like a plan?"

"Valkyries, huh?" Mardi said, raising an eyebrow. "Those sorority girls?"

"Our brother Freddie knew a few of them quite well," Freya said, her lips curling into a smile.

But as they were lifting Molly to go, she seemed to be trying to tell them something. Her eyes were darting frantically around the room.

"What is it? What do you want to tell us?" Mardi asked, a little crazed. "We don't have time! If we don't get you back to Fair Haven, you're going to die!"

She wished she could understand what Molly was trying to tell them, but she had no idea. What did Molly want? Her tote? She had it packed.

"It's under control, I've packed all your stuff," Mardi said.

Molly emitted a low moan.

"Poor thing," said Freya. "She must be in pain. Don't worry. We'll have you back to yourself in a couple of hours. Stop trying to talk now. You'll only strain yourself."

They picked her up and walked out the door.

But at the very last second, Fury jumped onto the dresser, knocking what looked like a phone to the floor. Fury batted it with her paws so that it skidded across the wooden floor planks straight to Mardi's feet.

She looked down. Of course. This is what Molly had been trying to tell her. "Alberich's phone! Of course! It probably holds all kinds of clues." Mardi leaned down to grab the phone and give the dog a stroke. "Fury, you're a genius." She winked up at her immobile sister. "Who knew you're as smart as my cat?"

* 40 *

BLURRED LINES

$\mathcal{I}$t might have been the calming ocean breezes or the general air of forgetfulness that infused North Hampton. Some force, either natural or supernatural, was causing Killer and Fury to forget their differences as August drew to a close. In fact, along with Jo's cat, Midnight, they formed a rather merry band around Ingrid and Matt's house, frolicking on the beach, chasing squirrels, and generally making the resident kids, big and small, feel that all was going to be right with the world.

Mardi was relieved to see that Molly recovered quickly from the spider venom, although she secretly thought that it would have been nice to keep her sister quiet for a day or two longer.

Mardi had helped Freya gather the herbs she needed for the antidote: feverfew, catnip, and angelica root. Then they had gone into the woods, scavenging for very specific toadstools and for the skeletons of snakes and the skulls of small birds. Observing Freya at her craft, Mardi was mesmerized. Maybe she could learn to do the same thing one day.

But she was with Trent now. He had asked her to meet him on the *Dragon*.

"Took you long enough," he said when she arrived.

"I drove here as fast as I could."

Then he was kissing her, and it felt so perfect and sweet and right, and Mardi wondered why she had fought it for so long.

Mardi soon lost her desire to get back to her old life in New York. Her endless nights of underground clubbing were fading to a blurry smudge in her memory. They seemed empty, weightless. She had succumbed to the charms of life on the East End. Could it be, she teased Trent one evening, she actually might want to return to North Hampton next summer?

"Of your own free will?" he asked, gently kissing her eyelids.

"Of my own free will."

Mardi felt almost sorry for Molly, who was not nearly so fulfilled right now as she was.

But Molly was adjusting to her new circumstances without too much drama. She was spending a lot of time helping Ingrid and Matt with the kids and tending to the menagerie of familiar animals now inhabiting the house. Fury, the pricy Löwchen, was, of course, by far the highest maintenance of the family pets. And since there were no options in town for outsourcing the dog's walking, feeding, or ridiculously elaborate grooming, Molly was doing it all herself—with Jo and Henry's enthusiastic help. It was a brave new world of responsibility for Molly. And Mardi couldn't help but hint that it was good for her twin to get down and dirty. Well, relatively down and dirty at least. When she shaved Fury's hindquarters, leaving the hair long at the front and around the ankles, Molly donned a navy-blue Gucci coverall to protect her clothes. And she never failed to wear Ingrid's gardening gloves for any kind of manual labor. Before putting the gloves on, she would slather her hands in lotion, "just like at the salon." She didn't care if her sister teased her. These days, Mardi's teasing only made her smile.

With very little ceremony, the Cheesemonger had closed down. Ocean Vines, the tony wine shop next door that Molly had been briefly attracted to on her job search at the beginning of the summer, was quietly expanding to take over the gourmet store's narrow space. Ashley Green, for one, could already no longer remember when she hadn't risen early to bake for her guests in her own kitchen at Rose Cottage, since there was absolutely nowhere in town to buy a decent muffin or scone. Only Jean-Baptiste, as he prepared to return to New Orleans for the fall, recalled, wistfully, that the raspberry and ginger scones from the Cheesemonger had been nothing short of exquisite.

It would have been a happy and relatively carefree time for the twins were it not for two things. The case back in New York was still looming. Dad had called to somberly announce that a September trial date had now been set. And, even more urgently, no one quite knew what to do at this point with the ring. For now, it was "safe" on Mardi's hand. She seemed to be the only person who could keep its evil in check. Something about her skin nullified the curse. But still, she wanted it off her body. Even if it stayed inactive, it put her in grave danger.

Molly had made it very clear that she would never wear the ring again. It was too bound up for her with the nightmare of her escapade in Montauk. Whenever she looked at it, its pattern seeming to move like a slithering diamondback rattlesnake, she felt a wave of horror.

"Promise me," she said to Mardi, "that when we have our accounts back, we'll come up with a different symbol to float to each other. I never want to see that thing again."

"Of course," Mardi agreed. But that was the least of their problems.

Mardi suggested to Ingrid and Freya that they bury the ring. But Ingrid pointed out that it might poison the soil, ruining crops and causing strange cancers and birth defects.

"Okay, then. Scratch that," Mardi sighed.

"What if we melted it?" Molly asked.

"It wouldn't do any good," Freya said, glancing at the

light on Mardi's finger. "It's not the ring itself but the Rhinegold that's cursed. The Rhinegold can assume any shape at all and still wreak havoc in the world."

The four witches were gathered in Freya's airy living room, sipping fresh-squeezed lemonade from tall glasses on the coffee table, which was nothing more than a simple glass cube. Because this room was so uncluttered, they felt they could think clearly here. Even the piles of Freya's excess clothes were neat and streamlined, like colored pillars in a work of minimalist art. This was neutral territory, slightly outside of space and time, removed from the living chaos of everyday life. It was a place for introspection, and perhaps even for reason.

Mardi, Molly, Freya, and Ingrid were waiting for Jean-Baptiste in order to have a final session. This would not be a memory session per se, since, thanks to Alberich's overpowering need to brag about his crimes and his hatred to Molly, the facts about the fateful New York night had finally been fully recovered. Instead, the witches had asked Jean-Baptiste to help with their remaining dilemmas: how to deal with the ring, how to use the evidence on Alberich's cell phone to prove Mardi and Molly's innocence so that the White Council would be appeased, and how to find out who had saved them from the jaws of death that night, sending them back, oblivious, into the comfort of their beds. Even if the god of memory did not directly provide them with the answers they sought, they hoped that his guiding questions and eminent wisdom would help them come to these answers in his presence.

There was a polite knock on the front door.

Mardi jumped up to answer.

"Hello, Jean-Baptiste. It's really great to see you."

"The pleasure is all mine."

He seemed to arrive everywhere on foot, no matter the distance, without ever having broken a sweat, jacket on, pocket square freshly pressed. He was the incarnation of elegance.

Mardi took a moment to appreciate him. "You're pretty cool for an old guy."

"I'll take that as a compliment." He smiled.

"Come in," Freya said. "We saved your spot for you." She gestured to the tan leather Eames chair.

"I believe," he said, taking his accustomed seat, "that the painful part of our work is now behind us. We are now faced, at present, with practical concerns. These are urgent, yes. But the urgency is of a different nature from before. I hope I can be of some assistance."

They told him that their first order of business was to find a safe place to keep the Rhinegold. They weren't sure how much longer Mardi's magic would be able to neutralize it. The pressure was too great. She wanted it off her finger.

Having listened carefully, Jean-Baptiste began by putting an open-ended query to the witches: "Is there anywhere on this Earth that you could conceive of hiding it?"

Ingrid answered him. "On this Earth, no. Midgard is too fragile an ecology to absorb so much negative energy. With all the global warming and pollution and strife already affecting this planet, a curse this strong would push it into chaos. We can't let that happen. Midgard won't support it."

"Wait a second!" Molly stood and started jumping up and down in her steep wedges.

Mardi winced. She wished her sister could be a tad more dignified. But once she had she heard Molly's idea, she stopped caring. Between exclamations of "OMG!" and "I've got it!" Molly was able to articulate a plan to have Trent ask the Valkyries to come back for the ring and take it for safekeeping into Limbo. "Let it curse people down there for all we care!"

"I never thought I'd say this, Molly, but you're brilliant." Mardi beamed.

Jean-Baptiste was more measured in his response. "Freya? Ingrid? What do you say to this plan?"

Freya answered him first. "I say close, but no cigar."

"Yes," Ingrid echoed. "You're on the right track, girls, but it's not so simple."

The twins cried out in protest together. For once they were able to agree on something, and instead of celebrating with them, Freya and Ingrid were going to poke holes?

"We don't exactly want the Rhinegold in Limbo. There are too many unsavory characters languishing there. And if the Valkyries make a big deal of bringing it down, Alberich might somehow get his hands on it again."

"But," Freya took up Ingrid's thread, "Molly's idea of hiding the ring in another world is an excellent one. And, since North Hampton happens to be located on a seam, we're uniquely placed to get it into the gloaming space that borders the Underworld. If we could find the entrance to the gloaming within the renovated Fair Haven, we could bury the ring there and know that it would be safely out of the way for centuries, or until we find a way to undo the curse."

"The passageway used to be in the ballroom," Ingrid continued. "They changed the paneling in the renovation, but I imagine that beneath it the connection is still intact. I'm sure that Tyr will help us find our way."

"Of course he will," Freya agreed.

"It seems," said Jean-Baptiste in conclusion, "that you have found your solution. And that the four of you have found it together. Bravo."

Mardi tingled with restlessness. Now that there was an end in sight, she wanted to be rid of the ring immediately. "Great! What are we waiting for? I'll text Trent right away. Let's go."

Molly grabbed her bag. "What she said!"

"Just a moment, girls." Ingrid stayed resolutely seated. Why did she always have to be so slow and deliberate about everything? "I know you are eager to rid yourselves of the ring. We all are dying to get it out of our lives, believe me. But, as long as we are fortunate enough to have Jean-Baptiste among us, don't you think we should let him help us come up with a way to prove your innocence in New York? After all, he guided you toward discovering what really happened that night. His instincts are invaluable."

Mardi had to admit that Ingrid had a point. She looked at Molly, who was gently placing her purse back on the floor, ready to stick things out a little longer. They both had realized by now that if they blew the police investigation, the consequences would be dire. The White Council had been quiet of late. No more warning notes to Dad. But this was not to say that the Council did not hold major punishments in store for anyone who threatened to reveal the covenant of its witches.

The twin goddesses of strength and rage looked to the god of memory for guidance.

"We have the phone that shows everything that really happened and proves beyond any doubt that we didn't kill them—in fact, we tried to save them—but we don't know how we can use it." Mardi spoke with a rare tentative quality to her voice. She pressed her tongue stud against her teeth in thought. It was so frustrating to have the perfect proof, and to have no way to use it. "It—it reveals way too much about magic to the mortals. The White Council would roast us alive if we introduced it as evidence. There's no way to prove what happened without doing exactly what we're supposed to never do."

"Yep," Molly summed it up. "We're pretty screwed."

"It seems to me," Jean-Baptiste mused, "that in this particular instance, Magdi and Mooi, you two have absolutely nothing to be ashamed of. In fact, if I were your father, I would be very proud of you. My advice to you is this: no matter what the ultimate outcome in the mortal realm, you have behaved overall with great honor and bravery. You risked everything. When the choice was before you, your true characters shone through. And since your arrival here in North Hampton, you have defeated both Alberich and the curse of the Rhinegold, two of the greatest scourges of our times. Your story is one of supernatural courage. And if I were your father, I would want to know it. And, as I say, I would be proud. Very proud."

"Well, when you put it like that . . ." the twins thought aloud, as one.

Immediately, they emailed their dad the video from Alberich's phone, along with a blow-by-blow of their exploits.

Within twenty minutes, Mardi's cell rang.

"S'up?"

"How about 'hello, Dad'?"

"S'up?"

"I see that some things are never going to change." There was a lightness to his tone that Mardi hadn't heard for a long time.

"Dad, I can tell you have good news. What have you done?"

"Well, first of all, I've convinced Headingley not to suspend you and Molly next year, provided there are no more bizarre incidents with flying lunch items and radical changes of hair color among the staff. I'm afraid this called for a very large donation on the part of our family foundation. We're endowing a scholarship."

"How nice of us. But did you look at the video we sent? Is there anything we can do?"

"You've already done it, Mardi."

"What do you mean?"

"Sometimes, believe it or not, honesty is the best policy. I've shared the tape with the White Council."

"Dad. You didn't! And, Dad, it's not called a tape. It's a video. You're, like, twenty-five years behind the times." She rolled her eyes. Dad was such a loser, but he was their loser. Molly, Freya, Ingrid, and Jean-Baptiste were all staring at her, the beginnings of smiles lighting up their faces.

"Darling, please hear me out. Because you two have taken such great risks, both to save the mortals and to fight the curse of the Rhinegold, the White Council has determined that it will, in turn, take a risk on your behalf."

"I don't get it."

"The Council is has given me permission cast a spell of oblivion around the deaths of the mortals."

"What, their families and friends are going to forget them? That's not right!"

"You're misunderstanding me. No one will forget

them. But people are going to soon be forgetting how exactly they died. It's a very complicated process of erasure, which is the reason it is almost never performed. There's not a lot of room for error. It involves going back and restreaming months' worth of media as well as entering the memories of dozens of witnesses to blur the lines. Luckily, the Council trusts me to carry it out. And if I blow it, it's on my head. So I've got my work cut out for me. The real estate deals are on the back burner for the next few weeks. I may not have always been here for you, girls, which no doubt explains a few things. But I watched what you did in that subway station. And now it's my turn to kick in."

"Wow, Dad. I never thought I'd hear you sing the praises of blurred lines. I'm impressed."

"Blurred lines? What are you talking about?"

Molly reached for the phone, and Mardi handed it to her.

"Dad, we have one more question. Maybe you can help us." Molly felt all the eyes of the room fall on her. "Who could have rescued Mardi and me after we were killed on the subway tracks? Who brought us back from the dead?"

There was silence on the other end of the line. A sigh. "I can't be positive," he said. "But I do know there is someone with strong ties to the Underworld who loves you very much and who may have called in a very special favor. Someone who thinks you and your sister should fulfill your destinies here on Earth, to make sure witches use their power for the good, to stay strong against the hatred of certain evil men."

Instantly, although she had never met her mother, Molly was flooded with certainty. "You mean our mother? She's looking out for us?"

"Always," he said. "Your mother is quite a force."

Molly looked straight at her twin. Their smiles locked. They weren't abandoned after all.

41

I'LL BE MISSING YOU

$\mathcal{I}$t was the twins' last evening in town. Labor Day. They were getting ready for their farewell dinner at Goose's Landing, which was opening that night, at long last, to great fanfare. The dock was strewn with fairy lights and ribbons in celebration. There was going to be a lobster bake under a full moon.

Trent would be there, of course, along with Freya, Ingrid, and Matt. Graciella had offered to babysit for Jo and Henry. Jean-Baptiste, his mission accomplished, had already headed home to New Orleans, so they would raise a glass to him as they ate. He had given each girl her own pocket square as a souvenir, suggesting that they carry them as handkerchiefs. Mardi's was jet black. Molly's was hot pink.

"Let me dress both of you tonight," Freya had offered. "That way you can pack all your stuff so you won't have to deal tomorrow."

At first, Molly had been skeptical. She thought she

had made it perfectly clear that she was not so into the vintage.

"Come on, Molly, I have some classic pieces that will look amazing on you." Freya winked a bright green eye. She was irresistible.

Half an hour later, Molly was wearing a pink leather body-hugging jacket and skirt.

"Oh, Fury!" Molly squealed, picking up her little dog and standing on tiptoes to admire herself in one of Freya's many full-length mirrors. "Check us out!"

"You can keep it," said Freya.

Molly didn't know how to thank her.

While Freya worked with Mardi on something more down and dirty to wear, Molly tried on several pairs of strappy sandals, finally settling on a simple white option that looked reassuringly new.

When Ingrid poked her head into the attic wardrobe wonderland to say it was almost time to leave for their reservation, Mardi gave Molly a significant look.

Molly knew it was time to bring up the subject that she and her sister had stayed up half of last night discussing. She had said she would ask, and she was going to be as good as her word. Molly took a deep breath and dove in. "Ingrid, Mardi and I have something we want to ask you, but we don't think we should do it in front of Matt at dinner. Can we have a minute now?"

Ingrid nodded kindly. Freya looked intrigued.

Molly continued. "Do you remember the night of the storm, when we were searching for Mardi on the water, and we found that little drowned boy, and you, well, you called on your mother and you were able to bring him back from the other side?"

"Of course," Ingrid replied softly, understanding now why they would not be able to discuss this matter at the dinner table.

"Well, here's the thing: Mardi and I were hoping you could do something like that again. For our friends. What happened to them was so totally unfair. And even though we didn't do it, our magic was involved. We want to make it right. Please, Ingrid? Can you and Freya please get your mother to help bring them back from the Underworld? They don't belong there yet."

Molly found she was crying. She looked at Mardi, then Freya, then Ingrid. They all had tears welling up in their eyes too.

Ingrid put her arm around Molly, while Freya took both Mardi's hands. The two older witches looked long and searchingly at one another and shook their heads.

"It's a beautiful thought, girls," Ingrid said gently. "But it's impossible. It's much too late. They have been dead too long. There is nothing of their souls left any-more in the mortal realm. If we were, by some miracle, to be able to bring some part of them back, the results would be disastrous."

"They would come back as zombies," sighed Freya. "Or, maybe even worse, as wraiths."

"So," Molly sniffed, "there's nothing at all we can do to show them how much we care?"

"Nothing?" Mardi echoed.

"Well," Ingrid said, "there is one possibility."

Freya gave her sister a questioning look.

"Freya and I could ask Joanna about the possibility of getting a message to them in the Underworld. A message from the two of you. I know it's not what you really want. But would that help?"

"You would do that for us?" Mardi asked.

"On one condition," Ingrid said. "Because getting a missive through the passages is not something we can just do on a whim overnight. If you are serious about this, you girls have to promise to come back to the East End next summer." She smiled, her bright blue eyes alive with mischief. "Think about it. The kids would be over the moon."

Molly and Mardi looked from Ingrid to Freya and back again. Then they all burst out in laughter.

Faintly at first, then progressively louder, a childish cackling mingled with their laughter. They followed the sound to find Henry hiding in a box of lingerie. He had managed to encase his chubby little body in at least seven layers of Freya's clothing, blouses, skirts, dresses, hot pants. It seemed an impossible feat.

"Hey." Matt's voice came from the foot of the stairs. "Sounds like you're having a ball up there, but can you bring it with you? I'm starving."

After dinner, Mardi and Trent took a long walk across

Gardiners Island Bridge to Fair Haven. They were quiet as they strolled arm in arm over the glittering bay, but both were stirred inside by a thousand racing currents. Was this really good-bye?

They barely spoke. Without discussing it, as if by silent agreement, they reached the end of the bridge, crossed the vast lawns of Fair Haven, and found themselves at the greenhouse. They opened its old-fashioned glass door and fell into each other's arms on the wrought-iron bench where they had first gotten acquainted, what seemed like an eternity ago. The hothouse atmosphere was heavily fragrant.

Mardi focused her dark gaze on Trent, committing his features to memory. It seemed impossible to say good-bye to this face. She would carry it off in her mind's eye and gaze at it forever. It was a crazy feeling. White hot. Had she found her eternal soul mate?

Reading her mind, he whispered, "Mardi, do you feel like hanging out together for a few more centuries?" His smile was radiant and kind. "I promise to age gracefully. You can trust me."

"When you put it like that, the nine months until next summer don't sound so endless."

"Yeah, but just in case you ever even think about trying to forget me, I got you a present that will totally keep my memory alive."

"Where is it?"

He kissed her full on the lips, murmuring, "It's hiding in plain sight."

She looked around the greenhouse for a clue. Freya's herbs were lush and overflowing. The giant ferns glowed in the moonlight. The plant life seemed riper and more beautiful than ever. But she couldn't spot anything specifically different. And within a few seconds, she found her eyes magnetically drawn back to his.

"I used to be scared of your eyes," she said, "of getting lost in them, of drowning."

"I used to be scared of yours too. I guess it's a healthy fear. You know, the fear of eternity."

"Have you shaken it?" She ran her tongue over his lips.

"Have you?"

She pressed herself into the muscles of his chest, willing her body to soften into clay in order to take an impression of him that would last until they met again.

"So, next summer?" His breath was hot in her ear. "You up for another spell in thrilling North Hampton?" He ran his fingers along the snaking curves of her rainbow tattoo.

"Maybe," she teased him. "I mean, this hasn't been nearly as dead a summer as Molly and I thought. But I guess what happens next summer kinda depends."

"On?"

"My present." She beamed gentle mockery at him.

"So that's how it is!" He laughed. Releasing her from his ropy arms, he stood. "This gift of mine is so much cooler than anything your sister will ever own."

"I like the way you talk. Don't stop."

He wandered over to the Venus flytrap. She noticed now that there was more than one. A second plant was flowering behind the original.

He reached beneath the leaves and pulled the plant up from the ground.

Mardi expected to see hanging roots and clumps of dirt. But instead he was holding a sleek black pot, from which the plant grew.

"You're kidding!" She had never been more purely delighted.

"I could tell you coveted one of these from the second you laid on eyes on mine. I can read you, Mardi Overbrook. I know what you want to eat and drink. I know what makes you feel good. I was put in this universe to please you, Goddess of Rage."

She took her exotic plant from him and began to caress it with her gaze.

"You're giving me a carnivorous plant to remember you by? What kind of symbolism is that?" She laughed.

"*Our* kind."

She really loved this this guy.

"Bye, Trent." She kissed him one last time, pulled away, took her flytrap under her arm, and raced off into the night before he could see her cry.

He knew not to come after her. "Good-bye, Mardi."

She could feel his deep blue gaze licking at her back like an undying flame. Through her tears, she smiled. Trent Gardiner wasn't going anywhere. He was the appointed guardian of Fair Haven. He'd be waiting here, beautiful as ever, when she pulled into town next June. Ever after, he'd be waiting.

The next morning, Molly climbed into the Ferrari beside Mardi. Matt had devised an elaborate system for strapping her three large Louis Vuitton suitcases onto the back of the car. Killer and Fury curled up together on a small dog bed at her feet. The Venus flytrap nestled beside them.

Everyone crowded around to say good-bye.

"Hey," Molly said as Mardi shifted the car into gear, "you found a keeper. We're coming back next summer, right?"

Mardi nodded. Her rainbow tattoo shone bright in the morning sun, and a green light twinkled from between her slightly parted lips. She was silent for a long time as they sped through the farms on the outskirts of town toward the foggy field of forgetfulness that they would need to pass through to get back to their real lives.

Finally, Mardi spoke. "You know, Trent took the ring to Fair Haven for us. He went through the passage in the ballroom, and he buried it in the gloaming. I didn't want us to know where exactly it lies. This way, we can never be blackmailed. We're safe now, Molly. The curse can't ever touch us again."

Molly felt a profound relief spread through her

body. But a question lingered. Their mother, the Rhinemaiden. Where was she now? Why had she left them only to miraculously protect them from afar? Molly had always assumed she and Mardi were abandoned. But now it was clear that their mother was watching and protecting them in mysterious ways. Molly furrowed her brow as she burrowed her bare, beautifully manicured feet in between Killer and Fury in their soft bed.

Once the Ferrari had crossed the misty borderline encircling the secretly magical town of North Hampton and the twins were heading west on the Montauk Highway, following signs to New York City, Mardi spotted another Ferrari. A black one. Brand-spanking-new.

Molly watched as her sister shifted gleefully into fifth gear, gunning it, leaving the douchemobile in the dust.

"Nice work," she told Mardi. "Let's crank some tunes."

"Now you're talking. What do you feel like?" Molly asked, realizing she truly no longer felt competitive. The ring's curse of discord was finally lifted.

Molly and Mardi were twin sisters. Identical. Together they could meet anything in their way.

Mardi smiled, her identical dimple deepening in her cheek. "You decide. Anything but opera."

A NOTE FROM THE AUTHOR:

When *Witches of East End* went off the air in 2014, the story ended on a cliffhanger. I asked Fox 21, who produced and owns the show, if they would be willing to let me tie up the story lines so that fans would receive some closure. To my delight, they said yes. (Thank you, Fox 21!!) I was told to keep a few of the story lines unresolved, just in case the show ever gets picked up again. (Hope never dies!)

I hope you enjoy the story, WitchEEs!!

xoxo

Turn the page for exclusive bonus content—the short story finale to the *Witches of East End* TV series!

MIRROR SOULS

✳ ☾ ✳

*W*hen Freya Beauchamp woke up that morning, she realized something was wrong the minute she opened her eyes. For one, she wasn't in her own bed. Granted, that had happened from time to time, but her days of falling into a stranger's arms at the end of the night were long behind her. Except the man lying next to her wasn't a stranger. It was Killian Gardiner, the love of her life, her eternal soul mate, the man she had loved and lost through time immortal. She took a moment to admire his broad, strong back, his thick dark hair, his long, muscled arms curled around the blankets.

Killian stirred, sensing she was awake. "Hey, babe," he murmured, reaching for her and pulling her into his arms. He tucked her head against his chin.

Freya sighed happily, wrapped in his warmth, pressing her body closer to his so that he moaned in her ear. "Minx," he whispered. After centuries of searching for each other, it was wonderful to know they would never be apart ever again. Still, it was odd to wake up with Killian in her childhood bedroom. She didn't remember coming back here the night before. And Killian was supposed to be away, taking yet another trip around the world on that boat of his. What was he doing back? When did he return exactly?

Now Freya was certainly confused. Her memory was fuzzy, but she was sure that last night she had gone to sleep in her own bed, in her own house, alone. The Beauchamp homestead was Ingrid's home now, with her family.

And as much as Freya enjoyed lying in Killian's arms, she was too agitated to remain there. She slid away from his embrace and tied a robe around her nightgown. Padding out to the hallway, she bumped into Ingrid, who jumped in fright at the sight of her.

"Ingrid?" she asked. "Is that you?" She wondered why she was having trouble recognizing her sister, then realized that it was because the Ingrid she knew was a tall, Nordic blonde who usually wore her hair in a bun, and the woman in front of her had long, flowing chestnut locks, a more youthful glow in her cheeks, and less of Ingrid's prim countenance.

But it *was* Ingrid. Freya was sure it was her sister, she'd know her anywhere . . . so what was going on?

"Follow me," Ingrid whispered, taking Freya's hand and leading her to a quiet corner where they could talk.

"I don't understand," Freya insisted. "You're you, but you're not you."

"Believe me, I know," said Ingrid. "I woke up this morning alone—and wanted to scream—where is Matt? Where are my children?" Ingrid had been happily married to the town police chief, Matt Noble, for several years now. They had two extremely adorable children.

"They're not here?" asked Freya.

"No—as far as I can tell—they don't even exist!" Ingrid pulled at her hair and worried her bottom lip. "I don't know what's happened. Is it a spell? We're in some kind of spell, aren't we? Have we been cursed? Oh, I knew I shouldn't have trusted that insurance agent who came to visit the other day. He was so shady I'm sure he was a warlock!"

Freya cast a glance at a mirror. It wasn't only Ingrid who looked different—she did too. Better, she would say, raising an eyebrow. She had lush, dark hair instead of her strawberry waves. She decided she'd wear it that way from now on. "I don't think it's a spell," said Freya. "I think . . . I think we woke up in an alternate universe."

"Not again!" said Ingrid, smacking her forehead. "The last time we did that we ended up trapped in Ancient Rome for years! *The smell!*"

"So we need to figure out why we're here and what's going on."

"Well, here's one," Ingrid said, opening her robe.

"Oh God," Freya said, staring at Ingrid's protruding belly.

"Uh-huh."

"You're pregnant!"

"Bingo."

"But if Matt isn't in this universe . . . then who's the . . . ?"

This time they both jumped. Ingrid pulled her robe tightly over her stomach.

"Hi, ladies," Killian said, appearing suddenly in the hallway and giving Ingrid a curious smile. He was bare chested, his pajama bottoms hanging low on his hips. "I came out to find you. You know I don't like to wake up alone, Freya."

"Hi, baby, why don't you get back in bed, and I'll be right with you."

"Don't keep me waiting!" he said, sauntering back into the bedroom.

When he was gone, Freya and Ingrid exchanged a glance. "Is it just me, or is there something different about him too?" Ingrid asked. She'd felt something spark between them when Killian had smiled at her. Something that made her terribly uncomfortable. Killian was Freya's, and always had been. Ingrid had never been attracted to him in her life. Of course, one could not help but find him attractive, but that wasn't the point.

"I know, right?" said Freya. "I felt it too. I'm not sure what's going on, but something tells me he's not from our universe. He's from here. But he's . . . different for sure." She looked at Ingrid's belly. "So . . . any idea who the father is?"

"This is going to sound so strange, but last night I had dreams of this weird blue guy. You know, like a

Mandragora? A sex demon?" Ingrid shivered. "With all those tentacles? Eww."

"Blue baby?" Freya laughed. "No way. Mandragoras can't reproduce."

"Really?"

"Trust me on that one," said Freya, whose turn it was to look uncomfortable.

"There's more," Ingrid said. "I got up early this morning, thinking I had to give Henry his bottle, but instead, I found someone else in the kitchen."

"Who?"

"Girls!" rang a familiar voice from the first floor.

"Mom?" Freya asked, her eyes shining with sudden tears. In their universe, Joanna had died, giving up her life so Freya could have hers. But in *this* universe . . .

They ran downstairs to find Joanna at the stove, making pancakes. She, too, looked different—younger and more vibrant—what was this universe, Freya thought, we're all so much hotter—it almost made her want to stay. Joanna was wearing tight jeans and an airy bohemian-style blouse.

"Mom!" Freya said, giving Joanna a huge hug.

"Oh dear!" said Joanna, laughing as she spilled pancake mix all over the two of them.

"It's so good to see you. You look amazing," said Freya, sticking her finger in the batter and taking a deep lick.

Joanna wiped her hands on a towel and regarded her girls. "You too."

"Mom, there's something you should know. We're not who you think we are—I mean, we are—but we're not—we're not the Freya and Ingrid from this world—we're from somewhere else."

To their surprise, Joanna took it in stride, perhaps because she was a witch and was used to paranormal shenanigans. In any event, the mystery was solved as their mother looked at them serenely. "I know. I brought you here."

Joanna sat her daughters down at the table. "I'm afraid I haven't called you here under the best circumstances. I used the Mirroring Spell to bring you both here, as it might be the only way to set things right."

"What's happened?" Ingrid asked, alarmed.

Joanna looked grave. "In this universe, we were banished from Asgard by my father, King Nicholas. He returned to this world for revenge, but we—the versions of yourselves who live here—we were able to send him back. However, we were too late to save Wendy."

"Wendy? Who's Wendy?" Freya asked.

"My sister. Your aunt. In your universe, she never existed, but she does in this one. Nicholas sent her to the Underworld. She's trapped there. We need to get her back before her soul is bound there forever."

Freya nodded. Sounded like the usual witchy dilemma. She was well acquainted with the Underworld and wasn't looking forward to going back, but if Joanna said they had to, they had no choice. "Okay. When do we go?"

"You stay here. Ingrid and I will go," Joanna said, pouring each of them a steaming cup of coffee.

"What! Why?" she asked, relieved to have gotten out of an annoying chore, but also hurt to think her mother didn't need her.

"Because there's something you have to do while we're gone."

Ingrid sighed. "What more could go wrong? I'm pregnant and have no idea who the father is, Wendy's in Hell, and . . ."

Joanna placed a plate of pancakes on the kitchen counter. "Dash is in jail. He's been in there for weeks."

"Dash? Who's Dash?" asked Freya, with a mouthful of pancakes.

Her mother disapproved of her manners but didn't mention it. "Right—you know him as Bran. He goes by his middle name here."

"Okay. Why is he in jail?" Ingrid asked.

"They think he killed someone."

"Did he?" Freya yelped. She wouldn't put it past Loki, the god of mischief, to do such a thing. But she and Killian had made peace with Bran in their universe. It was horrid to think he was up to his old tricks in this one.

"I don't know," said Joanna. "But he's not making sense. They're going to move him to a psych ward if he doesn't stop."

Ingrid frowned. "Why?"

"Because he says he's Killian."

"Wait—what?" Freya did a double take.

"He seems to believe he's his brother. And that the real Dash has stolen his identity—swapped souls into different bodies so to speak—quite a malicious use of the Mirroring Spell. So you need to visit him, see if he's telling the truth," said Joanna.

"But what if he *is* Killian? Then that means . . ." Freya looked up at the ceiling, where the guy she thought was Killian was sleeping in her bed. She had woken up in his arms! Had they done anything more? She shuddered. "I'll visit him as soon as possible." She would recognize Killian in any form, she thought. She would recognize his soul. She was sure of it, so why hadn't she done so this morning?

"Is it Killian up there?" Ingrid whispered, thinking that if he wasn't, then it made sense, although she had never been attracted to Dash in their universe either. She really felt ill, and it wasn't just the morning sickness.

"I—I don't know, I'm not sure," said Freya.

"I'm not done. Both of you need to be careful around town," said Joanna. "I have terrible news. I'm sorry, there's no way to say this but to just say it. Freddie's dead."

"Freddie!" Freya gasped.

"How? When?" Ingrid's face went pale, and tears were beginning to fill her eyes.

"We found him murdered in the living room," Joanna said. "And his killer had written 'Death to Witches' on the floor with his blood."

"Someone knows our secret," said Freya. "Poor Freddie."

"In our universe, Freddie is in Bora-Bora, swimming with the sharks," said Ingrid, to console them. "He's only dead here."

Joanna nodded, taking a shaky breath. She smiled through her tears. "Tell him to visit me here sometime."

"I'm sure he'd love that," said Ingrid. "Because—where we come from . . . um . . . never mind."

"Where we come from, you've been dead for a while, Mom," said Freya. "Don't worry, Freddie won't be the only one visiting."

"So why did you bring us here, Mom?" asked Ingrid.

"Because only a mirror soul can see the truth of the matter. You are versions of Ingrid and Freya, you know them and their lives, but can be objective as well. When we get Wendy back and when Freya solves the Dash-Killian problem, you will return to your universe and my Freya and Ingrid will wake up here."

Freya laughed. "So you mean we're here and they're there?"

"Well, I had to put them somewhere."

"All right then, let's make this happen quickly," said Ingrid. "Someone else is with my husband! I've never been so jealous of myself."

· · ·

Freya tiptoed back into the bedroom. Killian—or who-ever he was—was still sleeping. She tried to be as quiet as possible as she stood in front of her closet, figuring out what to wear, when she felt warm hands wrap around her torso.

"There you are, beautiful," Killian said, kissing her neck, and sending butterflies fluttering in her stomach.

Freya stood stock-still, unsure of how to respond, even as her body seemed to know exactly how. She closed her eyes, lost to the sensation of his kisses. He turned her around, so that she was pressed against his chest, and she ran her hands over his back, drawing closer to him despite her doubts. He growled low in his throat, and led her to the bed. Call her crazy, but these were certainly Killian's hands on her body and Killian's mouth on her shoulder.

"I've missed you," he murmured, as he tangled his fingers in her hair.

"Where have I been?" she teased.

"Not where you should be," he replied.

"And where should I be?"

"Here," he said. "You. Are. Mine."

Freya stared deep into his eyes.

Saw the desire there.

The domination.

The madness.

The man who was kissing her was not Killian.

Of that, she was certain.

She pushed him away roughly. "Hello, Dash," she said, and before he could move, she trapped him on the bed, holding him there with a spell of her own.

Wendy Beauchamp woke up in the River Styx, flames all around her. Oh man. She had given her last life to Tommy and now this. She didn't regret it, if only it wasn't so hot. Although she sort of loved how bronze she was getting. If anything, Hell gives you a killer tan.

The minute she arrived, she went to visit her sister Helda, who ran the place and kept the Book of the Dead. "Sorry, Wen," Helda said, closing the book. "You can't go back. You've used up all your lives."

"So, what happens around here? Are there any good bars? Cute guys?"

Helda rolled her eyes. "It's the Underworld, what do you expect? Welcome to an eternity of boredom."

So it was terribly exciting when Joanna and Ingrid suddenly showed up with a familiar green necklace.

"What are you doing down here?" Wendy asked. "And, also, took you long enough!"

"We came to get you, what does it look like? Sorry we were delayed, we had trouble with the time door," Joanna said in that big-sister way of hers. "Come on. Put this on."

"My necklace! It's green again!" Wendy said. As a cat with nine lives, her necklace glowed green as long as she had one extra.

"Technically it's not your necklace," said Ingrid. "Hi, Aunt Wendy." She had a cool aunt—this other universe was really so much fun. She wondered how long she'd be able to stay. She did miss her kids, but it was nice not to have to run after them all the time.

Wendy held up the necklace for closer inspection. "Whose is it?"

"We found another universe where you existed. And we asked her if she would give you half the lives she had left, so you could get out of here," Joanna explained.

"You did?" Wendy laughed.

Ingrid smiled. "It was my idea."

"You are my favorite niece, you know that, right?" She shook out her long, dark hair. "And I actually said yes?"

"Yes." Joanna's mouth quirked.

"How generous of me! So really I've saved myself. How many lives are in here?" she asked, shaking the charm.

"Don't tell, she'll be too reckless with them," Joanna warned Ingrid.

Wendy rolled her eyes. "I was just asking!" She put on the necklace, liking the familiar weight of her lives against her collarbone.

She was so ready to get out of Dodge.

• • •

The police station looked almost the same as it did back home: a bright, cheerful, charming place. When Freya asked to see Dash Gardiner, she was led to a small room. They brought him in, made him sit in a chair, and removed his handcuffs. He was wearing an orange jumpsuit and was skinnier and paler than she remembered Bran looking.

He wouldn't meet her eye, but when he finally did, her stomach fell. It wasn't Dash in there. It was Killian. Her Killian. God, she'd missed him.

"Oh, honey," she said, reaching for his cheek.

"Stop," he said, shaking his head. "You're not allowed to touch me."

"But I have to. It's the only way to fix it," she said. "Killian."

Dash's eyebrows rose. "You know! Thank God! I thought I was going crazy!"

"Shush," she said, turning to see whether the police officers were watching from the two-way mirror. When she was certain it was safe, she passed him a silver vial under the table.

"Drink it," she whispered. "Hurry."

He nodded. He emptied the contents of the small canister. He shuddered, choked, and almost fell off the table.

"Officer!" Freya cried. "Help!"

She would need their assistance for sure.

Because once the man across the table opened his eyes again, they were full of rage and fire. He was Dash again, back where he belonged, and would suffer the wheels of justice just like he deserved. Freya's heart pounded, wishing she didn't feel so guilty, especially since she'd kissed him just this morning . . .

Dash didn't seem to hold any affection for her regardless. "I hope you rot in Hell," he sneered. "And tell Ingrid if she knows what's good for her, she'll testify on my behalf at the trial."

"If you believe that, you don't know my sister at all. Face it, Dash, you're through. You're going to be in here a long, long time."

Ingrid was nervous. When they returned from saving Aunt Wendy, who really was a trip—she wished they had an Aunt Wendy in their world—she had gone through all of Ingrid's journals and discovered the truth. The Ingrid who lived here *had* been seduced by a Mandragora, but that wasn't all. She'd also been hopelessly in love with Dash.

Dash Gardiner, who knew? Ingrid felt her mirror soul ache even at the thought of his name.

But when she asked to visit him at the police station, they told her he had escaped. Knocked out two guards and ran.

Oh dear.

She fretted, putting her hands on her belly. That wasn't good news. What would happen to this child?

Later that evening, when she was outside the house, tending to the garden, she felt a presence watching her. She shaded her eyes and looked up.

"Dash," she whispered. "You can't be here." She straightened up and they were looking at each other.

He saw her stomach for the first time. "Oh my God. Is it mine?"

Ingrid nodded. "Your first, isn't it?" Loki's first child. His only. He had been in love with Freya forever, chasing a goddess who was meant for his brother.

Dash's eyes softened. He put his hands on her belly. "I didn't see—earlier—in the hallway. I'm sorry. I wanted to explain . . ."

She shook her head, tears coming to her eyes. It was too late.

"Ingrid, I love you," said Dash. "Run away with me. I'll change. I'll be better. I promise."

"You're a wanted man."

"I didn't kill him."

She wanted to believe him so badly. She saw the pain in his eyes, and the way he looked at her was the same way Matt looked at her back home. The Ingrid whom Dash loved, loved him back.

"Ingrid, please, I could have left hours ago—staying here to find you only puts me in more danger. But I couldn't leave without you. Please, come with me, with our baby. I want to be with you both. I want us to be a family. Ingrid, please say yes."

Back at home, Ingrid was married to an upstanding policeman, but in this universe, she ran away with a known criminal.

"Do you think our stars are still crossed?" Killian asked, as Freya lay in his arms. They had just finished making love, and he couldn't help but notice how passionate she had been, pouring her heart and soul into every kiss.

The thought of Dash and Freya together sickened Killian, but he had a feeling he had more than erased the memory of his brother.

"Mmm?" she asked. "What do you mean? Crossed stars?"

"Don't you remember? We discovered one of us always dies, in every lifetime we've had together." He raised an eyebrow. Had she truly forgotten?

She stared at him. "We do?"

"Yeah," he said. "We do."

Freya tightened her embrace. She looked up at him. "Then we better make the most of this life." She had returned to help straighten out his identity, to return his soul to his body. But there was nothing she could do about the stars. Even goddesses couldn't control the heavens.

Killian smiled. "Sounds like a good idea." He pulled the covers over the both of them and reminded her who he was once more.

. . .

When Freya woke up the next morning, she was back in her childhood bedroom. *Oh no, it didn't work.* She was still trapped in the alternate universe. Then she heard the sounds of giggling and laughter coming from downstairs.

She walked into the kitchen to see Ingrid, blond, with her hair in a bun, feeding baby Henry, while Jo, her daughter, helped make pancakes with her father.

"Hey, Auntie Freya!" the children called.

"Hi, munchkins. Hey, Matt. Ingrid? Can I talk to you for a second?" she asked.

She pulled her sister aside. "So, we're back now, right? We solved it?"

Ingrid removed her glasses and rubbed the bridge of her nose. "I think so."

"What happened while we were away? Have they said anything?"

"The children said I was much less strict the past few days, apparently many rules were broken." Ingrid rolled her eyes.

"I'll bet."

Freya shrugged. "Well, it wasn't like you didn't—"

"Not at all!" Ingrid protested, making a properly horrified face.

But Freya knew better. She had seen the way Dash-as-Killian had smiled at Ingrid in the hallway. Back then, she had thought Killian was still Killian, and she had kissed him almost to prove a point. That he wanted her and not Ingrid. But then it turned out Killian was Dash and not himself. It was all too confusing. "Come on. Didn't you kiss him? I know you did."

Ingrid smiled at the memory. "Okay, fine, but it doesn't count. Back in that universe, he was my true love," she said, prim as ever.

Freya smirked.

"Do you think I made the right decision for her? Going away with him? I just thought—a family should stay together," said Ingrid, fretting.

"We wouldn't be back here if we didn't make the right choices for them. Remember? Mom said once we solved it we'd be back in our own lives."

"Right."

"I miss Mom already," said Freya.

"Me too. But I heard from Freddie. He's coming back from Bora-Bora tomorrow. I told him we'd all go to the North Inn."

Freya gave her sister an affectionate squeeze. "Good. And just so you know, I'm glad that in every iteration of the universe, you're my sister."

Ingrid smiled and returned the hug. "You can't get rid of me that easily."

Together, the Beauchamp girls went back to the kitchen to make breakfast.